Philip Glazebrook
THE EYE OF THE BEHOLDER

This distinguished and elegant novel immediately sends Philip Glazebrook to the top of the list of those who are creating compelling and meaningful fiction. Both John Fowles' *The Magus* and Evelyn Waugh's *Brideshead Revisited* come to mind in reading this dazzling book, with its brilliantly evoked backgrounds of Italy, Mexico, Scotland and the Caribbean.

It is narrated in the first person by Ned, a minor foreign service official stationed in Rome. As the novel opens, he is visited by a strange girl, Amy, sent by his cousin George, who shortly thereafter appears on the scene himself. The contrasting and clashing temperaments of the two cousins give the novel its impetus; the retiring Ned and the forceful George, who runs the family estates according to his own unpredictable lights. They are closely linked by their past (their boyhood together at that estate, Saradon, when George was mysteriously responsible for his twin brother's death) and by their present (their odd relationship with the odd girl, Amy).

The prevailing mood of the book changes several times, reflecting in its coloring the changes of setting: gaily light-hearted in an Italian spring; dour and threatening in a Highland winter; charged with passionate tension in a Mexican summer. Against these backgrounds a subtle tapestry of lies and truth grows before our eyes.

jackals howl.

live, much as we began, trying to buy the children first class tickets for a train that doesn't run any more.

The Eye of the Beholder

BOOKS BY

Philip Glazebrook

THE EYE OF THE BEHOLDER *(1976)*

TRY PLEASURE *(1969)*

The Eye of the Beholder

PHILIP GLAZEBROOK

NEW YORK ATHENEUM *1976*

Library of Congress Cataloging in Publication Data

Glazebrook, Philip, 1937-
    The eye of the beholder.
        I. Title.
PZ4.G5554EY [PR6057.L35]   823'.9'14   76-11586
ISBN 0-689-10737-4

The Eye of the Beholder

"It might be a mere dream that he saw:
the imagery of a melancholick fancy
such as musing men mistake for reality."
Atterbury

I

THE SUN RARELY shone through the window of my office in the Embassy. Since the Italian spring is supposed to be one of the compensations for Rome's political unimportance this irritated me; I could have shaken my fist at the teasing wedge of sunlight, falling dustily for half an hour through my barred window, which was all of spring that came my way. Without, the April sun rode through the clear Roman sky, warming with its marvellous light stone pines and the roofs of palaces, cupolas, hazy mountains and the sea—warming to my particular annoyance the Ambassador's chauffeur, who seemed to have nothing in the world to do except sun himself below my window chatting to anyone who passed up or down the oleander-lined drive between the Chancery and the gate. His liquid, sun-steeped voice was like a blackbird singing at a prison window. I had never before been posted anywhere where the climate mattered: in Eastern Europe, come rain or shine, one does not envy the people in the streets. But in Rome the sun shone beyond the barred window like a lost gold coin twinkling down into the sea, unspent, wasted, gone beyond recapture. Not since I had stood at my window at school, on a summer evening after the fireworks, and watched the glossy cars of Old Boys making for London through the warm dusk, had I so envied the freedom of others. Then I had thought freedom came of itself when you grew up. Evidently it doesn't. It remains beyond the bars. All I felt like writing that spring morning was a letter of resignation.

However, I drank a cup of tea and set to work upon my project. At that time papers were circulated pinned together with pins inserted at random, left to right or right

7

to left, so that one frequently pricked a finger whilst trying to unpin them. My plan was to initiate a policy of inserting pins strictly from right to left, for only in this way could we safeguard HE's fingers from pricks. Such an innovation requires careful wording if it emanates from a Second Secretary, for enemies and rivals lie in wait to frustrate even the most humanitarian plans of their juniors. It is the Foreign Secretary who has the real power in these matters. Absorption in weighing each word of my minute had made me forget the chauffeur below my window, and the blue Italian sky, when my outside telephone rang.

"Hello, who are you?" asked a girl's voice.

"Who do you hope I am?" I enquired cautiously. I had a feeling—a fear—that this sunshaft of a voice was not for me.

"Well I hoped," she said emphatically, "I hoped you were George Tilton's cousin. I wrote your name down but my lovebirds ate it."

"How is George?"

"Didn't he write?"

"George never writes to people."

"He does to me. He didn't to you? Oh the embarrassment. Awful. Now I'll have to ring off with the embarrassment. Toodle-oo."

"Wait—wait. What was George supposed to write about?"

"About me," the voice said, surprised that there could be any question of other subjects for correspondence, "about Amy Gunnis. I mean I didn't dream of ringing you up except he said I must because he'd written all about me coming. He said he'd tell you to be kind to me because I don't know anyone. So you see?"

Because of the alluring presence which her voice projected into my office I nearly asked her to a dinner party I was giving the next evening. But, recollecting how odd George's friends could be, I asked her instead to meet me after lunch on Via Veneto. A diplomat grows wary of being exploited by his relations, who tell everyone they meet to "look you up" wherever you are posted, and my cousin George, knowing this, had in the past played various practical jokes of a sort on me: he had insisted, for instance, that his dentist should stay in my flat in Belgrade for nearly a week. It gave George immense pleasure to arrange such jokes and for all I knew this girl Amy Gunnis might be booby-trapped.

Nevertheless, for the rest of the morning my minute about pins did not absorb all my attention. Amy's voice had ruffled the tranquil, if sunless, puddle of my office.

It was George I thought about as I sat waiting on Via Veneto that afternoon. If only it was he himself who had come to Rome. Although his rare descents upon me abroad upset my routine and my flat—and my values—although he put me out and borrowed foreign currency and laughed at the Foreign Service, yet I wished he had come. Morose, gloomy and tyrannical as he was, alarming too, he took up the slack in life and created tension; a clock or time-bomb ticked audibly when he was there. I waited for Amy long past three o'clock in case she really was a close friend of his, and I had changed into suède shoes and a tweed jacket in case he had painted a ludicrous picture of me as the British Diplomat. George made me wary and defensive.

I saw Amy before she saw me: indeed everyone on Via Veneto saw her, for she had taken the unusual step of throwing her arms round the neck of a horse munching away at its nose-bag on the cab-rank and the horse, tossing up its head, had managed to upset its nose-bag all over her. Wet oats stuck to her hair and her face and her shoulders and dress, and quite a crowd gathered to pick them off her. Across the street I saw her, a girl in a blue dress laughing, sunny hair glinting, Italians picking oats off her; and I knew at once it was the messenger George had sent to disturb me. I'm afraid I turned my back on the scene in the hope that someone else would pick her up, or that she would go away, and I didn't look up from my news-

9

paper until I was aware of her standing alone, enquiring but resolute, by my table. A slow smile curved her wide mouth upward. She sat down. "I had an awful time with a horse," she said, "did you notice? It spilt its lunch."

"No! Really? What would you like to drink?"

"Could I have a few cakes? Ones with cream would be best. My!" she exclaimed, sliding herself to and fro on her chair, "oats in your knickers don't half prick."

"Just cakes?"

"I wouldn't mind a glass of sherry."

Congratulating myself on not having invited her to my dinner party I escaped into the café to give her order. But when I emerged a different thought struck me. She was beautiful. In the flurry of meeting her I hadn't noticed. She sat in the sun combing oats from the tendrils of hair which framed her full-cheeked milkmaid's face, and I crossed the pavement quickly in case anyone seeing her alone should sit down. She turned sea-blue eyes on me and put out a hand to touch my arm. "I'm sorry about ringing you up, but George made me promise."

"I'm glad you did."

"I don't know a soul hardly. And you forget what it's like to be lonely." She withdrew her hand and was still, catchable as a butterfly on a windowpane.

"Why did you come?"

"Is George your first cousin or what?"

I explained that our fathers were brothers and that when George's father—the elder brother—had been killed in the war, my father had taken on the running of Saradon, the family estate in Cheshire, until George was twenty-one. "So we were brought up together by my parents at Saradon," I finished.

She licked a smudge of cream off the tip of her nose. "George's mother?" she asked, as if for a card to make up a set at Happy Families.

"Died. His brother too, his twin, he was—well—killed."

"Is there a mystery?" she asked.

"Um—well—no, no mystery."

She studied my face. Then she said, "A lot of death about. George shows it don't you think? I mean the shadows near. The Grim Reaper——" she suddenly laughed, a lovely flash of laughter.

"Didn't he ever tell you about them all dying?"

"Oh yes he told me."

"Then..." I didn't see why she had asked.

"I thought he might be making it up. You know, like people do. Give themselves these riveting backgrounds I mean."

It seemed so curious a notion that I said nothing. Had I known her better I would have perceived that she imputed to everyone a dishonesty which, since it was in her nature, she thought all human nature shared. In fact it wasn't so very curious to suspect George of creating mysteries about himself. Nobody knew where they stood with George. His charades were elaborate and straightfaced. He sometimes believed them himself. Again I asked, "What brought you to Rome?"

"He's got a sister alive hasn't he? Dorinda or something, she's been spared."

"Leanora; yes, she's older."

"He's terrified of her."

"Oh is he?" I don't like strangers telling me what is or isn't the relationship between members of my family. The question of Lea and George bristled with complexity. Besides, I didn't want to look on Amy entirely as George's friend, and I didn't want her to look on me only as George's cousin. "Have you got rid of the horse's lunch yet?" I asked.

"Can you spot any left-overs?"

She turned herself slowly and fanned out her hair for inspection. She was strongly, almost heavily, built. It was the strength of a peasant girl who would survive anything the sun or the wind or the rain might throw at her: the vigour of nature coursed in her as a trout throbs in a brook. I picked an oat or two from her neck, but a charge seemed to leap up my fingers from her skin so I left the

11

ones which had lodged between her breasts. "That's the lot," I said. I noticed a clock. "I'll have to go, but give me your telephone number and perhaps——"

"Oh will you take me out? Quick, a pencil before you change your mind. I mean," she went on, writing intently with her face very close to the paper, "don't feel you have to because of George or anything. Is that all right?" She gave me the scrap of paper as though it were a child's exercise.

I stood thinking of my engagements for the next few days. I was wired in with diplomatic parties like a bird in a cage. I wondered if I could skip one and slip through the bars into the Roman sun. But before I could decide I was aware of a shadow across our table and I looked up into the cupid's-bow lips and white teeth of a young Anglo-Italian who stood simpering down at Amy.

"So, *cara*," he said in his tinny voice, "so this is what you do when you say how you must go home after our lunch to sleep, *é vero?*"

"Leonardo, do you know George's cousin?" Amy asked.

"Oh yes we met, *come stai?*" he said rudely and turned back with a shake of his black coxcomb of curls to Amy. "*Senti cara, che facciamo?* Oh look, all crumbs are fallen in your bust," he thoughtlessly picked out the oats and continued, "*ora che fai?* Come from this tourist place, come across the street to where we are, is much more chic, come. Your friend too if he wants."

His voice with its stagey Italian inflexion drew Amy to the kerb with him. I followed, thickset and uncomfortably pink in the sun whilst he was like a lizard in its warmth and she like a strong spring flower.

"I have to go back to work," I said, "but Amy—come to dinner tomorrow night? A dinner party. Will you?"

They were on the edge of the traffic, Leonardo's pale-suited form urging her to cross. "Ring me up," she called, "give me a tinkle, stating point of view. *Ciao caro.*"

I took a taxi to the Embassy, hoping that I wouldn't be summoned by HE in the suède shoes and tweed jacket which I now had no time to change. On the reverse of the piece of paper on which Amy had written her number she had begun a shopping list. It said in big letters "Buy food for lovebirds".

At the office I wondered why she had said she knew no one in Rome when she had just had lunch with Leonardo del Traffo and knew, presumably, his obnoxious set of friends who could be seen shouting at one another out of the windows of sports cars, or trooping in and out of night clubs, or making a great deal of noise in restaurants. I felt rather a fool for having been taken in by her disingenuous appeal. My resolve not to ring her up was helped by a rush of work caused by my Ambassador having accepted an invitation to say a few extempore words at a dinner that night, which meant that several of his staff had to submit draft speeches for him to choose from. When I was at last ready to leave, Amy rang up. "Can I really come to dinner tomorrow?"

"Certainly if you don't think it will be dull."

"You don't like Leonardo do you?"

"Not much."

"If only you could see his toe-nails, they're like ten little pearls. Doesn't that tempt you to change your mind?"

I relented, for there flowed such life and warmth in her voice. I gave her directions to find my flat next evening and made her read them back to me. On my way down to the gate to find a taxi I saw the evening sun ablaze on the pinnacles of San Giovanni, its great rococo statues afloat in the flooding golden light, afloat in the freedom as I felt myself to be. I wouldn't ask another man to partner Amy at the dinner, which was a farewell party for an Australian attaché; I didn't care if my table was unbalanced or not.

It was fortunate that I didn't ask another man because Amy never came. At nine o'clock the telephone's *interurbano* note cut through the din of Australian voices and I went into my bedroom to answer it. Amy's voice moped distantly into my ear. "I can't come my love."

13

"Where are you?"

"In bed in this awful room where I told you—can't you come and see me? Or I suppose you've got your party," she mourned. "I'm so sad and ill, couldn't you come?"

"Later I could if——"

"No I've taken all these pills, later's no good."

"What pills? What's wrong?"

"Bye my love, enjoy your party, bye." She hung up.

I was worried as I returned to my guests. Then I realized that there was a flaw in the conversation: Amy could not be in Rome, for the call had come from the provinces. She didn't know that out-of-town calls have a different ringing tone in Italy. This was my first experience of the careless incompetence with which Amy attempted to deceive people. I promised myself it would be the last.

II

MY BRUSH WITH Amy's world of tricks and delusions
was over in thirty-six hours, and left me valuing my everyday life more highly. It is wiser to accept the limitations
of temperament just as a bird once caged is wiser not to
stray. There had been something indescribably intimate
about Amy, an immediate contact and tension which my
acquaintances in the diplomatic corps didn't provide:
the tension between hunter and hunted from which the
cage-bird is safe. The danger of freedom receded like
hounds' music gone over the hill, and I was left snug in
my office with the sun beyond the barred window where
it belonged.

Three weeks later, in May, my cousin George rang up.
"Where are you George?" I asked.

"I seem to be in your flat," he scratched out in his dis-
pleased voice.

"In my flat! How did you get in?"

"I got the key from the porter of course."

"He gave you the key?" I was appalled. Obviously there
was no classified material in the flat, but one is supposed
to maintain security. "What are you doing there?"

"Hanging up my cloak and dagger. Ned don't try and
dramatize your incredibly boring life or we'll have to put
you back in the booby hatch."

It amused George enormously that I had once undergone
psychoanalysis. "I hope you're going to stay," I said.
"There's a room——"

"Yes I found it. When are you coming back?"

I looked at my watch. "It's six o'clock, I could get away
now and——"

"Give me an hour would you," he broke in. "And Ned

where do you keep the Coca-Cola? I've found the rum but I can't find the Coke."

"I'll bring some," I said. "Do you want to sleep? Have you just flown in?"

"And bring a few fags could you? You know they cost you nothing. See you." He hung up.

Nobody but George could have got the key out of the porter; George walked in and out of my life as he liked. I went downstairs and crossed the drive towards the cluster of Nissen huts under the pines which housed the overspill of Embassy staff. The cacophony of Roman traffic shot with the scream of horns, which closed windows kept out of my office, rolled up from the city like the clash of battle. *Fumum et opes strepitumque Romae....* In the shop I bought Coke and Chesterfields.

The storekeeper was a great one for chaff. "You walking out with one of the Yank lot then?" he asked, bustling through the smell of cheese and beer in shirt sleeves and braces. "Call that Marshall Aid do they, favouring the Britishers?"

"I expect so."

"Don't do nothing I wouldn't do." He stood like a jolly little model of John Bull, hands on the counter, whilst I signed the chit. "You know what Walter Raleigh copped in the States and I don't mean potatoes. Cheerio."

You expected to emerge from the shop into a London side street. Indeed a sign nailed to a cypress called the patch of tarmac "Trafalgar Square". Uneducated English voices came through the huts' windows. Whether it is insularity, or patriotism, or homesickness which creates this charade of England I don't know, but diplomats abroad can't do without it. The cosmopolitanism which is often imagined to be an attribute of the diplomatist is, where it exists, an attribute of his own temperament rather than a consequence of his occupation. My temperament doesn't have it. It seems to me that all natural barriers, be they mountains, seas or languages, should serve as warnings against over-hasty attempts to step beyond

16

what is familiar: to speak a foreign language "like a native", for instance, only encourages the speaker in the delusion that he is at home where he is in reality a stranger.

I knew, travelling back to my flat in Parioli, that George would be immediately more "Roman" than I. He would make me feel an absurdly British fuddy-duddy. Even though he spent half his year farming at Saradon, and the other half fishing or stalking on his property in Scotland, whilst I lived abroad, the facts didn't matter to George: he would give the impression of being a Roman, and he would take himself in. As the taxi neared my *largo* I felt the onset of a nervousness and irritability indivisible from dealing with George ever since, when I was about sixteen and he fourteen, our relationship had fundamentally altered. At that age I had first realized that George was much more important at Saradon than I was. Before, because I was the elder and because it was my father who ran the estate—and also because of George's involvement in his twin-brother's death—I had patronized him. Of course I had always known that he was the heir, but the truth of the fact—its implications—only struck me with the force of a reality when suddenly, at sixteen, the close horizon of childhood cleared to reveal the long cold vista of life itself. In that cold prospect I saw that Saradon would never be my home. My parents would move out and if I returned it would be as a visitor, George's guest. Everything was really his. He had usurped his slain brother's place, and he had usurped the place I had felt to be mine. I had not been able to adjust to this expulsion: hence my spell of psychiatric care.

Even after fifteen years I wasn't reconciled to it, perhaps because I had no home except flats in foreign cities. And I was wary of George in case he paid me out for all the years I had patronized him at school and at home. So far he hadn't, but I expected him at any moment to begin.

The door of my flat, which was on the ground floor, was bolted on the inside so that I had to ring the bell. Amy opened the door. Blonder, and beach-brown, she glowed against my dark hallway.

"Just going my love. Must rush," she kissed me in passing, "see you."

I went in. In a faded shirt and a pair of cotton trousers, lean, angular as bent wire, George squatted on my sitting-room floor cutting his toe-nails onto the back of *The Times* and scowling at the crossword. I say "scowling" because his habitual expression looked like a scowl: the thin compressed mouth was contemptuous, weight of anger seemed to crush the furrows into his brow, frequent movements of his hands to rough his black hair flashed impatience; he threatened and darkened his surroundings like a thundercloud. To my relief he seemed delighted to see me.

"Ned you're an angel," he cried, looking in my carrier bag, "Coke! Ciggies!—an angel from heaven that's what you are."

He loped away to the kitchen. I thought how his easy strides always made me feel cumbrous, a tug chasing a schooner. Following him on the hill in Scotland was worst of all. "Did you have a good flight from London?" I asked.

"Boring question." He clattered ice out of the tray, kicking cubes which spilled under the sink. "Now Ned, while I'm here I want you to look on me as a rich uncle. Treats and more treats. Tonight I'm going to take you to the most expensive restaurant in Rome, okay?"

"You mean you've forgotten to bring any money," I said soberly.

"Tomorrow I'm going to ring up my bank and arrange about it—but yes, I've run out of actual cash—oh God, don't look like that. You know I always pay you back. Don't spoil my annual holidays."

"Of course I'll lend you money, here you are." I chucked 20,000 lire onto the table. "You don't have to take me out with it if you want to have dinner with Amy."

"Oh, jealous are you? Well Amy's busy."

18

For some reason I was relieved. "I didn't know she was here this afternoon when you rang."

"Of course you didn't, how could you since I didn't tell you," he snapped, anger incipient. "Okay don't come out to dinner, I'll go on my own."

"Of course I'll come, I'd love to."

"That's my boy," he said, his brow clearing. "You pick the place, we'll feast till cockcrow—and fuck Amy is what I say. Do you know she hadn't been in the place five minutes before she started criticizing my toe-nails?"

"She has high standards in toe-nails," I said, recalling her praise of Leonardo's.

George looked at me curiously. "Well fuck her," he said, returning to the sitting room where he slumped in a chair and brooded upon his injuries.

I shook his nail-parings off *The Times*. "How's Saradon?" I asked.

"Weel Mr Ned—" it was the thin Glasgow whine of his housekeeper—"I'm trying to get Mr George to see sense and close the house."

I was appalled. "Close Saradon? You're not going to surely?"

"Part of it maybe."

"It isn't all that big."

"You only see it when there are people staying there. It's big for Mrs Winder and me. Fair too big Mr Ned."

This identification of Saradon with Mrs Winder annoyed me. "I wouldn't have thought Mrs Winder's wishes were all that important," I said.

"No," he allowed, "you probably wouldn't. But then you don't live there."

To that I had no answer.

For dinner I chose a restaurant where we could eat out of doors. George immediately became crotchety, hunching his shoulders, chafing his hands, glancing up at the sky between the spires of cypresses.

19

"Would you rather eat inside?" I asked.

"No, no." He sat silently shivering so that one could think of nothing except how cold he looked.

"We can easily go in if you're cold."

"Oh God are we going to discuss the weather interminably? Soup," he said to the waiter who appeared, "hot soup immediately and then I don't care, anything, you choose Ned. Except Christ, you're a vegetarian—here, give me the menu or I'll end up with a nut cutlet." My vegetarianism never failed to annoy George when we ate together. He chose steak tartare. "It's sheer escapism," he said, "it's no good pretending that the wheel of rebirth and destruction doesn't rule the world you know. The eater whilst eating is being eaten. You can't get away from that by nibbling cheese. You must face facts Ned."

I smiled. When he had drunk some wine and eaten several pieces of bread he cheered up. Living at his pitch of nervous tension food, preferably carbohydrates, was essential and immediately became more nervous energy. His height made him look gaunter than he was, and anyway I always thought of him as being emaciated because he had been such a spindly little boy. "Sparrow-shanks" the gardener, Pusey, used to call him. Because he had been so teased, especially by his brawny twin, he had written away from prep school for a correspondence course in body building—more and crueller teasing when we found out—and as he grew up he had filled out his frame. Still he felt cold and hunger intensely, in part due to the highly-strung temperament which, too, resulted from his relationship with his twin brother Tim; or from his involvement in Tim's death. What Amy had said was true: shadows hung about George.

I watched him tearing up the crusty bread. Nearby, waiters were roasting meat over fires of rosemary. Flame-light tricked successive masks onto his face, as the guttering of a candle lends expressions to a skull, and the scented smoke columned sacrificially upward under the gloomy trees behind him.

His hunger satisfied he asked, "Do you ever see Leonardo del Traffo?"

"In the distance."

"Rather a poor fish wouldn't you say?"

"There's a group of them with a lot of money in Rome. Vaguely neo-Fascist. Vague ideas——"

"Yes but apart from cash and politics, which don't interest me, what else have they got to offer?"

"If you rule out money and politics I don't know what's left."

"God what a fatuous remark!" he complained. "People are left. People—you know—or maybe you don't know any."

I said nothing.

"I mean what can Amy see in them?" he continued.

"They're the easiest group for a foreign girl to fall in with. If you tell an English girl you live in Rome she always says, 'Do you know Leonardo del Traffo?' His mother was English—they're all half-English or half-American or something, that lot. They act the stage Italian as a sort of tourist-trap for foreign girls."

"Christ, Amy's not a typist on a bus tour, what do you mean?" he demanded. I shrugged. I knew perfectly well that Leonardo's Englishness provided the home comforts of language and understanding to a girl like Amy whilst his Italian-ness provided the spice of foreign travel, but there was no point in telling George the truth.

"I mean she must like him, for some extraordinary reason," he went on.

"Liking or disliking only comes into it when you've got a wider choice than a foreign girl's got."

"That's obvious rubbish. I'd much rather see no-one than people I don't like."

"I know that's true of you George," I agreed, thinking of the rancour which his aloofness from local society caused amongst his Cheshire neighbours, "but most people get lonely. Amy doesn't strike me as a solitary."

"You don't know anything about Amy. Your judgement

is *ex pede Herculem* if I may make so bold. It's also the generalization of an ostrich—we all know diplomats can't choose who they spend their time with, it's things like that which would madden me about the Foreign Office."

"Most people have jobs," I replied mildly. "Practically all jobs entail maintaining friendly social relations with other people in the same line of business. You'll find that most people's 'friends' are professional contacts."

"Mine aren't thank God."

I might have pointed out that this was because he had never had a job, but there was no point in telling him this truth either. Having gulped a quantity of minestrone very fast he now, as usual, pushed away his plate as though food disgusted him and felt in his jacket for a cigarette. He always took cigarettes singly and rather stealthily from his pocket, perhaps to avoid offering them round, for he was always on the point of running out. "When are you going to leave the Foreign Office?" he asked.

"Not in the foreseeable future," I answered cautiously. George was adept at extracting confidences, and I had once or twice complained to him too freely about the irritations of the Service. Diplomats more than most people indulge fantasies of giving up their careers and becoming beachcombers or millionaires. I suppose there is more to react against in the Foreign Office.

"You really ought to," he said. "You've told me yourself most of your work would be done by a stenographer in commerce."

"Slips can be more important even at a low level in an Embassy."

"You're now claiming that spelling mistakes can cause world wars, which you know isn't true. You see that's the exact danger: the FO takes intelligent people and makes them do boring work, so what happens? You use your intellect to fool yourself that the boring work's important, like you've done. After years of that, when you've no idea any more what's really important, they make you an ambassador. But they can't give you any power, see, because

22

they know you haven't got any judgement any more."

"I know that's the way the argument goes," I said. Whatever I had been George would have tried to persuade me out of it—would have chivvied me out of any comfortable niche, if he could, with the arguments of Aesop's fox. "Probably my judgement is warped already, but——"

"So you agree with me," he said annoyingly. "I should get out. All the really clever people do. I mean I don't want to destroy your life's work at a stroke, but I do advise you to think carefully before soldiering on. I mean don't tell me you've got to the stage of thinking your ambassador is this marvellous radiant being have you?"

"Of course I don't, my judgement isn't that bad yet."

"Then how can you want to be an ambassador yourself? And how can you work in a profession you don't want to get to the top of? Answer me that." There was a good deal of the university debating-point in all George's arguments, so I didn't reply. Anyway he went on: "The only way you know you're in the right job is if you think the man at the top is infallible and blemish-free, like priests think of the Pope."

"And whom do you regard to be infallible and blemish-free?" I enquired, drawn into scoring a debating-point myself. "The head of the National Farmers' Union?"

He laughed, stretching his arms wide. "You're absolutely right. I'm a misfit in the world of the mangel-wurzle."

But George rarely laughed. It was impossible to talk to him without eventually being provoked into provoking him. Only during the early moves of a game of chess, or the early stages of any of the games he played with furious zeal, could you sit amicably with him. Came a point when the game or argument tended decidedly one way, and either he grew bitter or else he crowed. I remember him so infuriating me one Sunday morning before church, when I was about fifteen and he was beating me at croquet on the lawn at Saradon, that I clocked a ball with all my might in his direction and smote him on the ankle. His face whitened with pain. He limped away over the swelling roots of a cedar, a small reproachful figure limping the length of the house's yellow brick façade whilst the church bell tolled across the park, and painfully climbed the lavender-flanked steps of the drawing-room french window—to tell my parents, I supposed, of my brutality. But he told no-one, not even his sister Leonora.

Later I understood. An "accident" playing a game was too close to the subject of his brother's death—whose circumstances I didn't then know—for him to complain to anyone about a croquet ball hitting his ankle.

As a small boy (before he took the famous bodybuilding course) chess had been his favourite game, and now that he appeared to have recovered his fundamentally intellectual temperament—I mean by that the cerebral outlook which he had subdued as an adolescent mad on bloodsports—chess was again the game that suited him best. We played several times late at night in Rome when he came in from dining with Amy and I came back from a diplomatic party. I played because his nerves were standing out on stalks when he came in, and chess calmed him: it put his mind back in charge of his body, to shrink the world to a chessboard, and to concentrate his worries upon wooden men instead of flesh-and-blood.

Amy certainly upset him. Always bad in the morning he was now worse than ever, wouldn't open an eye when I took him coffee before I left for the office, but lay groaning in the dark, the bed too small for him, surrounded by drifts of books, clothes and newspapers. On the Sunday morning we had breakfast together and George said something which made me wonder about his life at Saradon. "I have an extremely practical tip up my sleeve," he said as he finished his boiled egg; "if you put your egg-spoon in the water you boiled the egg in, the spoon won't tarnish."

"How often do you eat your breakfast anywhere near a saucepan George?" I asked sarcastically.

"Oftener than you might think," he replied.

It was with difficulty that I could displace breakfast at Saradon from the dining room to the kitchen, in my mind. Routine at Saradon was fixed as an axis upon which the world turned. But it made me wonder.

In the evening when I came in from the office he would be gulping cornflakes with two or three of my books open on the kitchen table, and his swimming trunks in a puddle of water on the floor, morose and bearish. I had never known him put out so completely by a girl; but then he was so secretive that if he hadn't been staying with me I wouldn't have known that it was Amy who was upsetting him. I concluded from what he let fall that he had gone to stay with Amy when first he had arrived in Rome. Presumably she had turned him out. Although I was hurt that he hadn't chosen to stay with me first, I was obscurely relieved that she had made him leave; jealousy no doubt, but whether jealousy of George or of Amy I didn't distinguish.

Jealousy of whichever of the two of them it was it swelled angrily when I came in earlier than usual one evening and heard them laughing in my bedroom, which had a double bed. I went out and walked round the nearby zoo. What I couldn't understand—I hadn't any experience of my own to go by—was why George was still troubled by her if he was going to bed with her: I know that it was naïf of me, but I thought that people were promiscuous in order to release their worries and inhibitions. Those caged by temperament or conviction behind the bars of chastity do picture life outside as easy and delightful. I was indeed jealous, and I couldn't bring myself to go back to my flat until late that night. I found George cheerfully making a jam sandwich in the red nightshirt he wore. "I fear night starvation above all ills," he explained. "Been waltzing under the chandeliers I suppose?"

He caught me in his arms and danced me round the kitchen, taking long stooping steps with his hairy legs. When I extricated myself he continued alone, arms wrapped round his chest so that a hand gripped each shoulder blade, looking from the back as if they were the hands of a hidden partner.

"How do you do that?" I said. "You must have incredibly long arms."

He stopped at once. He hated any imputation of physical peculiarity. "Talking of deformity," he said as he wolfed his sandwich, "you're as white as a slug you know. You ought to come to the beach tomorrow. You must get some sun Ned. Yes it's decided: we'll collect you at one and I promise we'll get you back at four or whenever His Excellency blows the hooter. What's more I'll sing for you all the way in the car."

"There and back?"

"A medley of old favourites both ways, promise."

I decided to go because I wanted to see them together, although I knew, or feared, that seeing them together would rile me. When I got into their hired Fiat at the Embassy gate George did not look like singing. Amy had to drive because he of course had left his licence in England, and he had squashed himself into the back seat from which his voice pecked at our backs. They couldn't agree about anything. "What are you doing Amy?"

"Isn't this the way to Ostia?"

"I've told you we haven't got time to go to the sea. Is all speech useless?"

"Where do you want to go then?" she asked.

"I don't care, anywhere so long as I can get out of this seat."

"Do you want to sit in front?" I asked.

"Let us not waste the entire day with Musical Chairs."

Eventually they decided on a villa in the hills which had a swimming pool—at least Amy decided, for George answered all her suggestions by scratching out "Please yourself old sport." As we entered the cool of the villa to book a table George said, "Now we see why you've insisted on bringing us here."

Across the bright dazzle of water I saw Leonardo and his friends. They lounged aggressively, like a gang on a street corner, arms on one another's shoulders, water sparkling on sleek hair, gold medallions twinkling, sinuous bodies of men and girls brown and brilliant coloured in bikinis. My heart sank at the prospect of their vivacity. Leonardo walked towards us with his exaggerated litheness and clasped George's arm.

"Giorgio! Come with us, it's the best table over there, *vieni.*" He ignored Amy and myself.

"We're just going to eat," George said. "Or I am—I don't know if you would rather eat over there Amy?" he added with brow-puckered concern.

"We'll come over later," Amy said.

"An excellent solution. Then we can have our cake and eat it too," said George in his chilly tone.

The three of us changed, and then sat down at our table for lunch. In a bikini Amy was the colour of harvest, ripe and full, her hair light as the beard on barley; almost naked she came into her own, as if clothes were a sheet flung over a statue. George was dark, strong and lean beside her, somehow wintry despite the heat. The table was under a vine pergola, and beyond the terrace a splendid far-flung view extended over the hazy plain to Rome. It seemed like an earthly paradise, but still they quarrelled. "Oh George, I wish you wouldn't smoke all over the place at lunch," said Amy, wrinkling her nose and waving her hands. "For one thing it'll bring on your cancer."

"It's so bourgeois to be obsessed with smoking," George said. "It's got like the Victorians and masturbation, smoking's blamed for everything."

"Did I hear a vulgar word?" Amy asked, her eyes growing round with interest.

They then discussed masturbation at great length. For me the view, the sun through vine leaves, the heat, the whole opportunity—all shrivelled to waste. It was as though in a beautiful library one took down a book and found it crudely defaced. But they for the first time talked without quarrelling. Though I was careful not to show my repugnance George knew me too well. "You have contributed very little, what are your views Ned?" he enquired.

"It's such a dull subject."

"There's no such thing as a dull subject, there are only dull people discussing it. He finds us dull," George told Amy.

"Anyway my love," she said to me, "you can't think sex is dull."

"What you're discussing isn't sex," I complained.

"Masturbation isn't sex? I should say it represents at least eighty per cent of the diurnal sex experience of the population of the globe," George said. "You know that's true but you won't face facts Ned. Trouble with you is, you're still frightened of the Green Long-Legged Scissor Man."

"Who's he?" Amy asked.

"In Struwelpeter. Snip-snip if you don't hide it away."

"Rubbish George," I said.

"You evidently haven't read Professor Friedmann's work on the subject so there's not much point in discussing the matter with you."

One never knew whether the professors George cited existed or not. They were apt to, if obscurely. It was like a bluff at Poker.

"Great Heavens!" said George suddenly. "Look! Look who's there."

Across the pool, reading and rubbing his grizzle-haired chest, was stretched between two chairs an American actor famous for villainous rôles in horror films. George gazed at him reverently. "You don't see a talent like that every day of the week," he said shaking his head.

"He's a frightful old ham," said Amy, evidently irritated.

George ignored her. "I went the whole way to Chester to see *The Reliques of Baron Morag*."

"To Chester from London?" Amy asked.

"I live near Chester."

"Oh is Saraton or whatever it's called in Cheshire?" Amy asked without interest. I was astonished; not to have identified George with Saradon seemed to me not to have identified him at all. I wondered what on earth they talked about, or had in common. "Is that where Mrs Winder lives?" Amy went on.

"The egregious Mrs Winder. Indeed she does God bless her." George began to talk about his housekeeper, telling stories of her foibles illustrated in her purse-mouthed whine. He fantasized, creating for her the character of a delightful eccentric not recognizable as the grim sour woman I remembered. He made out that she had designs on all his male visitors, covering her advances under guise of bringing hot water bottles or early tea. I saw that he had studied her minutely, like the prisoner engrossed in a mouse for which he creates, out of his own need for entertainment, an enthralling personality. I think that he believed that she was an interesting woman.

"I bet it's you she fancies," Amy said. She didn't notice, or didn't care, that George compressed his lips angrily. "Tell again what she said about putting her feet in the Aga."

"I won't have her mocked."

"I thought you were mocking her my love," Amy yawned.

Amy wasn't at all alarmed by George. I thought of Harriette Wilson's derisive account of the rages of the Duke of Wellington—rages which had frightened half the statesmen in Europe, but not the courtesan who turned him from her door. Amy reminded me of Miss Wilson.

After lunch they swam, but I was fretting about the time and went to change into my suit. When I came out I stood by the pool. "I'm afraid I'll have to go," I said to Amy in the water below me.

"Why don't I ring up for you? I can say you're not quite up to snuff."

"It isn't a question of getting off work like a typist or something," I said coldly. She swam off neat as a fish through veins of sunlight which undulated over her body.

"You've got something specific to do this afternoon have you?" George enquired across the water.

"That isn't the point," I said.

He paddled lazily away. "There's no point in going to work just for the sake of sitting in your office. I should stick around and forget the cares of empire."

I was hot and red with irritation. I went into the villa to pay our bill. When I came out I saw George and Amy lying close to one another on mattresses, she under a large straw hat: I did not think they were talking until I came near and heard the peaceful murmur of their voices. I felt at my heart a grab of jealousy for this rapport between them which I didn't understand. Standing over them I heard Amy say, "I agree gym shoes are perfect for London, but what do you wear in the country?"

"Look I'm sorry but I've got to be taken back," I said. "I've paid the bill."

"Oh how trying you are Ned," George groaned. "You shouldn't have paid yet."

"I'd like to pay."

"No I mean we haven't finished. They have rooms here, we wanted a room to have a little rest. You could have joined us, couldn't he Amy?"

However outlandish, the suggestion was horribly exciting. But just then the American actor, whose chairs were nearby, called in his famously resonant voice, "One of you people want a lift into town? I'm heading in, take you, pleased to."

"That's very kind of you," George replied. "There you are Ned."

Amy had turned on her elbow to look at the actor under the brim of her hat. "I ought to go back too," she said; "would there be room for me?"

"Sure," he said, pushing his chairs aside and standing up, "let me just climb out of my bones and I'll meet you on the car lot."

30

Amy and he disappeared to change. George lay on his back with his eyes closed. "What about your driving licence?" I reminded him. He said nothing, tightening his mouth angrily. "I expect Amy's forgotten. I'll tell her," I said.

Then he opened his eyes. "For Christ's sake stop pestering people about the law Ned and leave me alone," he said savagely. His eyes burned on me. I went out to the car park.

When I got back to my flat from the Embassy that evening it was empty. George had packed and left. There was no note, but what touched me was that he had made out of his sheets and pillow an arrangement called at our private school, when we folded our bedclothes at the end of term, a "coffin". That was a note of sorts, for it reminded me how much past we shared, and I read in it George's wish to make his peace with me. I regretted the small ways I had shown my irritation with him, by keeping him short of Coca-Cola for instance, for the flat was empty and lonely without that tautness of his like a wound clock ticking.

I re-immersed myself as best I could in work which seemed for some time jejune and unsatisfying. Invitation lists for receptions had to be drawn up and squabbled over; letters of condolence to the widowed wives of Italian politicians had to be concocted in overblown language which debased all genuine feeling; tiresome English friends of Foreign Office bigwigs had to be met at the airport; occasionally the entire cabinet of a newly-independent African colony would swing and chatter into Rome. I remember ringing up the Minister For Naval Matters (as he styled himself) of one of these countries—to warn him that Geneva, where he planned to go next, was not as he supposed the capital of Switzerland—and being told by one of his many private secretaries that "De Minister is in de barf". George's strictures on the diplomatic life recurred to me as days filled with trivia dragged by.

It isn't that you have to think this trivia important, but you have to keep a zest for it, or at any rate be amused by it if everyday life is to remain worthwhile; and I couldn't be bothered to enjoy my running battle with the Military Attaché, all of whose additions to invitation lists I automatically crossed out; nor could I even laugh at the pomposity of the Minister For Naval Matters. The direction from which pins were stuck into pieces of paper was a subject I could raise no enthusiasm about as I sat behind my barred and dusty window which the sunbeams teased for half an hour each morning.

And then in June Amy rang up. She asked me to go for the weekend to a villa on the coast. "Whose house is it?" I asked.

"It's Leonardo's but he doesn't dare ask you. And you see my love I can't go if you won't come to befriend me. So I beg you on my poor bended knee."

I agreed to go. I was surprised how elated I felt. It was Friday afternoon and I had to meet her at her rooms in an hour—the rush was elating, minutes mattered as if the clocks had been set ticking again. When I told the Third Secretary that something vitally important had come up and he would have to represent me at the Japanese Musical Evening, I believed the lie myself. Though my heart quailed at the gang-like menace of Leonardo and his friends, at least the tension took up the slack and pulled taut a connection between myself and the sunny world beyond the window's bars.

When I arrived at her address on Via Regina Margherita I found a notice pinned up, written in her childish hand with its large round o's, which said, "Amy one floor up". It reminded me of the notices you see in Soho: my heart beat faster. It looked the kind of shabby building, cavernous stone reverberant with passing trams, where anything you put down would be stolen, so I carried up my suitcase and knocked on her door.

"It's open my love," she called. There wasn't a lock between herself and the street, nor a curtain or shutter against the roar of traffic which bombed the room through open windows. At the table she sat peacefully drawing. She held up her face to kiss me, and as I stooped I saw the drawings: charcoal sketches of myself, like, but so bald and fat that I was chagrined. If that was how she saw me, it took the wind out of my elation at going to the sea with her. I didn't dare kiss her.

"Like them?" she asked.

"You're very good at drawing."

She lifted the top sheet. On the pad below was a male nude. Again the head was mine. She sketched my striped swimming trunks over it. "Only guessing," she said. "Now I must pack my belongings in a light plastic bag for the adventure."

The noise of traffic was so violent that it was like a physical assault, the whole building shaking and rattling as if in some cataclysmic disaster. In a cage on the floor two small seedy birds huddled on a perch with their eyes closed. I looked out of the window for a moment and then turned to say something. Amy had undressed. She stood with her naked back to me, rather heavy in the hips, reaching for a dress from a hanger. When she had shaken this short smock over her head she turned and saw that I was watching. She gave me a look of complicity like a child that wants to involve you in being naughty. "No-one'll know will they?"

"Know what?"

"That I'm bare."

I looked away. "What about the birds?" I asked.

"We have to take them to my friend." Bending over the cage she asked them, "Why are you so peaky my loves?" She neither closed the window nor locked the door when we carried the birdcage and my suitcase and her plastic bag downstairs. On the pavement she said, "There's one thing I want to do, do you mind my love?"

"What is it?"

33

"You know George's mother is buried in Rome, well can we go and see?"

"Did George tell you?"

"Yes, but he wouldn't go."

George: he arose like a shadow between us. I knew that his mother's death was locked in the darkest recess of his mind. She had died in Rome a year after George's elder twin, and during that year she had never for an hour ceased to grieve for her son killed by George in the "accident" on the lawn at Saradon. I wasn't surprised that he wouldn't take Amy to her grave. "Yes I'll go with you if you want," I said.

We left the birds in a café where a child-waiter, evidently enslaved by Amy, who talked to him in a purring jumble of languages, took charge of them. The word *uccelli* was a great joke between them. In the street was an open Alfa Romeo which Amy told me to put the luggage into. I recognized the car with a heart-pinch of jealousy. "It's that actor's car," I said.

"Isn't it fabulous?" she enquired tentatively, as if trying on someone else's character and vocabulary. It didn't fit her; my jealousy ebbed because she evidently didn't think it "fabulous" at all. "Nippy too," she said in her own character as we bounded into the traffic.

At the Protestant Cemetery we rang the gate-bell and were admitted into the atmosphere which more than anywhere in Rome reminded me of a garden at home. Compost heaps and a potting shed, the smoke of a bonfire, and grass under tall trees; the soughing of the cypresses might have been the wind in the pines and cedars at Saradon. Amy poked her arm through mine; her fingers on my wrist communicated a tremor of fear which their pressure at the same time stilled, her touch giving and receiving both comfort and excitement. When we reached George's mother's grave there was a vase of decayed roses on the grass mound. Only George could have put them there. He had come alone. I had betrayed him by bringing Amy.

34

On the stone was lettered "Dorothy Tilton, of Saradon in the county of Cheshire".

Amy said, "I always wondered how you spelled Saradon."

That she should see the name, which figured so large in our family, first written upon a tombstone inspired me with foreboding. I had let her into our vault. When I looked at her, the tears were making their way down the side of her nose and on an impulse I put my arm round her. Unfortunately my hand caught the hem of her skirt and pulled it up round her waist. She struck out savagely at me—and then she laughed. "Sorry my love, I thought you were attempting a liberty," she said, pulling her smock down. She added as she looked round almost hopefully for watchers, "Do you think anyone saw?"

"I think they're all dead," I said, gasping a little from her elbow in my stomach. She had a hair-trigger mechanism in defence of herself. She never forgot her body; indeed she had only cried, I am sure, at the graveyard's threat to her youth and vigour which were all the world to her, for now she stepped happily away down the alley of tombs, reminded by the touch of a man's hand of her advantages over the dead.

Out of Rome on Via Aurelia the battering of the wind in the open car made it impossible to talk, but trailing a truck we couldn't overtake Amy shouted at me earnestly, "Is *Pilgrim's Progress* a good read?"

"On the sober side."

"Who's Giant Despair?"

"I'll lend you the book if you like."

"Oh I wish I'd read it," she cried. Then the exhaust howled as we tore past the truck, the wind tattered her hair, and once more we were isolated with our separate thoughts. The long straight road and the horizon raced towards us and fled by the windows. Looking out upon the winds with glorious fear, thoughts blown to shreds, I let the storm drive me where it would like a ship running free. I had never known that driving fast was such fun.

With the sun sinking we turned towards the sea and drove towards a solitary dark mountain against the west. Then again we turned, onto a dust track which climbed through rough maquis clothing the mountain slope, wild country in the dusk. Below was the shimmer of olives, and the silver sea crawling with light. I said to Amy how beautiful the olive trees looked.

"Oh show me the olive tree," she asked with that dishonest eagerness.

We soon reached the courtyard of an old farm amongst holm oaks and stone pines, a darker bulk in the dusk, and there Amy cut the engine. In upon the silence came stillness, and the scent of broom off the mountain. We sat in our places. The drive had been like the rush of air as you dive from a high board, succeeded now by the mysterious slow silence of the depths. There was the flutter of a night-moth's wing against the windscreen. Trying to catch it Amy said, "Do you think it matters?"

"What?"

"Us coming here together. I mean," she said, half-turning towards me, "we might be put in the same bedroom."

I tried to digest this idea. "Matters to whom?" I asked shakily.

"To George of course."

George. Everything was George's. I said nothing.

"If we are in the same room no hanky-panky. You see Leonardo's got this girl-friend so I couldn't come alone you see."

"I don't see, but don't worry, I won't attack you."

"Why, don't you want to?"

"That's beside the point."

"I don't see how it's beside the point. I mean either you want to have sex or you don't."

She made sex sound like a commodity or an operation. I said, "What I might want, and what I will do, are two different things."

Still chivvying the moth she frowned. I might as well have explained to the moth why a partition of solid air (as the windscreen must have seemed to it) should exist in the midst of apparent freedom, as explain to Amy the existence of a moral law. "We'd better go in now we're here," I said.

She blared the horn. Floodlighting burst from the house onto the courtyard and the shocked dusk retreated behind a wall of blackness. I watched Amy get out of the car and face the streaming brilliance, her features harsh with chiaroscuro, her skin flashing like shellac. Two figures, Leonardo and a tall girl, appeared arm in arm from a doorway at the top of a stone stair, casting gigantic shadows. Martial music of the Third Reich foamed through the door behind them. They waited for us to mount the steps; I would sooner have climbed a scaffold, though I did not yet know what crime I was to be punished for.

III

THAT WAS IN the month of June. In August I had some leave and went to England, where I spent a short time in London lunching or going to the theatre with fellow diplomats posted at home, or with contemporaries whom I regarded out of custom as old friends. They were no longer in fact friends, for an annual lunch and a Christmas card hadn't kept me in touch with the development of their lives; but I had no-one else to see, and our rather barren and regressive discussions about the old days which were all we had in common, whilst their wives sat politely smiling, had to pass muster as friendship. After a week I took a train to Hooton and a taxi thence to Saradon.

The perimeter of the estate was guarded by iron railings, curved over at the top and painted white, on a corner between the village and the house. Railings of this pattern, which as children we had thought was unique, were known to us as "Saradon railings" so that when we were car sick their appearance was a longed-for sign that we were almost home. Later, when I saw them elsewhere, they always made me homesick; and when I first glimpsed them on this particular corner on my way back from school, my heart would bound. As I passed them now in the taxi the sight of them filled me with homesickness unrequited, for the sandstone piers of the drive gates through which we turned no longer led to my home.

It was to be a family party. My mother and father were on their annual visit from Antigua, where they had gone to live when George came of age and took over Saradon —pottering off like a pair of dying elephants, ostensibly "for tax reasons" but in reality because my father, since he couldn't live at Saradon or the Scottish lodge, Ardnagour, had inflicted a beach bungalow upon himself and my mother as a fiery purgatory before their souls could wing back to the flat and rainy Cheshire landscape, which was their paradise. As well as my parents, it was rumoured that George's sister Leonora would try to spare us a few days from her exalted socializing.

Such were the complexities this family party presented that I had the taxi driver set me down at a point where the front drive branched to the kitchens and stables, and was screened from the house itself by an evergreen shrubbery of hollies and yews. Dropped like a paratrooper I could approach unannounced on foot. Rain threatened from the clouds pushed in from Wales, and the oaks in the flat park stood sorrowfully expecting the worst. Past the mirroring black window of the library I approached the porch, a landing-stage of yellow brick in the lake of asphalt. I wouldn't think of the day a kingfisher had dashed itself to death against the library window, or of the day George's brother had picked toadstools into our nanny's umbrella and put it in the porch for her to open over her head, or the day, or any of the days that wreathed Saradon with withered flowers, like the blown roses on George's mother's tomb in Rome. I bent down to open one of the two tall glass doors that faced me inside the porch.

It pushed in with its slight individual click. Like the click in an amnesiac's head which restores his memory, the click of the door flooded my mind with total, unstemmable recall of Saradon. There was no use trying to keep it out.

I carried my bag between the oak settles, the closed doors and dark engravings of the hall, knowing against my will what each contained, and mounted the curved staircase. The house as always was immutably still, and scented with its own fragrance from pot-pourri in Chinese dishes and the polish on furniture. On the long dim landing a wink of light gleamed like an eye in a copper fish-kettle. I knew the sound the copper made when you lifted the lid to look inside at hunt-the-thimble. I knew everything about Saradon.

Nothing stirred in the house. Mrs Winder must have heard my taxi but neither duty nor inclination led her to welcome visitors. That I looked out first for Mrs Winder was an acknowledgement that times had changed, for she had only been housekeeper for four or five years, but George had enshrined her as the genie of the place, and the place was George's. I walked towards my old room at the far end of the landing. I had always felt justified in having the "best" children's room—that is, not a disused nursery but a room at the front of the house—by merit of seniority; when realization came that George was the heir I had still stayed there, in guilty grandeur. I stepped over the bald head of the tiger-skin which guarded my room and opened the door.

Mrs Winder was turning down my bed, as was her invariable rule at whatever hour one might enter one's room. She had no doubt heard me arrive. She gave her customary frightened start. "Ah so you've come Mr Ned," she said dolefully through tight lips; "we didn't know just when to expect you, with the strikes."

She creaked about the room pushing ornaments fractionally out of place whilst we discussed the industrial unrest she feared, and I unpacked. Whatever other significance she might have, Mrs Winder embodied the Scottish counterpoint of Saradon, a refrain noted in stags' heads in the gunroom, in rodboxes labelled "Inverness", and in sepia photographs of Ardnagour on the billiards' room walls. Like James I's Scottish courtiers she complained about everything English in her thin voice whilst pocketing whatever she could lift. "Of course you'd be in the know now Mr Ned," she accused me, pushing her sour grey face and scraped hair towards me; "but we'll have no peace I say till these students and such are punished and put to work. Do you agree with these grants do you? I know I don't. Ah well I must away to my kitchen while I have a minute. Now you've come I must see what's to do. There's that many in the house already. You'll have heard who's here?"

"Yes I know who's here."

"We're all that surprised at Mr George."

"Thank you Mrs Winder."

She drew her mouth tight like a drawstring purse and her eyes sparked with vexation, but she went. I hate to be told things by servants but I did wonder as I unpacked who it was staying in the house that she disapproved of. I didn't bother to take out of my suitcase *Paley's Evidences*, which I had brought as a holiday task (and had read a good deal of in London), because I knew that I would re-read one of the dog-eared books in the bookcase, all relics of crazes, from *Cricket My Life* by Norman Yardley through Lancaster's *Art of Shooting* to *Merry Slimtails*, which was about mice.

Still reluctant to join the complexities of a family party I went down a couple of steps off the landing to the nursery lavatory. Attached to the cistern handle was a label upon which my father's faded writing still gave the order "Press down firmly ONCE". The hand was small and neat, the capitals rising unevenly as his peppery voice rose from his small neat figure when such things as plumbers' bills enraged him. When I went into the nursery bathroom next door to wash I was shocked to find it twice the size and gleaming with new pink enamel. Then I realized what George had done: he had included into it the old bedroom next door, his twin brother's room. Twenty years ago Tim had charged out of that room, shouting boisterously no doubt, to hammer George's bowling all over the lawn for the last time. Time hadn't obliterated memory. Perhaps workmen whistling, and pink enamel, had exorcized it. To see what else George had vandalized I walked softly along the passage. At the open nursery door I stopped short.

Amy was reading on the window seat. She sat against the grey light with her legs drawn under her and her hair, like the petals of a dahlia, flopping over her face. Her finger traced the words across the page. I retreated. The image I carried away was of a butterfly trapped against the nursery pane.

"We're all that surprised at Mr George." I was as surprised at Amy. I hadn't seen her since the last ridiculous incident of our ridiculous weekend together; I had insisted on being put on a train to Rome on the Saturday, and Amy had managed to get herself carried away on the train with me until it could be stopped at a wayside halt where the signalman, who was playing *The Gondoliers* on a gramophone, telephoned for a taxi to take us bumping back across the fields to the original station whence I started once more, hours later, for Rome. "Having crossed the R-hubicon" Amy kept singing, her voice creaming over with delight at what she called "the adventure". Back in Rome—indeed before my train reached the city—I began to think that I had behaved in an overwrought manner, and I sent her *Pilgrim's Progress* as an overture. But she made no sign. It had been an "adventure". An adventuress, she had forgotten it.

It wasn't surprising. When I looked at myself, straightening my tie in a looking glass on my way outside to meet the family at last, I saw what Amy had sketched, a plump unromantic puritan face. I accepted what my treatment by Amy had made apparent: this plain face was not someone else, was not an outrageous disguise, not just the appearance but the truth, myself as I was condemned to be. You aren't obliged to be grateful to girls who make the truth apparent to you. I suspected the motives of an adventuress who came as far out of her way as a family party in a country-house. So no doubt did Mrs Winder. I walked out between the camellias of the glass-domed loggia into the damp green garden.

A grass terrace surrounds a sunken rose-garden, then lawns extend under cedars to the ha-ha. Across the park you can see the rust-coloured dutch barns of the farm, and the meagre steeple of the village church, whilst away to the right the lawn curves out of sight to a croquet pitch from which came the excitable cries of Tiltons playing games. I approached them by a mossy path ribbed with tree-roots—cause of many a bicycling smash—and stood by the rose-twined summerhouse watching the game. At golf croquet George was playing the blue ball and the black against my mother and father. He was on all fours lining up a shot, crouched like a gloomy spider on the grass whilst they waited, my mother glancing nervously up at the sky and my father swinging his mallet in a meticulous arc. He was a small neat man. His pinched collar and tightly knotted tie prevented easy or quick movements of his head. The hair laid across his pate was thin and silvery. Yet despite the dapper neatness I saw now, there lurked, for me, traces of ogrishness in his bulging eye and domineering nose—the largeness and hairiness I remembered from his prickles and cigar smoke when I used to reach up my face to be kissed goodnight.

"Come along George," he rasped, "we'll be rained off else."

"I think it's spitting already," my mother conjectured, holding out her hand as if expecting God to smack it. "Or maybe not just yet," she added typically.

George paid them no attention whatsoever. Eventually he dropped his cigarette on the grass and played a fine in-off. I stepped onto the lawn. George saw me first. "Hallo Ned," he said, "you can be blue. We're three up and four to play, red's shot." He stooped for his cigarette.

My father's firm grasp—a diffident brush with my mother's cheek, and her hand squeezing mine—I was re-absorbed into the family and into the game. My mother's *sotto voce* questions were silenced when my father called "Come along yellow, we're all waiting. Now just try for position and don't get in my light."

Rain had begun to fall, pattering on my mother's macintosh hat, sparkling in George's hair, causing my father to button his jacket across his throat. I assumed the name of Blue, Black George's junior partner, and the eternal strife of Blue and Black against Yellow and Red descended upon the croquet lawn, as though the colours were ever-warring gods and we their avatars. The performance of the balls, as always at croquet, was consistent with their drivers' character: my mother's ball trailed along behind my father's, ineffectual on its own and only appearing at the hoop in time to thwart some tremendous plan he had envisaged, so that whilst Red huffed and puffed and stamped his feet Yellow apologized in her mild wailing tone, and Black crowed. Because the venom was directed against colours rather than against people it was not deemed unmannerly, but it was surprising the amount of malice which the game released in one's heart. Many an old score could be paid by knocking Red into the ha-ha.

"Hallo there!" my father sang out, making us all turn.

Amy was wandering over the lawn in a decayed burberry borrowed from the cloakroom and a yellow sou'-wester worn back to front.

"Come and take my mallet," my father called. When she floated up he said, "Forgive me, you don't know my boy Ned."

"Yes we do." It irritated me that my father played the host. I kissed the rainy cheek which Amy offered. "Do you want to play?"

"Oh!" George pursed his mouth and emitted his prim groan. "She doesn't know how to play."

"Better learn. Come along, turn and turn about." My father pushed his mallet into her hand. George had begun to shiver.

"Shall I pop it through the hoop?" she enquired.

"Bit of a long 'un, I'd go for decent position, about here."

"Oh play!" George groaned. "You know I have one less layer of subcutaneous fat than anyone living."

"I think I'll pop it through," Amy maintained.

"Here, half a tick, hold the mallet like so——" my father, in trying to alter her grip, pushed the handle of the mallet through her open raincoat into her dress and entangled it in poppers which unpopped to reveal her generous bosom. He fell back abashed whilst Amy squeaked and gurgled.

44

George shaking his head enquired in his scratchy tone, "Why is it Amy that wherever you go life is a continual French farce?"

Pinched and grey with sudden cold, for he never wore enough clothes, he fretted into the summerhouse where he wearily put down his mallet. The tension of the match had been unstrung by Amy's arrival, and tautness of another kind replaced it. The rest of us trailed behind him towards the house through the drizzling rain. Amy called, "Oh George, someone rang up, that's what I nipped out to say. Might he be called Gilbert?"

"Archy Gilbert?" my father broke in, always ready to bag a name; "I know old Archy Gilbert, why don't we have them over?" George stalked ahead, stooping occasionally to pull a grass-bent. My father went on, "Always like to rag old Archy."

"It isn't Archy Gilbert," said George over his shoulder. "It's a friend of mine from London."

"Probably the son is it?"

"I doubt it. My friend's a darkie."

Although this was probably not true it silenced my father. The party split to attack the house by different entrances. Amy and I were left together. She suddenly laughed. "What's funny?" I asked with caution.

She waved the sleeves of her mac at the house in the rain. "It's such a ridiculous house. You'd think it had been whipped up out of jelly and stuff like an enormous pudding. Nice I mean, but a joke."

I looked, but I didn't see what she meant. "It was built in 1886 by my grandfather," I said antagonistically.

"When he'd made his pile in Liverpool?"

"There was a smaller house here before." I saw no need to tell her that the smaller, Regency house had not belonged to my family. My grandfather had bought it and pulled it down when he had moved out of Birkenhead in the eighties. All that remained of the older house was the stable block.

At the cloakroom door Amy said, "By the by I've got

your book you lent me. If you come I'll give it you."

She kicked off her gumboots, threw her raincoat on the floor and padded ahead of me down the flagged kitchen passage which, by the back stairs, was the shortest route to her bedroom in the old nursery. It was the route a child would have taken, past the servants' hall and pantries and store rooms, and thumping up the wooden back stairs; it wasn't a visitor's route. In her room nursery pictures looked down on the virginal bed and a mouse scuffled in a cage. I wondered how long she had been installed. "What happened to your birds?" I asked, thinking of her room in Rome shaken by traffic.

"They died the poor loves," she said, searching for my book. "I think it was old age. They began to look very old, also I think they had sex too much, all their feathers fell off with the exertion. Here's the book."

I took my copy of *Pilgrim's Progress* and leafed through it. It smelt of sun-oil and the covers had curled in the sun. "You read it?" I asked.

"Some bits. Enough to see."

"See what?"

"Why I wanted to read it was because George said the only character in *Pilgrim's Progress* who's married is Giant Despair."

George married: jealousy's miserable pangs pinched my heart. Amy married: pangs just as miserable followed the thought. Watching her comb her fingers through her hair I said, "Do you remember that Giant Despair had fits in sunshiny weather?"

"Did he?" She whipped her skirt up to tug her shirt-tail down just as though I wasn't there. "George is a love here isn't he?" she said. "Much more himself."

I said, "At one time or another he's been a lot of different selves in this house."

"We'd better go down for tea."

She picked up the book I had seen her reading on the window seat and went downstairs ahead of me.

In the long aquamarine drawing room the silver kettle

hissed over a spirit lamp amid porcelain on the lace-clothed table. By the table stood Mrs Winder without her apron; maybe she had put on earrings, or powder, or a brooch, for she was indefinably spruced-up in some way and it struck me that she intended staying, possibly pouring out tea. Perhaps on the previous day some incident had occurred, for my mother too hovered competitively about the tea-caddy. I thought I saw George from his chair make a single negative gesture with his finger at Mrs Winder; at any rate she left the room and closed the door with a thump of mahogany. Without looking up from *The Times* crossword George said, "Do make some tea for us Amy."

Whilst Amy commandeered the tea-making equipment he sprang up, left the room and returned in a few moments with a sugar basin. There was already sugar on the table, and I wondered if he had gone out to make peace with Mrs Winder. Impossible to guess at their private relationship, their everyday life which this family party disrupted, but I determined to keep my eyes open for signs that the Saradon we all saw, life in the old style which was real to us, was in fact a charade. George's tip about egg-spoons had put the idea into my mind. Leonora who knew everything (and had engaged Mrs Winder) would know. Whilst my father pottered to and fro bringing us all cups of tea I asked, "When is Lea coming?"

George rattled his paper but didn't reply. My mother suggested, "Lea is awfully vague isn't she?"

"Vague?" George said, always proprietorial about Lea. "She's not at all vague, she's forever sending telegrams. Contradictory ones mind you, but each a model of clarity."

"What I mean to say is," my mother complained, "we knew she was in Antigua on her friends' yacht in February —didn't we darling?"—she couldn't believe anything without my father's help—"but she didn't look in on us."

"Do you call that vague?" George wondered. "Or

perhaps you're using it in its rare or obsolete sense, meaning to wander or roam?"

To turn into a dictionary was one of George's tricks for making people wish they had never broached a subject which annoyed him. Presently he crossed the room licking jam from his fingers and took out of the lacquer cabinet a tape-recorder with which he returned to his chair. "Now," he said, "I know how musical you all are so I'm going to play you rather a rare opera if that's agreeable."

"What's it called?" I asked.

"Its title is *Emilia di Liverpool*. It's by Donizetti and I'll——"

"Oh no George dear, don't you think you're mistaken? Donizetti didn't write an opera called that, did he darling?" my mother applied to my father, who merely raised two buttery hands by way of reply.

"I assure you that he did Aunt Joan," George said, running the tape to find what he wanted. "I'll just fill you in on the plot: our heroine Emilia has been seduced in Rome so she very understandably joins an establishment in the mountains near Liverpool where one of her duties is to rescue travellers who have fallen into the Mersey. Picture her surprise"—he wagged a finger—"when one such traveller turns out to be her wop seducer on his way from Rome to London. That's the bit I'm going to play you. We start with a chorus of Liverpudlian mountaineers."

My father was already at the door, vaguely excusing himself with duties hinted at. I suspected George of a fraud. "I'm surprised anyone wrote an opera about Liverpool," I said.

"God!" he complained, "the way you all run down Liverpool. And you ought to be on your knees blessing its stones. Every time you traipse off to Rome or Antigua it's Liverpool money that pays. You'd be nowhere without Liverpool, none of us would be. I tell you, when the history of global civilization is finally seen in perspective do you know what'll stand out biggest? Liverpool and Birming-

48

ham and Manchester will. Far bigger than Athens and Rome—far bigger. Manufacturing and world trade started around here, who the hell's Thales of Miletus compared to James Watt? There ought to be dozens of operas about Liverpool; but anyway there's this one, so listen."

He pushed a button and the Liverpudlian mountaineers, if he was to be believed, swelled in like applause upon his tirade. I recognized that George owed two allegiances, one to the classical education that had formed his mind and one to Liverpool for financing that education. So did I, though I'd never thought about it; the time George had for introspection made him doubt his identity, made him wonder whether he was really a farmer, an heir to a Liverpool fortune or an honours graduate in Greats. He had too much time in which to wonder who he really was.

I watched him sitting in his chair either distracted from the music by the crossword, or from the crossword by the music. Amy had opened the bottom drawer of a walnut bureau where family photographs had always been kept—I was surprised that she knew this—and my mother had come to sit beside me. Her hurried whisper began in my ear whilst she scratched at a silk cushion with her nails. In order to shut off her monologue—and to close my mind to her remote life in Antigua, which was thorny with worries I couldn't alleviate about servants and neighbours and my father's heart condition—I asked, "Is this opera really Donizetti?"

When she turned her careworn face upward to listen, the light corrugated wrinkles in the leathery skin she had acquired in the Caribbean. I was shocked to see how old she was. "If it is I never heard it before," she said.

Was it genuine or not? There were no books in the house to refer to. It might as well have been sung in Esperanto for all one could hear of the words. It would have been typical of George to impose a deception on us for his own amusement; but no less typical of him to have recorded an opera no-one had heard of. As with Saradon itself—the whole question of whether the Saradon we saw

49

was an elaborate charade—George specialized in making the ground beneath one's feet quake with uncertainty. He urged you to "face facts" but then muddled the facts with fantasy so that you didn't know where to face.

He and Amy were both lying on the floor showing each other snaps from the photograph drawer. On the sofa beside me was the limp purple book Amy had brought downstairs, which I picked up. It was extracts from the writings of Mary Baker Eddy. Out of it slipped a picture postcard of Saradon upon which she had written *"Carissimo uccelo d'amore* I only wish"; it was addressed to Leonardo del Traffo, in London. Of course I made the connection between Emilia's wop seducer, in the opera, and Leonardo; but allegory only added another dimension of doubt. Leafing through the book I read a sentence or two. "The foam and fury of illegitimate living and fearful and doleful dying should disappear on the shore of time; then the waves of sin, sorrow and death beat in vain." I thought of Amy's finger tracing the words across the page, and I wondered what on earth she made of them, for people who read with difficulty, as she did, don't accept the written word as glibly as do fluent readers. They tend to think that books are true. If anyone ever confused or redrew the boundaries between reality and illusion, it was surely Mrs Eddy.

One morning a day or two later my parents and Amy and I were eating breakfast at the large dining-room table when George appeared. He always looked rumpled and sleepy in the morning, moving tentatively as though his feet were asleep, his face more creased than ever and darkened with beard, and he made his way at a snail's pace to the sideboard, there to stand under an enormous brown watercolour wondering, apparently helplessly, what to eat. Already Mrs Winder had paddled in and out bringing us each a boiled egg separately, to emphasize no doubt the extra work which guests entailed, and she now opened the door bearing George's egg. Because they did not speak I wondered if they had already met. Possibly she took him early tea. Very slowly George was upending a cornflake packet. When it proved to be empty he set it down wearily.

"Cornflake packets," he said, "come to an end very abruptly, whereas in a tube of toothpaste you can always squeeze out enough for one more day."

There was consternation: Amy was on her feet, my father peered into the corner cupboard where cereals used to be kept, my mother looked round for a bell to ring. I was struck by the perspicuity of his remark about toothpaste, though it seemed another sign of under-employed intelligence that he had considered the matter at all. He had carried his coffee and egg carefully to the oval table in the bay window where he sat down alone to contemplate them. In a moment, looking furiously out of the window, he said, "I must be the only landowner in creation to be sung at every morning by blackbirds with flat voices."

From the fireplace, standing with his thumbs in his waistcoat under another big brown painting, my father called across the room, "Don't know about blackbirds, devil of a lot of magpies about. There's a little beggar out there now."

George aimed two fingers through the window. "Bang you're dead," he said, then returned to stirring his coffee.

"You won't have any partridges you know," my father pursued. His almost paranoiac hatred of vermin had caused the estate to resound summer and winter with the explosions of his gun.

"Probably not," George agreed. He cautiously opened his egg. "I'm not shooting here this year anyway."

"No—but—ahem!" My father controlled his rising voice and bulging eye. "Well, up to you, but it's always seemed to me that shoot or not, please yourself, you've got a duty to your neighbours you know, keeping vermin down."

"Yes, George dear," my mother chimed in, "there is your duty dear."

Amy said, "Poor little birds."

It was on her that George turned. "I couldn't care less about the birds. It's me I care about, how I feel. I don't want to spend my winter covered in blood strangling half-shot pheasants with my neighbours, nor do I want to spend my summer killing crows for my neighbours. All the bloody ganging-up, I'm sick of it." In the silence he ate his egg. Then he said, "Do you remember the Gaunt School, Ned?"

I did. It was a prep school near ours which always fielded teams of gigantic thugs with hairy legs and deep voices. George sighed as though he regretted delving up the memory.

"What were you going to tell?" Amy urged. We watched him at his separate table against the plate glass, grey light, grey trees and doubtful sky behind him. He pushed away his egg.

"My first match when I got in the rugger team was against the Gaunts. I was full-back and my moment came when the Gaunt forwards broke loose and charged down on me fly-hacking the ball which I was supposed to fling myself on and save the day. Can't be too bad, I thought, other people do it. My brother Tim would have. So I did. To my surprise it *was* too bad, awful—I swore to myself I'd never do anything so stupid again. But, this is the point, in the bus back our skipper Mason said this thing, he looked round the two or three people sitting near and said—very confidential tone, 'We're the only chaps who can say we played any real football this afternoon'. I was hooked. You know that elation you get from being chosen? Your strength is as the strength of fifteen because there *are* fifteen of you treading all over people's faces—ugh! What kind of game is it to grab strangers' bodies and fling them in the mud? It's gang hysteria. So are blood sports, especially hunting. Gang hysteria. I tell you, if I ever take up shooting again it won't be for my neighbours it'll be for me. And woe betide the world if I do."

Surprisingly mildly my father objected, "But George rugger teaches boys what boxing teaches, that it's not the end of the world if you get roughed up a bit, knocked about you know."

"It teaches callousness, which I think is the end of the world. Physical brutality—next thing is, you're bayoneting people and blowing flesh and bone to fragments. Because progress had bred brutality out of civilized men, team games had to be invented to breed it back in again. You must see that. It is impossible to have too great a respect for the human body. It's the particular—fragile, sacred—temple of individuality. It holds us the way that eggshell holds its meat. We're all of us sitting quite alone inside our eggshells, and I don't want anything to do with smashing even a magpie's, just because of gang hysteria."

I agreed with him though I said nothing, knowing that he wouldn't want an ally. My father rather sourly repeated the catch-phrase, "Make love not war and all that I suppose."

"Love's just as bad, making love," George said. " 'Love consists in this'—I've forgotten who said it—'that two solitudes protect and greet and touch each other.' It doesn't consist in mucking around with people's bodies."

My father cleared his throat. "Any news of Lea?" he asked.

"But George 'touch each other'," Amy pleaded.

"Didn't I see a cable, was that from Lea?" insisted my mother. She and my father were like compères steering a panel away from obscenity.

It was difficult to tell how George and Amy were getting on. You never saw very much of other people at Saradon, for we all had independent ways of spending the day. I never hear that phrase from the Collect, "That we may pass our time in rest and quietness", without seeing again in my mind the tranquil rooms and garden-walks of Saradon. It had reabsorbed me in its continuum; I neither struggled against its embrace nor tested it for fraud, but was content to be unobjective as an embryo in the womb. Small ripples reached me from George and Amy. Through an open door one morning I heard Amy, with her arms full of washing, say to George,

"But do you want me to take it to a launderette my love?"

"Amy, not only is Mrs Winder not your personal servant," George replied earnestly, "she is my life's blood and I will not have her upset."

His life's blood. I passed by. At other times to see them together affected me with loneliness. From my bedroom window I watched Amy jump the ha-ha to where George stood waiting; she fell, and he lifted her with slow tenderness. Intensified came the restless longing, the sense of life uselessly passing, which the Roman sun just touching my office window had ignited. I gazed after them as they walked away across the park, and when the trees hid them my loneliness was complete. To my parents I felt apathetic, avoiding them out of habit: between George and myself stood a distance, greater than usual, filled I suppose by Amy. The kitchen, once a refuge from the ephemeral loneliness of childhood, was so filled and altered by the ambiguous presence of Mrs Winder that I never went near it. She was not the servant of the house, in the sense that cook and parlourmaid had been, but the keeper of the house, the housekeeper, and in my fixed view of Saradon no such position existed. Perhaps because of the torpidity of my own life I regretted, even resented, change or growth in others—as I resented my mother for looking so old. With a sense of the utter futility of the occupation I read *Merry Slimtails* at the window of my room until I saw George and Amy returning from the farm.

Not that I wanted to be with them: there was no point. Instead I ascended the curious Florentine tower which rose from the roofs of the house to give an airy view of the flat country, on the one hand as far as the grey line of the Welsh hills and on the other, far off, the murky bulk of Liverpool cathedral. I thought that George was happy

—for someone of so black a cast he looked happy, like a raven on a sunny day. He seemed to have come to terms with himself; but then, as I had told Amy, in his life he had been divers selves. Tramping the sounding deal floor of the tower between its four glass walls I could overlook the whole landscape of his childhood, could look down on each of his successive selves as I looked down on the pleached fruit-trees of the walled garden or the foliage of cedars or the slate roofs below me.

George's father, whom I hardly remember, had been a thorough-going Englishman who rode straight to hounds, outwalked his stalkers, was welcome everywhere for his cheery temperament, and solved problems quick as Alexander's sword blade; George's mother worshipped him, though, whilst he lived, she wisely took George's part so that a balance was kept between George and herself on the one hand, and her husband and George's elder twin on the other. This was necessary as Tim grew up. A trait of character which was no worse than insensitive in the father was in Tim a coarse, boorish, bullying nature which delighted in taunting and belittling George every day of his life. The maxim *de mortuis nihil nisi bonum* closed our mouths upon the subject, but Tim was a brute. I remember one Boxing Day—my father was in the army and we lived in a rented house near Aldershot but came always for Christmas to Saradon—when, in a snowball fight which as usual with Tim turned vicious, he forced handfuls of snow down George's neck, dragging him along by the collar until George's limpness bored him and he turned, to my terror, upon myself, or to stoning the gundogs through their kennel-bars, or shooting robins with his air gun. Early in 1945 George's father was killed fighting in Italy and all the devotion, all the hopes of George's mother focused upon the twin who most resembled him, Tim. It could be said that she abandoned George. He came to the prep school where Tim and I were already prefects, and I remember the satisfyingly adult feeling which was to be had from discussing George as a "problem child". He

55

wet his bed and sucked his fingers, crept about the school by himself and was constantly in trouble: one could only dissociate oneself from having such a wet relation by treating him more harshly than others did. Yet he could disconcert me: I remember finding him crying after he had been beaten, and telling him, "You really must take a brace and grow up." "Grow up in school?" he retorted. He saw beyond our horizon. But I think he came to realize, perhaps when his mother's dereliction left him quite unsupported, that the horizon of school and games fences in an inescapably complete universe; I think his letter to Charles Atlas, applying for a bodybuilding course, was the first step in manufacturing a purpose-built character as artificial, and for years to be as autonomous, as Baron Frankenstein's monster.

Then one summer's day he killed his brother Tim.

Killed, or murdered? Looking down from the Florentine tower onto the lawn where it had happened I tried for the thousandth time to visualize the event. Rarely allowed to bat, George had been bowling to Tim, trailing after the ball which Tim hit all over the garden and over the ha-ha into the park. Pusey, the gardener who had now retired to his cottage in the lane, told me that they were quarrelling. I think he had seen and heard everything. I think that Lea too knew exactly what had happened: perhaps the shared secret made the special bond between George and his sister. George might have thrown the ball at his brother from close range. He might have hit him with the bat, or with one of the iron pegs which secured the net. Despite Charles Atlas he can't have been strong enough to kill Tim with a fair, bowled ball unless his twin's skull was unusually fragile. I thought of the "eggshell" George had talked about at breakfast.

The mystery or conundrum of the "accident" remained. Grow as he might, change as he would George carried the guilt in him. He only owned Saradon by that "dolorous stroke". Probably no-one thought about it now as much as I did; possibly the psychiatrist was right in saying that jealousy of George's ownership made belief in his guilt a psychological necessity to me.

After Tim's death, and his mother's death in Rome a year later, my father, who was George's guardian, left the army and came to live at Saradon. George developed his purpose-built character, captaining rugger teams and learning to shoot and hunt, growing to resemble or imitate his brother and father as if his usurped inheritance obliged it. He presented to the world a tough and insensitive enough façade to withstand the burden of what he had done: perhaps it was the only way he could survive. It isn't difficult for someone clever to masquerade as a thorough-going bully-boy if it serves his purpose in keeping the world at bay. Gang hysteria can be used to such a person's advantage and protection. Now it seemed—there had been signs of it ever since his majority, when my father had pottered off to Antigua—that he was dismantling this manufactured character to reveal, if not the true George, at any rate a different rôle. I hadn't Amy's certainty that he was "himself", but he was certainly sure of his part.

An instance came one evening when he and Amy were playing croquet against my father and me in a break in the summer rain, and my father suddenly shouted, "Hoy! You there! Off that gate!"

Amy and I turned to see two children swinging on a gate on a footpath across the park. They took no notice so my father bellowed again. George, who had not looked up, said, "Your shot red."

"See those kids? They'll have that gate down."

"Yes George," said Amy hotly, "do tell them to get off."

George wouldn't look up. "If they bust it it'll have to be mended that's all. You won't have to mend it. Do play, red."

My father played his ball. "Got any forrader with having that blessed footpath closed?" he asked. It had been his hobby-horse for many years, his real motive (hatred of anyone setting foot on his land) disguised behind the usual

57

locus standi, that trespassers will let the stock out. He recounted his campaign to Amy, who sympathized surprisingly fiercely.

"It is interesting to note," George said when he had played his stroke, "that one of the first things that that great socialist William 'Topsy' Morris did when he became a landowner was to close a footpath which ran too near Kelmscott for his liking."

"So what?" Amy asked.

"Insecurity. Insecurity about what you own is a recognized sign of a fascist nature. Haven't you noticed that in your fascist friends, Amy?"

Perhaps because Amy had ignored me I liked her less. It is particularly irritating when people imagine that if they have charmed you once you will stay charmed without further exertion on their part. I noticed blemishes—that her upper lip was unpleasingly loose, so that her gum showed when she smiled, and that she shaved her eyebrows to make her eyes appear further apart—and I was glad to find her trite. I convinced myself that George too must think her jejune.

After lunch on the last day of my week's visit we had drunk our coffee in the glass-roofed loggia outside the morning room when Amy, pulling the glazed green leaves off the camellia behind her chair, asked, "Couldn't we have a little outing George? See the sights?"

"Do you know any sights Ned?" George said.

"You could go to Parkgate."

"Been there," Amy replied.

"There's always Liverpool," I suggested jokingly, "the Athens of the North—according to George."

George chucked aside the newspaper. "Come on, we'll go to Liverpool," he said, rising from his wicker chaise-longue. "I'll just take the coffee things to Mrs Winder and meet you at the garage. You come too Ned, it'll cure you of mocking your origins."

When Amy and I reached the sandstone coach house she said, "Has George shown you the new upstairs?"

"Upstairs where?"

"Come and look."

She led me into a disused garage which had housed the electricity generator, through a dark tack room heaped with dusty junk and up a steep stair to where the groom's quarters had been. Here all was transformed. A long raftered room lit by skylights stretched the length of the building, an apartment furnished with sofas and easy chairs and colourful cushions, one wall lined with bookshelves, the others hung with rose-red hessian, a littered desk, hi-fi speakers, all the signs of constant, comfortable occupation. In stepping through the junk-filled tack room which hid its entrance I felt I had stepped like Alice into a looking-glass world. Amy had gone to the far end of the room where stood an easel and a jar of paintbrushes. George did not paint. She called me, but I was anxious to get out of the room. It was hidden from view, there were no windows to give it away from outside, only skylights; and hidden from my view of Saradon I wanted it to remain. Nor did I want to see how she had depicted George in her painting. On whichever side of the looking-glass reality lay, I did not want to step through it from the side I was used to. I retreated through the tack room into the coach-house yard.

George drove us through the drizzle with his cap pulled down over his creased eyes, and a cigarette smouldering between lips whose shape you never saw, so thin and tight did he clamp them. The wipers flopped to and fro. In Birkenhead Amy saw a sign to the Mersey Tunnel and asked if we were going through it. "No," George said, "though it's one of the wonders of the world, we're not."

"It *was* a wonder George," I said. "It's not any more."

"We're going over by the ferry," George continued. "I want Ned to see how his grandfather went to work each day. It's very salutary for grandees of the diplomatic world to remember their connection with Trade."

"Probably good for landed gentlemen of leisure too," I said.

"I don't forget my origins," he retorted. "Now this is Hamilton Square, fine Georgian houses as you can see." He waved out of the window in proprietary style.

We parked the car at the Woodside pierhead and went into the vaulted ironwork of the ferry station. It was like walking into late-Victorian England: the architecture, the lettering of the signs, it was a period piece. Even the wording of notices was indefinably archaic: "Frequent Electric Trains to Town", and so on. The ironwork over the wooden slope down to the quay was the sort of thing people preserve in museums. I couldn't make out whether George's affection for it was pride, unaware that it was dead as the dodo, or nostalgia. When we went aboard the ferry he wouldn't let us sit inside, and since only I had brought a macintosh I had to lend it to Amy, and my hat as well, for the wet and draughty voyage across the Mersey. The boat pushed through slopping wavelets towards the wharfs and gloomy black buildings of Liverpool gauzed by rain. Up and down the river derricks stood gaunt as dead trees against the low misty horizon. Leaning on the rail George was entranced.

"Smell that," he said, appreciatively inhaling the strong sea-going smell which is unique to warehouses and big ships; "that's money in cash, real golden guineas—you don't smell that in the Stock Exchange."

Between us Amy's hands poked out of the sleeves of my mac to perch on the rail. She said, "It's like the pong in Venice."

I wondered if George knew what I knew, that Amy had gone to Venice with the American actor whom we had met at the swimming pool outside Rome. I was phrasing a question which would bring the matter out—I felt I owed Amy nothing—when my hat blew off her head. It cartwheeled on the water, settled, and bobbed cheerfully away, swooped upon by gulls. Amy watched with her hands clapped to her blowing hair and her mouth a delighted O.

"That's the best-spent hat that ever was," she said; "I wish we had another."

When we stepped ashore under the murky waterfront edifices—the Liver Building with its great windows and Moorish domes as much like a cathedral as the cathedral itself—George set off rapidly. Amy kept beside him but the crowd brushed me off their flank. Walking behind I noticed that five or six of every ten people passing turned to have another look at the two of them—just briefly the pinched preoccupied faces turned under their umbrellas, and glanced, and hurried on. George and Amy belonged elsewhere than the grey streets in the rain. George thought he belonged in Liverpool, but he didn't. He was pointing out shops whose names had been familiar to us all our lives and her face, with her hair streaked against it by drizzle, looked eagerly this way and that like a tourist among ruins. I heard her say:

"I love it when people are all under umbrellas. It's like in cartoons when people have gloom-clouds of worry drawn in over their heads. Oh what's over there George?"

"Some frightful new shopping precinct they've built."

"Oh can we go?"

Reluctantly George followed her up the steps into an arcade which had been erected since I was last in the city. It might have been built especially for Amy's visit, as cities are changed overnight for royalty, so did she revel in the brilliant lights and the echoing Valhalla of pop music. Heaven to her, it was my idea of hell, and George's too. Eventually we emerged and stood amid the grimy grandeur of Liverpool's public buildings whilst cars and buses sloshed by. "What do you think of that?" George shouted at me through the traffic's noise.

I looked at the black peristyles glooming upward into the rain. "Athens with soot on it," I said. "They're only copies George, it's only imitation grandeur."

"Let me tell you this," George shouted, "you look at Pittsburgh, go and look at Mestre, look at any industrial landscape in the world and what you'll see are copies of the landscape of the Black Country. Okay so this is Athens with soot on it: the soot's what's important. We didn't copy soot from anywhere, we invented it. Soot is England's contribution to world civilization. Soot—aah!" He inhaled like the Bisto kids. "Do you want to go in the Walker Art Gallery?"

I was extremely wet. I looked at my watch. "Not particularly."

"God you phoney! And I bet you're in and out of the Vatican sopping up culture every day because culture's only to be had abroad."

"All right let's go in."

Just as we were about to cross the street Amy plucked George's arm and pointed to an unsavoury-looking café by Lime Street station. "Couldn't we just have a pot of tea?" she asked. "To freshen us up."

George turned on her. "Tea?" he demanded; "instead of pictures, tea?"

"Just a pot or two," said Amy unperturbed. She stepped out into the traffic towards the café.

George hesitated, which was rare. "Do you want tea?" he asked me.

I did, but I didn't say so; and to my satisfaction he shouted to Amy to meet us in the gallery. I thought her intractability must annoy him. They seemed to have no tastes or objectives in common. It seemed to me, judging by the waves of irritation emanating from George as we walked through the first rooms of the gallery, that Amy had cooked her goose. I looked at the pictures, but it was the names of their donors or collectors which seemed to interest George. "He was grandfather's partner at one time," he said; or "Those are the people whose daughter your father used to take out." Uninterested in his living neighbours, dead family connections enthralled him. He walked restlessly ahead. Soon he said, "Ned I can't go round with you if you're going to make these awful cultured comments people can hear. Meet you in the entrance."

When I had made my way round the rooms I hung about the entrance but saw neither George nor Amy. Eventually an official whom I asked told me that a man like

George had left some time ago: I realized that he had defected to Amy's café for a pot of tea. There was nothing for it but to tramp back through the rain to the ferry. I travelled inside on the boat, and although I examined my fellow-passengers carefully, thinking of my grandfather's daily crossing to work, not one of them seemed anything like so grand a personage as he was rumoured to have been. Or perhaps my grandfather had looked quite ordinary on the ferry, a businessman like those nursing parcels and briefcases on the seats around me, saving up his grandeur for his home circle.

George and Amy were sitting in the car talking when I opened the door and got in. George was saying, "...due entirely to the climate. Hallo Ned, you took your time."

Struggling out of my soaked jacket I said, "We agreed to meet at the gallery."

"Ned you mustn't expect people to behave like robots," he complained.

"How is it due to the weather George?" Amy continued their conversation.

He started the car. "The damp is essential to cotton-spinning because when the air is dry the fibre breaks. So never complain about the rain."

"Oh rubbish George," she said.

"Is there anything coming your side?" he asked her before driving into the Birkenhead traffic. It was extraordinary to me that she got away with telling him that he was talking rubbish. But then I did expect people to behave, if not like robots, at any rate logically: how else can you deal with the world? When George drove us past the Saradon gates I asked, "Where are we going?"

"I want to call on Pusey, do you mind?"

We all got out at the cottage in the lane where the retired gardener lived. Visiting him had been a penance for us as children, for he was a tyrannical old man, always sarcastic. In the 'twenties he had walked up from Somerset looking for work, and, quite irrationally, living now in pensioned ease, he scoffed at everything modern as a

63

degeneration from those harsh days. Beside the concrete path, borders hurt the eye with asters and pom-pom dahlias bedded out with municipal neatness. When George knocked on the back door sundry bumps and stirrings sounded within. The old man let us in and limped slowly back to lower himself into a windsor chair at a table against the kitchen window. There he sat in his collar-less shirt, his waistcoat and trousers no doubt an old suit of my father's, his hands large as two trowels on the table, his leonine head rather noble with its nimbus of white hair against the net curtains—there he waited in the kitchen which smelled sharp with carbolic, a stony idol expecting propitiation.

"Pusey," George said, "I want you to meet my future wife."

I don't know how Pusey or Amy responded: I was aware only of my own response. George's statement rang in my head like a death sentence. A long cold vista stretched ahead of me, a corridor whose every door had slammed. Possibilities of I-don't-know-what, doors I could have pushed open, George slammed. Along the corridor I must walk. The bleakness of my confrontation with the reality, aged sixteen, that George and not I would have Saradon, was repeated. George took all, locked in my face every door. He had taken everything, always, just as he had taken his brother's life because it stood between him and inheriting the earth.

Or so it seemed to me. The facts, so I had been told by the psychiatrist when I was sixteen, were straightforward. All children confronting reality think that they have been expelled from Eden, and look for someone to blame, as Adam blamed Eve, and Eve the serpent. I had been warned then to recognize and repress the symptoms of paranoia. So I escaped from the cottage with the excuse that I was wet and cold, and would walk back by lane and farm and park, perhaps for the last time, to the house which used to be my home.

In the vacuum of reality I saw clearly. In the cool rainy

light I saw Amy's character without her sun's dazzle blinding me. Engaged, her tentacles were sliced. As I withdrew, proximity no longer distorted my focus, and I saw her mind plain as a face you draw back from kissing.

Plain: she was obvious, not extraordinary at all. Anyone could see why George attracted her. Added to his magnetism were his possessions, money and houses and "position", and of course he attracted an adventuress who appeared from nowhere with a doubtful accent and no relations anyone had heard of. I wondered about her origins for the first time, seeing her shorn of tentacles and dazzle; before, it hadn't seemed to matter where she came from. Married to George she would be surprised how much it mattered, for although George might pretend that only his sister Lea cared about caste, he cared for Lea's opinion, so it came to the same thing. I knew that Amy did not realize how integral to George his position was, or how inseparable he was from what he possessed. Until I took her to his mother's grave she hadn't even known how the epicentre of his life, Saradon, was spelled. Now the letters would be branded on her flesh as stock is branded with its ranch-mark. Saradon and Scotland, order, his position and his past; however George had chosen to appear to her, these made up the iron framework of his life. Witness his interest in our family connection with the owners or donors of the pictures in the Walker Gallery: that inter-connection was the framework, museum-piece or not, which was the infrastructure of his life, bolted rigid as the Victorian ironwork of the ferry stage at Woodside. Into that iron vault tripped Amy blithely. She would not so easily trip out. When she found, as she would, that her frivolity and speciousness and inconsequentiality jarred like an urchin tittering in church she would run from door to door. But she would not find them open. Like a fish that grabs the bait in order to catch the fisherman, it was she who was caught. The eater eating is eaten: she was bound to the Wheel. Her belief that life was composed of "adventures" was really an attempt to evade causality, to avoid the consequences of her actions; it was a specious hope that the structure of life is not an interconnected framework but a succession of isolated incidents—a picaresque novel of which she was the heroine. Impaled on George's leister she would find it was not so frivolous. It served her bloody well right.

All this I saw plainly as I walked through the clear water-colour light towards the garden and house which would soon be Eden for another generation of children. What I couldn't see, and could only imagine, was the trivia of why people behaved as they did: had George, for instance, proposed to Amy in that dingy café, at the very moment when I thought her insistence on tea had disgusted him with her? Did people "propose" nowadays? And why had he told Pusey first, before telling even me? Could it be that the idol-like old figure had some arcane power over George, some knowledge of guilt, a hold gained because only he had watched George kill his brother? Where my intellect was lost, my imagination conjured spectres.

No. Tim's death was an accident. I wouldn't admit the flux of doubt into my mind again. Rather I would face the long cold vista of reality. I had the key to Amy's character, and that was enough as a talisman against her attraction.

IV

I WENT BACK to Italy earlier than I had intended and then, after a few idle days in Rome when there seemed nothing to do—except that I took the trouble to verify that Donizetti had indeed written an opera entitled *Emilia di Liverpool*—I returned to work before my leave was officially up. The comforting polemics of minutes, and office rivalries, had of course continued but, like radio serials when one has missed a dozen episodes, they seemed to have got very little further on. The by now bulky file on my Pin Insertion campaign had been returned to Registry in my absence marked by the Military Attaché "No further action required". I reactivated it.

Time passed. A deckle-edged card printed in silver script invited me to George's wedding at Sevenoaks "and afterwards at Fairways, Ightham Drive", but I didn't go, and I heard nothing of them. Nor did I go, as I had half-intended, to Antigua for Christmas with my parents: my Ambassador had planned a Christmas party so that his staff shouldn't feel homesick, and to have avoided home-sickness by actually going home would have earned a very black mark. Paper hats were issued, a comic long-playing record of a person imitating racing-cars amused us after supper and, observing *précédence*, we linked hands to intone "Auld Lang Syne". I pictured not Christmas in Antigua but the long aquamarine drawing room at Sara-don glistening red and green with "armed and vernished holly", its ceiling dazzling with reflected snow, our presents piled in separate chairs, and the bells across the frosty park.

One January afternoon I had to go to the railway station to meet a member of the royal family and dignify her journey to the airport. Because the train came in at the wrong platform the station-master and I flew about the station like panicky chickens until an enormous quantity of leather luggage indicated the presence of royalty. What with the bowing and scraping I didn't take in the members of the entourage until a cool and slightly sarcastic voice said, "Hallo Ned, been running?"

I looked up into the elegant hawk-face and grey eyes of Leonora, watchful, sardonic, armed at all points against emotion or surprise. Unique amongst my relatives, she never bothered me for help or favours, but it was typical of her to appear in this way, and in royal company. Ordinarily I should have travelled to the airport with the illustrious personage but Lea arranged things so that I found myself perched on a jump-seat in one of the cars, facing herself and two of her languid companions.

"You weren't at George's wedding," she remarked in the same abrasive voice as his. "You missed a laugh."

"A laugh?"

"You haven't met the new relatives. George tells me you dote on his bride, true?" The two clear brows arched. "Of course you do, one could see at the reception that she had any number of 'beaux' as her father would call them. My dear her family is the most surprising collection. Gabriel please keep your elbow out of my ribs," she complained to the lordly man beside her.

"Yes Gabby," chimed in the other girl, "even if you can't keep your paws off the senoritas or whatever they call themselves in this bloody dump."

The two of them, from their tone married to each other, wrangled about an incident in the villa they had been staying in near Venice, Gabriel braying with apparent satisfaction at her accusations and Lea impartially acid. I gazed out of the window in a seemly, absent way. I thought of the unreality of my position in the car and wondered, as I often did, what on earth was real life. Hardly this. Then Lea's voice asked,

"You heard about George's accident?"

Turning, I materialized so to say on the jump-seat. "No. I've heard nothing."

"My dear typical of George he broke his ankle. Limped up the aisle on two sticks. In and out of clinics ever since, the despair of medical men. Furious when one quotes that quatrain of du Bellay's."

"How did he do it?"

"It's really too touching—fell downstairs taking Amy her breakfast in bed, can you beat it? In my flat I'd lent them to be engaged in. The facts had to be doctored for the in-laws. My dear the father! Sixty Players a day—arms yellow with nicotine—mad on golf—thanked me for my 'costly gift'——"

"Who is this fascinating fellow?" Gabriel asked.

"Not your type Gabriel," Lea told him crushingly. I suspected that Lea, who had moved up a social class, was riled by George's move down. Claiming George's in-laws as relatives was her way of taking the bull by the horns.

"What does your new relation do?" I asked her.

"When he isn't teeing up for a round with the Hon. Sec? I believe he's what they call 'a big noise' in some department store," she said. "Do you know he offered Robbie Afflick a discount in soft furnishings? Called him 'your lordship' Robbie swears—wasn't it typical of George to have Robbie as his best man? Great excitement at Fairways. Poor George."

"I shouldn't think George cares," I said.

"Shouldn't you?" She rested mocking eyes on me. "He wrote me a very droll letter about his Christmas at Fairways. I'll leave it with you if I've got it." Then she turned to talk to Gabriel and I, out of politeness, asked his wife (who had been staring crossly out of the window) if she had been long in Italy.

"What?" She stared through me and turned to her husband. "Gabby listen, do we rate the VIP room do we? Because you know I can't stand bloody airports with my agoraphobia. Don't they usually organize a little man from our Embassy?"

Lea nodded towards me. "He is the little man from your Embassy."

"Oh then you'd know," the girl said to me. "Is the VIP room laid on?"

At the airport there was the usual fuss about the Press. One cannot do right: having been instructed that this was a private visit I had not told the Press; but evidently the royal personage expected to be news, so I had to find a couple of photographers who were meeting a starlet's plane and encourage them to mill round my party taking photographs, a two-man mob for them to complain of, the men ambling about with long blue velvet-collared overcoats flapping open, the girls comparing dates for future parties with diary-pencils at the ready. Handing them over in good order on the tarmac to the plane's cabin-staff required a great deal of shepherding. When I said goodbye to Lea she pushed a letter into my hand.

"George's Christmas at Fairways," she explained. "It'll make you laugh. Goodbye Ned, will we see you at Ardnagour in August? Try to come; dull as it is I don't want to be swamped by George's in-laws."

She clipped away alone towards the plane, ahead of the rabble but behind the royal party. If she was alone it was because she had moved upward out of her sphere, impelled to climb ever higher by her too-fastidious eye for the faults in everyone she knew. With her family she gave the impression of a great actress consenting to watch amateur dramatics; to watch, but not to perform. One felt apologetic for not being special enough to elicit a display of her talents. Left by her father a "competence" —it exactly described the way she managed her affairs— she had turned it over to a friend in the City who had made her comparatively rich. The ease of the operation rather irritated me.

Still, I thought as I returned through the airport to my Abassador's Rolls, going up in the world would be quite as disquieting as going down, for the world she lived in seemed to me every whit as unreal as the world of Fairways. It is best not to move at all, then you know where you are. I was in an ambassadorial Rolls, as I would one day have a right to be on my own account if I stuck to my last, insulated from heat or cold by Sundym glass, floating behind a chauffeur into Rome whilst I read George's letter.

My dear Lea (he had written on the deckle-edged paper his in-laws favoured) living as you do a life totally insulated from reality you would scarce guess at the joys of Xmas in Sevenoaks. The moment we arrived it was into our finery (Amy's half-brother Terry, who hopes to go into second-hand motors, sported a plastic-leather jacket, a style all the go in Sevenoaks) and away we went in the new Jag to the Golf Club Christmas beano. Elfin lights—paper chains—I gasped with admiration and ordered gin-and-limes all round. Hampered by my broken limb ("Energetic honeymoon old boy?" nudge nudge) hampered I say by my deformity I couldn't dance, but made one of a genial circle round Pa-in-law (as he kindly allows me to call him) whose wife, like mine, seemed a close friend of several male members and was pointing a shoe in the Gents' Locker Room. How we laughed the hours away! All too soon I felt I should tear myself away. "Seen Amy?" I enquired. "Looked in the car park?" came the witty riposte. You and I may think that morals are a little loose amongst our buck-teeth-and-headscarf neighbours in Cheshire, but sister dear, that car park! Every Jag bouncing like a trampoline.

And so on: the letter scratched across several pages in George's school-masterish hand. Leonara evidently wanted me to sniff the bouquet of exasperation direct from his letter so that I wouldn't attribute the malice to herself. So indivisibly linked were George and Lea in their abrasive, flint-and-steel relationship that it wasn't disloyal of him to write mockingly; but I wished she hadn't shown

71

me the letter. I had hardly speculated about Amy's background until now. She didn't need a social context, for individually she carried off her vulgar streak, but George's letter showed me its provenance. What before had been a scrap of light fluttering in the sun he had transfixed with an entomologist's pin, and labelled "Common White".

Lea, who did nothing impromptu, had shown me the label so that Amy's flutter wouldn't dazzle me again. All Lea's allusions were worth following up, so in Rome I looked through Joachim du Bellay for the quatrain she had mentioned apropos George's broken ankle on his wedding eve.

> *Et si mon desir n'eust aveuglé ma raison,*
> *N'estoit-ce pas assez pour rompre mon voyage,*
> *Quand sur le seuil de l'huis, d'un sinistre presage,*
> *Je me blessay le pied sortant de ma maison?*

One March morning I picked up the ringing telephone and heard Amy's voice chuckling in my ear: "Mrs Newly-wed calling my love, and I've got a treat stored up for you. Can I come and stay?"

"What's the treat?" I asked cautiously.

"Me, I'm the treat."

"Isn't George with you?"

"Can't leave him behind nowadays. We're in Sicily having our honeymoon, blush blush, and tickling all over with Cupid's darts, and—*piccolo uccello?* Do I hear you not immediately asking us to stay? I'm going to hand you over to George now." I heard her shouting for George.

"Hallo George," I said when he came on the line. "Where are you? When do you want to come?"

"What?" George sounded at his most querulous. "I'm in Palermo I'm told. I don't know why Amy brought me to the telephone, it was her idea to pester you. Hang on." I heard him shouting for Amy.

"When do you want to come?" I asked when I heard the receiver picked up.

"Didn't George tell you? Tonight, our plane gets in about six is that okay? I suppose you could book us a hotel except old meany hates paying, you should see the dumps we stay in. I've got loads of presents for you."

"Of course you must come and stay. But why are you having a honeymoon so long after your wedding?"

"It's only my honeymoon. George says it isn't his."

My servant had gone by the time I got back to my flat for lunch, so I prepared for their arrival myself, making up my own double bed for them since the spare room had only a single bed. As I toiled about with clean sheets I wondered if I should invite one or two people to supper, but aside from the difficulty of getting diplomats to dinner at short notice I couldn't think of anyone whom they would both like. It brought me up against the divergence between their two characters. Ask the French Cultural Attaché for George, and Amy would have objected to his warts and bad breath; ask Leonardo for her, and George would have spent the evening reading back numbers of the *Listener*. What they had in common was a mystery to me. A bed to share would have to be the extent of my hospitality. *"Si le desir eust aveuglé leur raison..."*

When first he limped into my flat that evening, and tapped with his clouded cane across the marble floor to sink carefully into a chair, I was struck, as he no doubt intended me to be, by George's gaunt frame and exhausted face. Amy glowed brown and radiant behind him, carrying in her matched cases (I remembered the plastic bag she had packed for our weekend together) whilst I, of course, paid off their taxi. In the sitting room George had his foot on a stool and his head, eyes closed, racked painfully back. Opening one of her cases Amy said, "Now my love here's your costly gift."

She handed me an exceptionally vulgar little figure which, if stuck in a bottle's neck, would dribble liquid through its penis. I laughed uncertainly. The trouble was, I

73

could imagine such articles in use at Fairways. And "costly gift" was Amy's father's phrase. George had opened his eyes to complain, "Amy you already gave me that object once, if not twice."

"I know but I secretly bought it for Ned. I only lent it to you because you were so cross that day. Anyway you didn't treasure it the way Ned will. Oh Ned my love it's so pleasing to glimpse you once again——"

She gave me another warm-lipped kiss on the corner of my mouth before running off to the bathroom. Her presence hadn't been in George's letter, only her background. It was her presence that counted. The comatose figure in the chair had closed its eyes.

"Drink George? There's rum and Coke."

"O-o-oh!" came the thin moan, "poison to my system. The medical men in Agrigento forbade stimulants. They were very interested in my case as you will be when I put the facts before you." He grew more animated. "Let me——"

"He was only airsick in the plane," said Amy as she came in. George relapsed. "You've given us your room my love," she continued; "now let's plan——"

"Airsick she says." George groaned. "Look at my hands. Airsick indeed."

He held out his shaking hands whose palms were blotched with a rash. Amy said, "It's only an allergy to the sun George, you know the doctor said it'll go."

"But the sun has always been my friend," quavered George.

"He's been like this ever since he hurt his ankle," Amy told me; "honestly you'd think he was falling to pieces."

"Sorry about your ankle," I said, "it must have been very badly broken if it still isn't right now."

"Sinister presages never right themselves," said he darkly. "Of course it was very badly broken. When my wife says hurt she means spiral compound fracture of tibia and fibia."

"God it was a laugh at our nuptials though," Amy

74

gurgled. "Oh George you know you laughed."

He laughed now, if thinly. "For a bit I did. Not as long as you though. But then it isn't your ankle. Nor, unfortunately," he added with feeling, "is it Mary Baker Eddy's ankle."

I looked at Amy, remembering her book at Saradon, and saw her face cloud. "Anyway it's getting much better," she said. "You'll be right as a trivet soon, won't you my poor cripple? You sit comfortably and talk to Ned and I'll have a tub—oh do tell him George about that man and the tub—and tell him about the plan—then we'll think where to go for dinner." She left the room.

"Ned can you believe that my broken ankle is due to Error?" George asked.

"Error?" I was still thinking of the *sinistre presage*.

"Erroneous belief in the reality of matter," he explained impatiently.

"Does Amy?"

He sighed. "I'd have thought a husband suffering agonies for four months would have persuaded her out of it. But she's so inconsistent. You can't persuade inconsistent people of anything."

"She sounds cheerful," I said. Amy could be heard carolling in the bathroom.

"Only since she decided to come to Rome."

"Sicily wasn't much fun?"

"Depends what you call fun. If you're interested in Greek architecture and mediaeval methods of agriculture it's fun. Not if you want to waste money and 'meet people'."

"What about the man and the tub?"

"Some bore Amy picked up."

The oppressive shadow of George's temperament descended and extinguished any hope of cheerfulness. It seemed to me that a broken ankle which hadn't healed after four months gave credence to the Christian Science doctrine of psychosomatic ills rather than disproved it: unless of course he'd been foolish enough not to have it

75

medically set, which was possible if he was out to destroy Amy's belief. He sat morbidly examining the rash on his hands.

"Tell me about 'the plan'," I asked as brightly as I could.

"Oh just an idea of Amy's."

"What about?"

He sighed. "She wants me to write song lyrics."

"Lyrics for pop songs?"

"What's so strange about that?" He pounced on my incredulity. "I've always written them. Didn't you know that? It's just a question of bothering to market them." I knew that George had a connection with the music scene, but I'd imagined it was no more than a wayward interest in people and happenings totally different from his own world. "I can't think why you're so surprised," he said, nettled.

"It's just—wouldn't you say that pop lyrics are rather jejune?"

"No I wouldn't say that, not even if I pronounced the word correctly. It's not a French word Ned, it's from the Latin for fasting. No," he said, rising from his chair, "the working of Denmark Street evidently isn't your long suit. Don't you rather like my cane? I felt it was time for a psychotherapeutic crutch of some sort. If I am to be a permanent invalid," he added darkly, limping out of the room.

It was hard to make out his real feelings about his various ailments. George's attitude towards his physique, from the days of the Charles Atlas course until his lecture about the body's sacred fragility at Saradon last summer, had always been one of curiosity and interest. Since his wedding he appeared, as Amy said, to be falling to pieces. Amy, with or without the help of Mrs Eddy, had the congenitally robust person's non-comprehension of the troubles and worries—be they psychosomatic or physio-logical—of hypochondria.

Presently Amy came into the sitting room sparkling

76

like Cinderella on her way to the ball in an expensive dress and quite a lot of family jewellery. She sat down by the telephone, which she eyed as an alcoholic eyes a bottle, sideways and with longing, whilst she fiddled with her earrings. "I had my ears bored," she said; "agony but George wouldn't let me wear these till I did, and silly I thought to have them sit in the bank."

"Quite." No doubt there had been great gloating at Fairways over my grandmother's jewellery. Thinking of Lea I told Amy about my encounter with her, and when George reappeared Amy said, "Tell George."

But he stopped me. "Yes Lea wrote and told me."

"I didn't see the letter," Amy said.

"No you didn't," he agreed.

One could almost hear Amy wondering what the letter had been about. Artificially she said, "I was telling Ned about the agony of getting my ears bored."

"Pierced Amy, not bored. Boring is something else you do," he said.

"Oh pierced, bored, who cares, you know what I mean my love."

"It's incorrect. It's an incorrect truth, just as bad as a correct lie."

"What's a correct lie?"

" 'I am dead.' Correct but can't be true."

"Goodness you ought to be a schoolmaster."

"Perhaps I will be."

It seemed time for someone to comment on George's clothes. "Isn't that your nightshirt George?" I asked.

"Upon my soul I believe you're right," he said.

"I'm afraid there's very little food in the flat," I began, looking from one to the other of them. Amy was silent.

"A water biscuit if you have one, a morsel of anything. You and Amy must go out now she's all dressed up." Amy stubbornly refused to look at him. "Yes out you go, somewhere flashy. Take some money Amy, you'll have to pay your way now you're married."

Amy turned on him. "George you know I wanted—you

saw me putting on—my God why did we ever come abroad?"

"For your honeymoon Amy."

She suddenly laughed, ruffled his hair and laughed. "You old fraud, you think you *are* dead but I know you're shamming. Come on Ned let's blow."

We left him with his hair standing on end, in his nightshirt, examining the rash on his hands which he turned carefully to and fro as a necrophiliac examines his trove, with fascinated disgust. That Amy dared ruffle the tyrant's hair showed her power.

"Poor George," I said as we left the house, "he does hate being ill."

"Trouble is he hates himself," she rejoined, "he hates his ankle for going wrong and now his hands. What do you do with people who don't love themselves? It's obvious you've got to start by loving yourself."

"I thought it was charity that began at home."

"Love is charity. Now," she went on, her voice dropping from its strained note, "we'll get a taxi and I know just where I want to go, I promised myself and I'll pay. Come on my love, it's a treat."

She put worry behind her. I thought how lightly she had once treated George's health, joking him about smoking and cancer. She might have known that his hypochondria was not the molehill it looked, but a mountain in the distance: Amy was no surveyor. Yet if you surveyed your friends' characteristics through the objective lens of a theodolite (as, say, Leonora did) whom would anyone marry? How did people arrive at the decision to "propose", when there was so much to be taken into account? In the light shed upon her by George's letter to Lea I could read Amy's motivation in marrying George. Her dress and her jewels were the plunder. What the letter hadn't explained was why George had proposed to Amy.

In the chosen restaurant she ordered the most expensive dishes and set waiters scurrying this way and that. Behind the charade of queenliness she winked at me over the wine-list. "Sicily's so cheap you can't imagine," she said; "couldn't spend any of George's money."

I asked her how she had liked the Greek architecture.

"The temples are a bit wonky."

"Well they're quite old," I began sarcastically; then I saw the sly gleam in her eye, and stopped.

"Darling I know they're old, I know they're unique, I know Mr Baedeker measured them from top to toe—what more's to be said about them?"

"Say they're wonky," I agreed.

"There were black bees in the holes in the columns," she said, "and flowers all around, you never saw such flowers. And George stumping about asking some old peasant how many kilowatts of olive oil you got from every hectogram of fields." She laughed, adding, "He got quite cross with the flowers for using up the rain and me for picking great armfuls."

I imagined the scene, the vale of flowers around the temple at Segesta and Amy picking, like Persephone, the hundred-headed narcissus. And George: "Forth-rushing from the black abyss arose the gloomy monarch of the realm of woes." To Tartarus the king of the dead had taken his bride. Later on I asked Amy, "Are you going straight to Saradon when you get back to England?"

She looked obstinately downward. "Darling the future's the future, it hasn't happened yet. Tell me," she looked up, "rather a snappy idea for George to write songs don't you admit? I mean he's as musical as can be and he's got a twelve-volume dictionary, what more do you need?"

"I'd have thought—I don't know, he might find it difficult to write what they call schmaltz. After all these years writing alcaics and hexameters. And a twelve-volume dictionary—rather an encumbrance I'd have thought."

"I get your drift old fruit," she said absently. Then she revealed her hand: "But I mean—and I mean—and another thing would be we'd have to live in London. Part of the time," she pleaded.

79

"What with Saradon and Scotland? Have you been to Ardnagour yet?"

"No, but I've booked fishing lessons and bought special clothes. Does he," she enquired, "does he stay up there long usually?"

"Three months or so. More when he stalked."

"Thank God he's given up stalking. Well I suppose there are neighbours. You'll come won't you? Do. I want there to be friends in case the Scotch are all like Robbie Afflicted—how can George dote on such a crumb?"

"I don't think he dotes on him." Robbie Afflick was a large beefy boor whose Scottish lands marched with Ardnagour.

"Then why have him for a best man?"

Evidently she hadn't plumbed George's taste in social comedy, the only explanation I could imagine for pitchforking Afflick into Fairways. She sat staring round the restaurant and moodily twisting her wedding ring.

"One of the things about being engaged," she told me, "is that no-one makes passes at you. Do you think they will now I'm married?"

"Do you want them to?"

"There's no other way of telling if people like you. It really rattled me being engaged, like catching leprosy, the untouchable bit."

"How did you get engaged Amy? Was it in that café in Liverpool George proposed?"

She laughed with delight. "George propose! Oh wouldn't it have been lovely if he had? Dusting the knee of his trousering as he arose."

"But he must have asked." Unless she had.

"Never. He told that old gardener man I was his future wife and that was it. I was. Oh I wish he'd proposed." She was in high good humour. "Drink up your coffee my love and we'll go dancing. Shall we?"

Her mischievous look of complicity worked. I wanted to dance with her. "Shouldn't we ring George?" I wondered.

"You can, you know he'd let you do anything. Come on."

She had calculated, rightly, that flattering my influence over George would smooth out my qualms about taking her to the nearby nightclub. I say "calculated" because as soon as we entered the place I realized, with that familiar pinch of the heart which Amy specialized in, that I had been manipulated. Out of the maelstrom of strobe lights and heat, undulating as if the blast of music swayed his reedy figure, Leonardo stepped forward.

"So Signora Tilton, you see I get your postcard."

Grasping his slim arm Amy beatifically closed, then opened, her eyes whilst a smile upturned the corners of her mouth. The cat had got the cream, and purred. She had planned not only that she should be in Rome, but at this place at this moment. George and I and Leonardo had all complied. Of course she purred.

For an hour or more I sat across a little table from them, or rose when they went off to dance and sat down again and waited for them to return. I might as well not have been there, except that it was awkward, coming and going like the Cheshire cat's grin as I was spoken to or ignored, just as I had done on the jump-seat of the car taking Leonora to the airport. This was worse: to be imposed upon by royalty, or even by African cabinet ministers, was part of my job, but to play the gooseberry for a half-bred Italian and a girl from Sevenoaks was extremely poor amusement. Besides, I was jealous.

"Don't you think it's time you went back to see if George is all right?" I said as Amy and Leonardo returned once more from the dance floor.

To my surprise she agreed at once. Gathering up her bag with slow sleepy hands she said, "My poor love of course you're bored if you won't join in the fun."

"That's one way of looking at it."

"It's the truth. You never join in the fun. *Ciao carissimo.*" She kissed her fingers and touched them to Leonardo's lips. He bowed mockingly and strolled away, more unconcerned than she. You could see that there was competition between them as to which should play the moth, and which the candle.

In the taxi Amy's hand crept into mine and she murmured, leaning against me, "Quite like old times isn't it?"

"When did we ever come back from a nightclub in a taxi?"

"My love don't be so literal. Have you forgotten our whole night together? Leonardo hasn't."

"Oh that," I said. That was an example of a correct lie, that we had "slept together" at Leonardo's villa.

"'Oh that!' Charming! Well even if it doesn't mean anything to you I wouldn't go regaling George with our adventure."

I made the connection: I wasn't to tell George she had planned to meet Leonardo. I wouldn't have done anyway, knowing that in some roundabout way he would have contrived to blame me, but I let her lean her softness against me like a bribe I accepted.

Presently she said, "Wasn't it funny meeting poor Leonardo like that?"

"But Amy you sent him a postcard." I was insulted that she thought it necessary to spell out the word blackmail.

"He'd have been there anyway. He lives in that place."

Useless to talk. I let her lean against me. She didn't so much lie as disregard the facts, or re-work them into a more useful pattern. She didn't know what was true; whatever suited her views would serve as truth. And she had never been made to pay for being caught out in a lie because the full penalty is rarely exacted from attractive people. Harriette Wilson is forever telling how she "deceived" her lovers with lies they can't possibly have believed, but which they forgave her because there was nobody like her. I forgave Amy. But I wasn't married to her: someone once said to Harriette Wilson, "Had you been my wife, by Heavens I'd have murdered you long ago." Amy would be wise to take George's temper more seriously than she had taken his hypochondria.

Whilst I paid the taxi Amy took my door key and ran ahead to let herself into the flat. "George George!" I heard her calling eagerly.

She met me as I came in. "He's not here," she said.

"Oh I expect he's——" I wondered how to reassure her.

"Dash it all. We needn't have come back if we'd known."

As usual we had hold of the opposite ends of the stick. Wearied by misunderstanding her I said goodnight and closed my bedroom door. For some time I heard her scuffing about the flat, and telephoning, before silence descended.

Just as I was going to sleep the sprightly tap of George's stick passed my window. By the time his footsteps had turned the corner and entered the block they had degenerated into the limping shuffle of an old man. Knowing George as I did I was sure that this loss of vigour was not conscious deceit but an impromptu worsening of his physical condition brought on by the power of the unconscious will. It was necessary for him to suffer at times an immensely complicated broken ankle—God knows why—and so he "really" did. A Christian Scientist would call it self-mesmerism. Whilst Amy had no regard for academic truth, bending facts to her momentary needs, George had a fierce regard for it; but the trouble was, his unconscious will had doctored the facts which his brain believed. George lied only to himself; Amy lied to everyone, but as the teller of fables lies, or a storyteller spinning yarns. If you ever had to decide which one of their versions of an event had actually happened, it would be like working out a brainteaser. I heard Amy, who must have been listening for George's return, run barefoot past my door; then her low vibrant laughter and George's chuckle when they met. I compelled my imagination not to picture them, and fell asleep.

In the morning there was no sound from their room by the time I had eaten my breakfast. I tapped on their door softly when I was ready to leave. No-one answered so I looked in. Beyond George's shaggy black hair on the pillow the swell of Amy's breasts in the half-light fascinated and yet alarmed me like snow-slopes revealed by the dawn. Then I saw that she was watching me.

"When you want breakfast just tell the servant," I whispered, backing out.

"Stay my love."

"I can't."

I closed the door and went out to the Embassy. If I got to the office later than nine-thirty it was always to find that the lavatory on my floor of the Chancery building had already been occupied by the Minister, who not only suffered from a stomach disorder contracted in the East but also smoked a pipe, a combination which made the lavatory uninhabitable for the rest of the morning.

V

ONE AUGUST MORNING I clumped out of the gun-room door at Ardnagour, encumbered by waders, into the concrete back yard where cars were parked. Amy called me from a Land Rover in which she was sitting amongst the fishing rods with her mongrel puppy on her knee and the radio playing. I climbed in beside her.

"Listen!" She held up a finger.

I could only hear the tinny blare of pop music, crackly and remote in the Highlands as if the world it sang of was on a different planet. "Is it a song George wrote?" I asked.

She turned the volume down. "Now listen."

From mighty pipes against the pebble-dash walls of the yard came the gush of a lavatory being flushed: one, then another, and another yet, until the courtyard resounded with a tumult of waters. As the roaring downpours became gurgles, and the gurgles mere trickles, one could hear bolts drawn back upstairs and down, and the clash of nailed boots on wood or stone.

"Another day free from the terrors of constipation for the Tiltons," said Amy as she turned up the music again.

It was true that we suffered from constipation. Like Luther in the tower privy at Wittenberg (and Lutheran in temperament we were) my family wrestled sternly with excremental devils behind locked doors each morning. The cannonade of the water pipes was celebratory, like the monsoon downpour after drought, a freeing of the waters. Amy probably didn't suffer from constipation; and nor did her puppy which, if Mrs Winder was to be believed, had made a mess in every room in the house.

Ardnagour was a Victorian lodge, stern stone against the stony hill, its main rooms large, ponderously furnished, ceilings encrusted with margarine-coloured plasterwork and flock walls hung with enormous engravings; behind these pompous beginnings the house disintegrated into a ramble of passages and larders from whose damp dark it was always surprising to emerge into the vast stillness and silence of the hills. The glen was utterly silent, for the only road was a private track and the river flowed at the base of the opposite hills, half a mile across peat and bog cotton beyond the bay windows of the lodge. From the floor of the glen hills rolled upward on every hand, patched with birch copses or stands of pine, to stony tops or outcrops far above.

I had come North for a long weekend from London, where I was temporarily posted now that my tour in Rome had ended. I hadn't seen George or Amy since they had stayed with me in March. The first morning of their visit George had rung me at the Embassy to say that much as he wanted to stay Amy insisted on leaving that day: then Amy had rung to say that George had booked a flight that afternoon without telling her. Neither knew the other had telephoned me. Call it independence, call it lack of co-ordination, but it was evident that the erosion of separate identities which must take place if two individuals are to fuse into a unit—if George and Amy were to become "the Tiltons"—hadn't so far affected them. For all their disparities my father and mother were such a unit, locked together like the partnership, indissoluble if irksome, of red and yellow at croquet. I had wondered, travelling North, how George and Amy would function with a house to administer and guests to entertain, for, as well as my parents and myself, Amy's half-brother Terry was staying, and Leonora was expected from the Borders that evening. That they had kept on Mrs Winder was my first surprise, for I wouldn't have thought that there was room for a housekeeper, even if she had been George's "life's blood", in a household which now had a mistress.

Later on in the morning I was sitting amongst the stones in the birches' shade watching George fish down a pool.

I don't see the logic of fishing, since it seems to me that you are either bored by not hooking a salmon or worried to death by playing one, but tradition ordained that everyone (except my mother) fished at Ardnagour. In hot dry weather like the present spell this entailed driving five or six miles down the glen to a beat which was supposed to hold fish in low water, so one couldn't sneak back to the house. I paired with George because he fished tirelessly himself and didn't chivvy me into the water the way my father did. The less propitious the weather the more insistent was my father that you should fish, just as a cold sea and a bitter wind had made him insist on us bathing as children, and had indeed goaded him into the water himself. He was safe upstream, teaching Amy to fish. The amber water lapsed, George's rod glanced, the long line balanced in the air to hiss like a bowshot far across the pool, and I was almost asleep when Amy and her puppy came tripping along the heather bank. She was sporting yellow trousers low on her hips, a shirt knotted across her tummy and enormous dark glasses.

"I've escaped," she said; "Terry's having a lesson now. I didn't catch a single one." She sat on the crumbly bank just above me, giving off lush wafts of scent and sun oil.

"I'm sorry if my father's being a bore," I said. I well remembered his peppery ways as an instructor.

"It's the sun that's maddening him—did you hear at breakfast when I said hooray the wireless man telling there was going to be sun and stuff? Nearly bit his porridge bowl in half."

My father was at all times obsessed by weather. He only kept a five-year diary (so George said) in order to contradict people when they said what a good summer it had been two years ago. At Ardnagour, to complicate matters, "good" and "bad" weather were reversed: the spate river needed rain to bring the fish up, and, since fishing was the object of existence there, we all scanned the sky for clouds and hoped that the frequently tapped barometers would fall to "Much Rain". Because Amy so delighted in the sun I had particularly noticed our obsession with rain. The sun blazing down upon the bald hills was cursed as an implacable deity who drank dry our springs, burnt the track to dust and the rocks to bleached bones, and parched our very hearts of charity. Cursed by drought, like the subjects of the Fisher King, we longed for the freeing of the waters to bring salmon from the depths of the sea.

"Has George always been a mad keen fisher?" asked Amy, lying on her back with her puppy on her chest. Before I could reply I had glimpsed the dark, even sinister, head and tail of a big fish as it rocked in the current at George's fly.

"There's a fish," I told her. "Look."

"Where where? Oh George did you see?" she shouted.

George had turned to wade a few steps upstream so as to come down over the salmon's lodge afresh. "He can't hear you," I said.

"Oh yes he can. He can hear, he can hear me. He just doesn't listen anymore."

We watched his unhurried rhythmic action lay the line again and again across the sliding water. In a glide between two rocks the fish took. I saw the floating line straighten, a coil of it snake out of George's left hand, the rod-point lift and arc as he set the hook. Only when the salmon ran and the reel-ratchet squawked did Amy realize. Then she leaped to her feet.

"Oh he's caught one! Ned look. George, George! Pull George! Can I net it? Come on fishy—come on George. Oh you idiot you've let it go!"

Indeed the line drifted slack from the straightened rod. Immediately, as evenly as before, George began again to cast. But excited by Amy's cries the puppy had started barking at him from the shingle, and Amy was shouting at the puppy. George reeled in and splashed his way out of the river, the nails of his boots grating on stones as he approached. "It is not Blackpool beach," he said through the uproar. "We may as well go and have lunch."

"Aren't you thrilled my love? Cool as a cucumber you

looked out there alone with the killer whale. You're certainly king of the fishers all right." George walked across the heather to the track, Amy hopping beside him. "But why did you let it go?" I heard her ask.

"Because it bit my finger so."

I walked up the track behind them. Against the sun so he said (though the rash on his hands looked to me much improved) George wore a tweed cap, and against rain which never fell from the cruel blue sky he wore a water-proof shooting coat, and against the river he wore black waders, making in all a sombre figure, a gloomy monarch clashing over the stones of the track which wound up-ward through his wasted kingdom above the sunken river. The wet prints of his waders dried immediately in the dust. Beside him Amy seemed dressed for a different hemisphere. "And who is the third who walks always beside you, Gliding wrapt in a brown mantle, hooded..." I don't know why the lines edged into my mind, but when they did it was Tim I thought of, for this glen, and spilling the blood of its salmon and stags, had been his idea of the earthly paradise.

We came up with my father and Amy's half-brother by a pool where the flat black water, scummy, glittering with light-points, made a turn under an overhanging bank. Amy shouted down to them, "George nearly got one."

"Nearly isn't quite," said my father gruffly. He was sitting in plus-fours and a flannel shirt teaching Terry to tie knots.

George gave his rod to the ghillie, a craggy individual eating his lunch in the shade of the Land Rover. "It was only a sea trout," he said.

I knew it wasn't. Then the ghillie McLeod called, "You've no barb to your hook Mr George."

My father smacked his forehead with his hand like a cricket captain who sees his star batsman get out through a careless shot in a crisis.

"That's life I suppose," said George, looking into the picnic basket from which Amy and I had already taken our lunch packets. I had a suspicion that he fished with barbless hooks deliberately, perhaps to take the blood out of blood sports, for he was too meticulous to have lost the barb without knowing it. From the picnic basket he said in a hurt tone, "I see there is no lunch for me today."

Confusion reigned. We looked everywhere imaginable for George's lunch whilst he sat with his chin on his hands and waited. One by one (except for Terry who had eaten his) we approached and laid propitiatory contributions from our packages on a piece of greaseproof paper at his feet.

"Trouble is Mrs Winder's gone bonkers with the Heeland air," Amy said.

"Ah yes it must be Mrs Winder's fault," George replied.

Amy didn't apologize for the catering lapse, indeed I hadn't the impression that she was responsible for the household, less so than my mother, who was continually anxious about subjects such as bread and milk which were traditionally tricky to arrange at Ardnagour. Possibly Mrs Winder had issued no lunch for George as a sanction of some kind. Conceivably Amy had disposed of it. She continued to talk about Mrs Winder to Terry but George didn't listen, he sat apart from us and began a murmured conversation with the puppy.

Of Amy's two guests (her dog and Terry) I preferred the dog, a merry creature which she had called, not unpredictably, Rover. I didn't take to Terry. Although only a half-brother he bore a resemblance to Amy as unkind as a caricature; you saw developed in him the coarseness she so nearly had, the thickness her grace carried, the commonness which her style overcame. What I mean to say is that she was obviously related to this fat lout. My father treated him in the breezy manner of an officer to an NCO, always having at his command, to fit all cases, one of the stereotyped army relationships which appear so quaint in Civvy Street. With my mother I hadn't discussed Terry, steering her away from the subject, which she pined to broach, because I didn't want to hear the aspersions which any discussion of the brother would have cast on the sister. George was so charming to him, and so wooden-faced when I asked some question about him, that I saw he wouldn't be drawn. The preceding evening George had done something which no-one from Ardnagour had ever done before, he had gone out in Terry's Alfa Romeo for what Terry called "a noggin at the pub".

A sleepy silence followed our picnic except for George's conversation with Rover. Amy I think would have liked the animal to have attached itself exclusively to her—the creatures she had owned hitherto had all lived in cages in her bedroom—and George's friendship with it irked her. She called to him, "Why keep telling him he's only a dog George? You'll break his little heart."

She went over and picked Rover up. George said, "He's got to face facts. He's living in a fool's paradise."

Amy whispered into the puppy's muzzle as she carried him off, "I'll tell you all the facts you need to know my little angel."

Rover would be puzzled, I thought, if he ever tried to reconcile Amy's version of "the facts" with George's. Seeing George idle my father offered him *The Times*. "Want this for your crossword?"

"He doesn't let himself do the crossword till after tea," Amy said, as if George's small disciplines were to be laughed at.

Typically, Terry took the paper. "Just have a dekko at the motor page," he said. He sat scratching his belly, which strained through his shirt, and whistling at the prices asked for second-hand cars. His mouth had a coarse, fleshy look of rapacity. I was glad that he was not and never would be in a position to do me the slightest harm.

My father read the label inside his hat until the message began to bore him. Then he clapped it on his head and stood up. "Well George, where are you planning to send us all this afternoon?" he asked; adding, "Tell you what, I suggest I deploy downriver, take Terry, Amy too if she wants, and you go on up. Ned you happy to carry on as George's half-section?"

No-one moved. It seemed as if the sun had overthrown the military dictatorship. George said, "Yes I'll go up. Anyone else is free."

Amy and Terry had been whispering. "Can we take the Land Rover back?" Amy asked.

George, who had started to walk up the bank for his rod, stopped. "But how are we to get back if you do that?"

"Oh I'll come for you."

"But I don't know when I'll want to be fetched."

It was final. He walked away uphill with the rod springing on his shoulder. "I thought you said we were free," Amy called after him, but he had gone, hidden by the hill. "It'll be okay in a minute here," I heard her say to Terry.

My father tramped away downstream attended by the taller figure of McLeod whilst I, a wallflower as usual, was left near but not close to Amy and Terry, who sat murmuring intimately together and pitching stones into the black river. Amy had kept hold of her puppy so that he shouldn't follow George, and occasionally she still glanced up the glen to see if he might yet attract the dog away. Or perhaps she felt, as I did, overlooked by a presence, by eyes lent to a raven in the blue above, by ears picking up whispers off the wind, by a watcher in the silent broken landscape which had engulfed George. She and Terry whispered like conspirators against a king whose spies were everywhere. Excluded, I picked up George's spyglass in its leather case and ascended the track with the idea of spying the hill for deer.

After half a mile I sank exhausted onto a heathery outcrop which caught any breeze that stirred. Even the sound of water on stones from the river below seemed burnt up by the sun. The very moss was shrinking off the rock as cooked flesh shrinks off the bone. Solitude was emphasized by the sharp wild eyes which I knew were watching me from the corries. Defensively I took the glass from its scored case to spy back at the deer. As usual I couldn't see any, for I lack the hunter's instinct, or blood lust, which attracts his eye to the quarry. I do not feel the bond between hunter and hunted. Bored I turned the glass down-river to the pool where we had picnicked, and there I held it steady on the scene I spied.

Amy was swimming. Now her blonde head flashed in the pool, now her flank glanced silver as a fish as she dived and vanished until again the sleekened head broke the water in a necklace of splashes. She swam for a long time while I watched, so joyous and free that the whole glen was happy and the sun had its point, its focus. Then she eeled naked out of the river onto a smooth rock, and crossed the stones with the light-tripping action of a hind: salmon-like in the river, deer-like on the hill, Amy was more akin to the quarry than kin to the hunters. Then an ambiguous scene took place. Terry, who had been hidden from me by the bank, came forward into my view, his hand seized by Amy. Perhaps she was cajoling him to swim, for she began to unbutton his shirt. But he either broke away from her or pulled her after him (I couldn't tell which) into the dead ground under the bank. From there they did not emerge.

I still had the spy-glass to my eye, and was pondering interpretations of the scene enacted so clear and close, yet in reality, without the lens, so remote, when I was frightened out of my wits by a hand grabbing my foot.

"Spying?" asked George's voice.

"No—yes, spying for deer, yes." How long had he been watching? I shut the glass. "Did you get a fish?"

"I haven't been fishing, I walked up to Drumnakeel," he replied.

"I thought it was derelict." Drumnakeel was a croft high in a strath which climbed out of the main glen, a remote shieling used long ago as a shelter where anyone stalking the highest beat of the forest could lie the night.

"It was."

"You don't use it do you?" I asked.

"You never know what you'll need next. Shall we walk on down?"

"Just give me time for a breather." I didn't want to stumble on the scene under the bank which I had spied upon. "Have you a plan for Drumnakeel?"

"It was something for McLeod to do, patching it up. Apart from poaching," George said. Involuntarily he added, as if ardour for the place he had seen made him speak, "It's fine and wild up there. A world apart. Nothing could touch you up there."

"Do you remember we were never allowed to go there? The roof's dangerous or something."

"Not just the roof," he said. "But McLeod says he and Tim stopped the night there once when they were caught in the snows hind shooting."

"Funny to think of snow up here," I said, squinting up into the heat of the sun.

"*Où sont les neiges d'antan?* And where oh where are the rains we used to have?" sighed George.

Silence and heat filled the glen. Wrapped in a brown mantle, hooded—Tim was near, it was his kingdom still. Always in league with the gaunt and taciturn McLeod, whose hands and clothes were never without the stains of blood, Tim had killed hinds and stags and fish with a thirst for their blood which no amount of killing slaked.

Presently George stood up. "We'd better go down," he said, "Terry and Amy must have had their fill by now."

"Their fill?"

"Cockneys in the countryside get bored."

As I kept up with him tramping down the track I asked, "Will Lea have arrived, or are you going to Inverness to meet her?"

"Oh!" he moaned with a world of pain, "she can hire a car, you're always telling me how rich she is. Oh it's so upsetting when Lea comes. Inspecting things and moving the furniture and asking why we haven't any decent playing cards. Oh how trying it all is."

When we reached the turn in the river we found Amy

alone dangling a fly in the water. She ran up to us barefoot waving the rod and kissed George. "I thought if I could just catch a little one," she said. "Can we go now? Terry walked with Rover. Rover adores him."

In the Land Rover George asked, "Did you swim?"

"I was tempted," she said, "but I thought it would frighten the fishes. My love it's so poignant of you about Terry."

"It's an investment like any other," said George as he drove us down the stony track. "I'm glad you're pleased though," he added, turning his dark smile on her.

"What's the investment?" I asked.

"George is giving Terry the money to buy a share in this garage thing he's in."

"Oh Amy I wish you'd get things right," George scratched. "If you must know Ned, I am advancing Terry a niggardly sum at an extortionate rate of interest."

"It comes to the same thing doesn't it?" Amy said. I feared she was right. She encircled George's neck with her arm and laid her head on his shoulder—her hair still wet from the swim she had denied having—as we jolted along with dust powdering in through the windows. I formed a picture of the entire family from Fairways rifling his pockets whilst she held his neck in a half-nelson.

Far down the glen, almost at the iron gate and cottage beyond which the outside world began, we came upon my father angrily hurling his fly at the river whilst Terry and McLeod watched from the bank. We collected them and returned up the track towards the lodge.

From a certain turn you first see Ardnagour at a great distance, the house miniaturized, the tumbled immensity of the hills all around. I could just discern the glitter of a car at the far-off front door. George groaned. When we drove up to the house he parked behind the strange car instead of in the back yard where we always parked. He got out and shouted through the open window of the drawing room, "Lea can you move your car please."

She came to the window with her tea cup and saucer

in her hand, very fastidious in the wilderness, and greeted us all except George. Then she enquired drily, "Why do you want my car moved George?"

He pushed his cap about his head like a man sorely tried. "Because it's in my way of course."

"Move it yourself then." Lightly she dropped the keys onto the gravel and turned inward to resume her tea.

Lea's presence had the effect of shrinking George into a younger brother. It had always been so, she had always been able to diminish his standing; I remember once when George and I were arguing late at night and Lea had swept into the room in her dressing gown, aged about eighteen, to say, "For goodness sake George shut up and go to bed, you're keeping the whole house awake with your childish shouting." George had withered into silence, as humiliated as he had ever been by Tim's bullying. He was extremely wary of her, knowing that she had once understood him through and through and would never let him forget it, the scornful elder sister crushing his attempts at acting the grown-up. She made him intensely competitive too; at Happy Families nothing could exceed the acerbity of his tone when he asked, "Tell me Lea, is Mr Bun by any chance at home? Thank you. And Mrs Bun? Ah yes. And Miss Bun too? How satisfactory." Yet she was the only one of his family left alive and he loved her: against his will, to his exasperation, I think he believed that she was omniscient; certainly he was very much influenced by her opinion, and her opinion of Amy would be of conse-quence.

In my bath that evening I could hear through the parti-tion wall taps being run and the scamper of Amy's feet on the lino floor of hers and George's bathroom next door. From the landing I heard Lea rap on their bedroom door and ask Amy if she could come in. When the taps were turned off I was surprised to hear the murmur of both their voices come through the splashing of Amy in the bath. I couldn't hear what they said, only voices talking; perhaps they were discussing George, for when he entered the bedroom and called Amy the conversation stopped. I pictured George confronted by the two of them when he looked into the bathroom, Amy amid the steam, Lea on a cork-seated chair. He went out, banging the bedroom door, and his footsteps receded. In the bathroom the low feminine voices began again. Intimate as their tone sounded—Lea's voice asking questions to which Amy's responded eagerly—I would have been suspicious of my visitor had I been Amy. Lea's method was to collect information, make a judgement and then close her mind to any evidence offered subsequently, just as she wouldn't admit the evidence for George having grown up. It was her recipe for omniscience, that she had once and for all decided the issue.

As I soaked in the peaty water amid the brown pitch-pine I remembered how dauntingly masculine the sound of my father bathing next door used to be, mighty sluicings and spongings like an enormous salmon leaping, I used to think, compared to the tiddler I had looked to myself in the bath. Now, no doubt, the steam next door smelled of feminine essences as Amy lay divulging her secrets to Lea, and it was my father, waiting to bath after me, who had shrunk to a tiddler. Everything had altered; I wondered if Lea, by driving George out of his bathroom, meant to force him to recognize how fundamentally marriage had changed his life, and how much he must cede; for nothing could bring one up so short against the realities of marriage as finding two women gossiping about oneself in one's bathroom.

Mrs Winder was Lea's protégée, for Lea had hired her for George—possibly why he had kept her on, as if his elder sister's appointments were irrevocable—and she acted as Mrs Winder's spokeswoman in the front of the house. "George this dog of yours is getting on Mrs Winder's nerves," she told her brother in the drawing room before dinner.

George made tetchy sounds and rattled his paper irritably.

"Come into the hall a minute will you? George!"

He climbed to his feet and followed her, sighing. Through the open door I saw Mrs Winder grimly at work on her knees on the carpet with bucket and rag. "I'm sorry about the messes Mrs Winder," he said. He told Amy who had just come downstairs, "You really must clean up after your pet."

"Don't dirty yourself Mrs George," said Mrs Winder. "It's not him going to the toilet I mind, it's what I'm paid for, but it's my wee pussy he goes for Miss Leonora, aye he comes in my kitchen and barks till Fluffy's that scared Mr George."

When she had clanked away with her pail they came into the drawing room, Lea saying, "I'm sorry Amy, I thought it was George's dog."

"You know what it is," Amy said to George, "it's all because we made her put our beds together instead of having the table with the wee potty in between. It's not decent Mr George," she whined.

"It's foolish to be paranoiac about the cook, Amy."

"Cook! Nanny more like. Anyway I'm only saying what you said, you know she thinks we get saucy up there. Imagine her and her mystery husband indulging—Och, can I give you a wee pokey Mrs W?"

"You're no mimic Amy."

She wasn't, but she kept at it during dinner, perhaps as an outlet for her spleen against Mrs Winder; and her brother Terry, thinking in his dull-witted way that Mrs Winder was a general butt, assumed a Welsh sing-song in which he repeated Amy's imitations. My father, accustomed by untalented company to taking the intention for the deed, was prepared to laugh whenever anyone attempted a comic accent, but George only straightened his cutlery and cleared his throat, whilst Lea made her mouth smile at Amy, her grey unmoving eyes amused at a different aspect of the scene. Mrs Winder was like a bone Amy worried.

George's "life blood", Amy's bone of contention; she was blood and bone of the household, grafted onto it by Lea and now ineradicable. Especially in Scotland she was the *genius loci* or, rather, the chauffeuse of the time-machine which carried us all back willy-nilly to "the good old days". The thick soup she sent in to us, with mountains of potatoes and overcooked greens, and meat for those who ate it, were in keeping with the massive furniture and chocolate-brown paint of the dining room, a diet for the stout sportsmen whose photographs, amid their dead salmon and stags, stared with sepia solemnity from the gun-room walls. By a force of habit we accepted that this regression into the pre-war world was a holiday; but to Amy it must have seemed like a prison, and Mrs Winder the wardress.

One by one the next evening, after another hot and fishless day on the river, we assembled in front of the house for our annual expedition down the glen to Robbie Afflick's lodge, Killaneen, for his birthday party and dinner.

To end the wrangle about who should travel in which car Leonora said, "Come on Amy, let them sort themselves out; can you drive me in your brother's car, then neither of us will get filthy in the Land Rover? Since George seems to have lost my car keys which I carefully gave him," she added as she got into the Alfa Romeo.

"Can I try, Terry?" Amy asked.

It irritated me that she should pretend to forget. As he stepped forward I said, "But you've driven a car like that Amy, you drove me to the sea in Italy in one."

"Show me the gears and things Terry," she said.

George said waspishly, "You can't expect her to remember every little adventure she's had, you know."

"No," Amy rejoined, "and Ned has so few adventures it's sad I can't remember his one. Off we go."

They shot off scattering gravel and George stooped for Lea's car keys, which were where she had dropped them out of the window. Handing them to my father he said,

"You drive. Lea's car would be almost certain to fall to pieces if I drive it."

We all crowded in and motored sedately down the track, children in the back, my father and mother in the front. The evening light coloured the clear hills with rose. My dinner jacket felt hot and tight, like a school suit at the end of the holidays. Killaneen lay at the head of a sea loch into which flowed the river we fished, and as we dropped down from the bare peaks towards its groves of oaks, and saw the roofs of the house amongst lawns and policies and garden walls, I always felt uncouth, one of a marauding band from the mountains about to enter the valley-dwellers' world. The Afflicks had at one time owned the whole extent of forest and river and hill; I was very much aware that my grandfather had only bought Ardnagour from them in 1908, which seemed much more recent in the Highlands than it did in Cheshire. As we drove between the lichened oaks of the drive a steep-pitched gable of the house seemed to sneer at us like a long superior nose. On the lawns, against coloured herbaceous borders, the leisurely groups strolled under trees. When my father parked our car George got out and walked quickly off into the garden.

We followed, my father tightening his bow tie, my mother adrift in her filmy dress, tacking slightly as if into a personal head-wind, and Terry slicking a comb taken from his blazer pocket (he hadn't brought a dinner jacket) through the cow-lick of his hair. With George and Lea and Amy had gone the distinction of our party. I slipped round behind some rhododendrons so as to enter the gathering by an ellipse, on independent terms.

There is no harm in making oneself agreeable, circulating with a glass in your hand, lighting girls' cigarettes, opening and shutting your mouth at people to whom you have nothing to say. Diplomats are practised at it. With a large ebullient girl named Susie I discussed salmon and grouse and the chances of a spate, whilst all the time I was aware of the clean hard line of the hills behind her head, and of Ardnagour high in its glen, and of the highest and furthest outpost of all, the desolate strath of Drumnakeel. That remote silence was why we were here, why we met and talked; it was the point of our coming North, undiscussed yet in our minds, just as the implicit point of a diplomatic reception is not the food and drink but a high unspoken ideal.

There was no harm in the party, unless you expected to meet someone interesting. My father was perfectly happy, for as far as he was concerned, since the moment he first sat next to another boy on a school bench, neighbours were by definition friends; and my mother asked nothing more than that there should be what she called "peepul" at parties, a requisite well-supplied at Killaneen so long as she skipped the stalkers and ghillies asked along in their blue serge suits for Robbie's birthday. George's mistake at Saradon, and the reason for his unpopularity there, was that he expected his neighbours in Cheshire to be as diverse and intelligent as his neighbours in Peckwater Quad at Oxford.

It wasn't a mistake he made in Scotland though, I thought as I watched him circulating the lawn. In the Highlands the strength of an older order prevailed, we were parvenus who had bought Ardnagour with our Liverpool money, and rather than expecting his neighbours to be like him, George became like them. I too felt the distortion of a looking-glass world: Killaneen wasn't civilized, it represented nothing I admired, but in the Highlands it was reality and its values ruled. In the lodges congregated a species shot at in the south who migrated north to regroup and breed, like mute swans, on estates which were so enormous, though desolate, that the territorial instinct had full range. These waste lands were really kingdoms.

Over the massive shoulders of Susie, whom I found (at any rate in this looking-glass world) rather attractive, I saw George talking to Robbie Afflick, a big breezy fellow whose laugh boomed round the garden. George, lean and saturnine, stood with one foot advanced towards the hefty, kilted bulk of Robbie's figure as if their conversation was a sparring bout. For years George had allowed Killaneen to stalk the Ardnagour ground, and to fish the river when he wasn't up here, all of which Robbie took as of right, like an overlord's right over a satrapy; and the relationship of their two figures on the lawn looked one of suzerain to surrogate. Or if you looked again, without the distorting glass of Scotland, George was like a racehorse beside a Clydesdale, as I said to Amy who came up to us just then.

"Yes he's terrifically strong," she said, "I've been chatting him up. I love his kilt, I can see why people feel like a grope up your frock."

I don't know which of these remarks drove Susie away. I was rather irritated that Amy had so changed her opinion of the boorish Afflick, which she had done, as was usual with her, as soon as she had established a sexual connection. She needed to grasp what to her was vital, rather as cavemen drew images of their quarry on the rocks. I remembered the sketch she had made of me in her room in Rome before we went to the sea. Not that I was her quarry. Robbie strode towards us calling loudly to Amy; wouldn't she have a crack at an eightsome reel?

"I don't mind showing a leg if you will," she said. "I don't know the steps or anything."

"Dead easy. Jolly good. Come along."

Amy tripped away and I watched Robbie tramp amongst the girls. He sowed a flutter of excitement, like a man scattering corn to hens, and before long each of the girls he had asked to dance had found someone who would push them seemingly against their will towards the piper, who was a kilted shepherd. Robbie and his father, George and our ghillie McLeod were the men, and with the four girls they joined hands beneath a wide oak on the lawn. Beyond them, beyond the garden, faded the twilit prospect of sea loch, mountain and sky. Now the shepherd drew the first sustained plaint from his pipes; so long as that melancholy cadence lasted, so long as one saw the poised and solemn dancers in their Druid's circle, and the evening star brightening over the oak, there was harmony.

But I am afraid that when the dance began it was a shambles of shrieks and giggles and girls hopping woodenly up and down, though all the while the music played soft and sad to the mountains and the sea. It was Susie who danced first, and I was about to turn away for shame.

Then into the circling figures entered Amy dancing alone. It was as though the melody had been a flame creeping unnoticed through dead leaves, and now struck fuel, and burst and blazed, for in Amy the music flamed to the sky. There was the fascination of fire, and the menace too. As on the hills of Greece she might have danced as a maenad, so she danced to those pipes with the sea behind her and the star above. All the while she smiled like a dreamer on the men she danced with. I hadn't noticed that George was her partner, momentarily in the reel, until an old woman leaning on her stick beside me shook her muttering head, "Aye," I heard her murmur, "aye, they're sair in love those two."

I looked to see if I could read the scene the way she did. But surely Amy danced for herself. It was herself she loved. Wanton as a maenad she danced with any man who entered the circle, but to please herself alone. Now it was McLeod who twined through the figure of the reel with her, his hands grasping hers, and still she smiled. The old crofting wife could just as truthfully have said that it was McLeod she was in love with.

All of us from Ardnagour remained to dine with Robbie and Susie (who was apparently his girl-friend) and with Robbie's father, a four-square old party whose countenance was port-coloured and broken-veined by whisky and weather. As we sat down and shook out our napkins round the gleam of the table in the dark dining room the ten of us gabbled away quietly at first, like ducks in the marge of a pool which reflected silver and candles in place of stars and moon. Then George launched out. His voice scoring a furrow across the mahogany pond set the ducks quacking all around in protest, for they had been agreeing (like Mrs Winder) that the government should punish strikers with frightful severity.

"Seems to me much more sensible," George suggested, "just to pay the dole to people who don't want to work. I mean pay them to stay away, then they can't cause trouble at the mill."

My father's laugh was very like an angry quack: "You wouldn't get a blessed soul come in to work at all."

"I doubt that. In fact I know it isn't so," George proceeded to convince himself; "you've only got to look at all the people you know who are quite rich enough not to work who work all the same. There are plenty of eager beavers, quite enough to operate automated factories. It's the ones who don't want to work you've got to pay to stay away. I don't see the difficulty about that."

"The whole principle of paying people not to work is wrong," Robbie said, shaking his head, "totally wrong George."

"I don't know, the working class has invested in England same as us and I think they deserve a divi," said George. "We all live on divis from our ancestors' investments."

More headshaking from my father. "Quite different. We provide capital."

"Work is capital isn't it?"

"Oh, theoretical socialism!" My father raised neat hands in despair.

"You turning out a bolshie are you George?" called Robbie's father down the table.

"You don't lead a very socialist sort of life if I may say so George," rejoined my father. "Bit like your pal William Morris closing down the footpath." He often took years to make a riposte to a stroke that rankled.

George smiled. I think he caught Amy's eye. "No-one knows what sort of life I lead," he said with great satisfaction.

"What do you mean George?" Lea asked him caustically,

not silenced as the others were. "There's no particular mystery about your life."

"Not outwardly no. Not for those who judge the yolk by the shell."

Amy said, "George thinks no-one knows what anyone else is like."

"I don't think that at all Amy," he complained. "As usual you put a much subtler thought in your own over-simplified terms—which is exactly what I do mean; Amy hears me say something, understands it in her own terms and then thinks that's what I'm like. But in fact she's made me up, she's dreamed me up to suit herself."

Lea said, "If that there king were to wake you'd go out —bang!—just like a candle."

There was a terrific quacking of "What? What?" round the table which George ignored: "You're absolutely right Lea. Only the Red King's real, and everyone is the Red King on their own board, so everyone's real to themselves, dreaming up the other people they need in their dream."

"Do you mean I'm the girl of your dreams?" Amy asked. "How lovely."

Lea however rejected an alliance with George just as he had rejected one with Amy. "You flatter yourself if you think that's a subtle thought George. It's called solipsism, quite well known."

"Oh you're always calling things names Lea," George complained, "you're not a bit interested in understanding things, just in classifying them. Trouble with you is," he added sharply, "you eat the menu instead of the dinner."

Into the silence which his asperity caused my father remarked to Robbie, "Jolly good salmon this, get it this week did you?" To my mother Robbie's father boomed, "Tell me Joan, what do you make of all these chappies in bands stoking 'emselves up with dope eh?" He cupped a large red ear in her direction. Belatedly Terry had piped up "I agree with George"; but no-one listened, for the ducks were back in the reeds, the two Afflicks and my parents quacking agreement, and comfort, on the subject of drugs.

Like the whistle of wings in the night above their pond sex and drugs disturbed them. I knew their troubled feeling that there were wild birds flying in the great spaces above the clouds, following the sun. But I wouldn't throw in my lot with the quackery in the reeds.

I turned to talk to Susie but George, on her other side, was talking to her already. For a time her hand clasped the table's edge beside me like an anchor she had cast out to save herself from drifting onto dangerous rocks. But it dragged away from me as she succumbed to whatever siren's song George sang her. Her robust shoulders were shaken at first unwillingly, but soon eagerly, by laughter as their smooth slopes turned more and more against me. I could hear his voice, the dry scaly rustle of the snake twined in the Tree, offering her what fruits I couldn't overhear.

The table was appallingly badly seated. As a result of Robbie's jovial request that we should sit where we liked the outcome was as unsatisfactory as Musical Chairs. Lea, next to my father, sat in totally self-possessed silence, the slightly humorous arch of her eyebrows leading you to suspect that the food, conversation, guests and furnishing might one day make an amusing story for illustrious ears. Next to her, opposite myself, Amy and Terry sat together talking secretively. Their intent faces suggested that they were scheming, for the distrust I felt of Terry extended to Amy when I saw them together. Earlier, at the party, I had heard him negotiating a price for his Alfa Romeo, telling the young man who wanted it that he was changing it for a "Maser". It was perfectly obvious where George's "investment" would go. Now, as I watched, he filled his own and Amy's glass from a bottle of hock he had trapped in front of him. The two of them gave me the impression of a couple of adventurers bivouacked by the road to enjoy whatever pickings the neighbourhood offered whilst they planned tomorrow's assault on a soft world. Amy looked up and saw me watching. She winked. But I looked away, I wouldn't accept conspiracy, or sympathy, or whatever the wink offered. After all it was I who was amongst my own kind. I pretended to listen to Robbie's conversation with my mother, though his shoulder too was turned on me. Still Lea talked to no-one; but the table was too wide and too ill-seated for us to join forces in our isolation.

When at last the meal was over Robbie's father led the men outside to stand in a row peeing on the lawn. He said to George, "What's your view of this permissive business George? You know any people who take drugs do you?"

It evidently preyed on his mind. George answered obliquely, "Musicians have always taken them since jazz came in. They need them at the pitch they work at like climbers need oxygen."

"Climbing's totally different," my father said.

"I was making an analogy not a comparison," George told him.

"Oh ah? Still don't see what mountaineering's got to do with kicking up a frightful racket in a night club. You done any climbing ever Robbie?"

"So you approve George do you?" Robbie's father continued as we came indoors. "Regular drug fiend is he?" he asked, clapping me on the shoulder.

George never had learned that in company where academic discussion is unknown you are thought guilty of any crime you defend. He wouldn't quack agreeably for the sake of peace and quiet, he would try to establish fine distinctions regardless of the fuzziness of his interlocutor's head; so of course he ended up misunderstood and suspected. We were led into the smoking room for our port.

It was a barbarian's den. Bloodstained clothes and mole-traps and cartridges littered the table under a bulb drizzling its yellow glare onto our heads. The air smelt thickly of the dogs asleep on a torn horse-hair sofa. A chocolate-box painting of a naked girl simpered down between two stags' heads. The only neat thing in the room was a glass-fronted gun cupboard in which gleamed a line of blued barrels.

107

"Good sort of room to have, this," commented my father.

"Well it's a man's room," Robbie's father answered.

He was bustling in a drawer whilst his son slopped port into glasses and now, wheezing with jollity, he extracted a clockwork contraption which he wound up and put on the floor. It was a man and a woman made of painted tin who creaked through the actions of sex at our feet. Their unlovely jerks made me think of the girls who had danced the reel. My father stooping down said, "Get it in Paris did you I suppose?"

"No no Jack, you can get this kind of nonsense in London now you know, great advances since our day what? Now they've done I'll just pop 'em back in the drawer, don't want the girls seeing, what?"

"Permissiveness evidently has its advantages," said George drily, but I'm sure no-one made the connection, or followed his logic.

"Show you where I shot that switch bugger I was telling you about George," said Robbie, chucking a pair of bloodied plus-fours off the table. Exposed was a plaster-of-paris model of the Ardnagour and Killaneen ground. It was a yard or more square, the peaks eighteen inches high, white as snow, a cold pure object like a chunk of Parian in which the sculptor had begun to shape his purpose. Miniaturized, the concept was graspable. On the hill itself, where the ice had scratched hieroglyphs on formlessness, the lines of glen and loch and mountain were scrawled too enormous to read; but above the model you could stand like a god, and almost read his icy mind, almost hear the wind howling over chaos before he began. I saw the black dot marking Ardnagour, the blue river like a vein, the blue lochs; far above them in the snowy wastes another black dot marked Drumnakeel, and still there was league upon league of wilderness beyond. It made me realize the extent of the desolation which we treated so familiarly as "the view".

Stabbing his finger at the cast Robbie was describing his

108

stalk to George: "Finally came in over here and got the bugger in that corrie there. Hell of a party getting him out, left a good half of his meat on the scree." It looked as though blood had welled from the white hill where his finger jabbed. In fact it was port.

In George's eye as he listened, revolving his glass in his hands, was a distant light. I thought of Aldous Huxley who, having quoted as "the earthly paradise" a description of a hawking, hunting, rumbustious squire, says of himself, "With what longing do I gaze upon the scene through the bars of my temperament." So George gazed on the scene he pictured on the hillside. Or so I interpreted his gaze until he said, "By the by Robbie you don't mind if I shoot hinds on Ardnagour this year."

"You shoot hinds?" Robbie looked taken aback. "Course it's yours."

"I thought you'd given up shooting George," I said.

"Seem to recall a lot of guff about you disapproving," heckled my father. The flushed winey faces turned on George.

He stilled his trembling hand. "I don't disapprove of anything," he replied coldly. An icy trickle of anger dripped into his voice. "Surely I can do as I please?"

Into the silence Terry spoke. "There's money in it George. Deer-meat's worth a bomb if you've got the contacts. That guy in the pub——"

"We're not necessarily trying to make a profit you know," my father told him; and having silenced Terry he asked Robbie's father, "Tell me, what have the dealer chaps been offering you for your birds down Perthshire way?"

Before long, as was inevitable, the conversation returned to the weather. This brought another facet of George's character into action, his capacity to bore people by knowing more than they wished to hear. When he wondered about the weather, George bought meteorological books and read them from cover to cover; what he had never realized was how trifling and superficial is people's interest in the weather, even if, like my father, they discussed it all the time. Now he explained to us at great length how the Gulf Stream worked. I confess I'd always vaguely imagined it to be a warm-water current blessing our western shores, but it is not so simple: upon the Gulf Stream, it seems, there rides towards us a current of air which picks up water from the Stream and holds it in suspense until, upon the air-current striking our west coast, the heat hitherto employed in carrying vapour is released to warm the air; one gallon of rainfall (George told us) gives off enough heat to melt forty-five pounds of cast-iron, and the heat derived from rainfall in the west is equal to half the heat derived from the sun.

By the time George had finished telling them all this his audience was practically asleep. Again I thought of Huxley yearning for the barbarian dining hall where Squire Hastings stirred his flagon with a rosemary sprig; for all his intentions George didn't belong in that earthly paradise, or in this smoking room at Killaneen. If he stalked Ardnagour it wouldn't be for reasons they understood: for sport or sociability. It wouldn't be simple, it would be complex: a complex charade. Even the heat derived from rainfall would not melt the bars of his temperament and admit him to Squire Hastings' paradise.

Unless I was quite wrong about George, of course. Unless, as he had said at dinner, I was the Red King dreaming up the cousin I needed for my dream, giving him the bars which in reality encaged myself.

The next day, a Sunday, I was to leave by the night train from Inverness. I expected various difficulties about transport to the station, for George was apt to groan and sigh and wrinkle his brow when matters of logistics were raised. "Oh why can't you drive Ned," he asked me after breakfast; "you just haven't come to terms with twentieth-century life if you can't drive."

"Well I can't and that's that, so how am I to get to the station?"

"This endless administration. When to go to Inverness, whether to take the dog, what to do about the damp in the roof—God, married life is nothing else."

"You had to think about it before you were married."

"I know, I know. But it's discussing it that's so boring." He had been sidling towards the dining-room door, and now slipped out.

After lunch Terry motored away to hand over his Alfa and collect the other man's car which he had already sold on the telephone, so he kept telling us, for "a very fancy price" in Sevenoaks. Amy was photographing George in the hall, posing him against a set of antlers so that in the photograph the stag's horns would appear to sprout from his head. Chuckling with delight she peered into the view-finder and waved her arms as if directing a cast of thousands.

"Now George just think for a moment," I said, "can you take me to the train?"

"Oh Ned are you still worrying about your train?"

"I know my love," Amy suggested; "how about we take Ned and the car which has got to be oiled and then—wait for it—nip into the cinema? We could have a pie at the Station Hotel," she tempted; "you know your tummy's crying out for a change from home cookin'."

"Everyone else would want to come," George objected.

Through the door into the drawing room came Lea's voice: "We've no need to go where we're not wanted."

"Why are you listening at keyholes Lea?" George called.

"Sorry I came now," continued Lea's voice.

"I suppose if she insists on coming we'll have to take her," George said, hoping I think that Lea would go with them.

"I'm not coming," Lea's voice stated.

"Good," said George, "with any luck she'll have gone by the time we get back. I suppose we've got to go have we?"

When the time came to leave, George drove me in the Land Rover and Amy followed in the car which was to be serviced. On the way down the glen I asked George how his song-writing had progressed.

"Everyone I need to meet is always in an aeroplane," he said.

"But you're working at writing them?"

"I don't start at nine and end at five if that's what you mean by work," he said testily.

Presently I asked, "Are you staying up here much longer?"

He peered at the hot blue sky. "No point if it doesn't fucking rain."

"Good for your harvest at Saradon."

"It must rain," he insisted. "I can't stand this accursed country with its bones sticking out. I want to see the burns white again the way they used to be. The river running full with rain, that's what I love. It always was, before."

"Before what?"

"Long ago." The door of his mind closed in my face.

It was hard to see why a spate was of such importance to someone who fished with the barb filed off his hook. The drought meant something deeper to him, there was some iron-hard block which he thought the rain could melt or loose; but what? I intended asking him what he had meant when he had said at dinner, "No-one knows what sort of life I lead." But I couldn't. The question was too large to be framed. Soon we were through the iron gate and onto the public road where, as far as I was concerned, other preoccupations took over. He drove on, his mouth clamped, his profile austere against the burnt landscape passing.

"You'll go to Saradon when you come down?" I asked after several miles of silence. "Or London?" Amy had talked of London.

"I don't know Ned. I do not know," he repeated, "I don't know what I'm going to do."

As though this answered all the questions he might be asked for a number of years he again drove in silence broken only by cursing at tourists who dithered in and out of passing-places on the single track road. It made me remember his forbearance over the children swinging on his gate at Saradon, in those days before his engagement, when he had seemed happy. His tolerance of people-in-the-street was a barometer of his spirits, and now the mercury was low. Thinking of those wet summer days at Saradon I asked, "George when exactly did you propose to Amy?"

His hard face cracked in delighted laughter. "You live in a world of your own Ned, you really do. Words like proposing and courting don't describe how people behave any more. People don't do any of those things like sofa-setting nowadays you know."

"People still end up married though."

"Yes they do." He thought for a moment. "You're quite right, it's the same old end grafted on the new means of getting there. Quite true. You ought to be married you know Ned. We must find someone you can court."

He had cheered up. As far as Beauly he questioned me about the Foreign Office examination, suggesting that my old-fashioned notions and deportment must have been of instant appeal to the examiners. He broke off when we passed a bearded hippy thumbing a lift, which always made George miserable. "Oh I can't stop and there's no room," he groaned; then he braked.

"Are you picking him up?" I asked.

"Amy is," he said irritably, watching in the mirror. He drove on, slowly enough to keep Amy in view, not listening to anything I said. Past the turn to Kiltarlity he braked again. "Now she's turned off with him," he said flatly. He sighed, and drove in silence to the station forecourt at Inverness.

"I hope Amy's all right," I said.

He watched me lift out my suitcase. "You know the

113

way in Malory all the knights ride about seeking what strange adventures might befall?" he said. "Amy's entire life is like that. Her entire life."

I followed him into the station, where he bought any number of magazines and presented me with *Playboy* and the *Economist*. Perhaps he delayed at the bookstall so that Amy should catch up with us, as indeed she did, running into the chilly stone vault of the station and gazing about at strangers until she saw us.

George mimicked her before she could speak: "'I've had such an extraordinary time'—come on, bore us with your adventures."

She wasn't at all crestfallen. "For that I won't tell you," she said, walking with us to the London train into which mail-bags were being loaded. I believe she forgot such incidents as soon as they were over; what she liked was that they happened, reminders that the world existed, and she in it like a butterfly in a sunbeam. She examined the lists of occupants posted on each sleeping car we passed. "Oh Ned," she called, "you've got Susie on the train."

"Susie?"

"You can't have forgotten. The big attraction at Kil-laneen? Now Ned you've got to take this seriously," she said, "hasn't he George?"

"Certainly," George agreed. They both peered at the list. "Now Ned, you are but seven doors from the lady of your aspirations. Your chance to do a spot of courting has come sooner than we hoped."

"Oh George, give him some advice my love. Ned needs help. Think of a plan."

As we climbed aboard the train to find my sleeper George pondered. Seating himself on my bunk he scratched his hair under his cap. "Now let me see," he deliberated. Amy and I sat down beside him.

"Pay attention Ned, he's a terrific seducer," Amy advised me.

"The first thing in your favour," George began, "is that many a lady finds the motion of a train extremely conducive to thoughts of a saucy nature. Now your second advantage is that I have studied this particular lady, so——"

"Woke me up about nine times to speak of her beauty, didn't you my love?"

"——so you needn't waste time the way others on the train will. They'll all be at sixes and sevens, but you—now: during dinner, crossing the Findhorn would be good timing, introduce the topic of rubber clothing. Slip into your badinage that you wear rubber drawers for——"

"Remember to tell Ned about the man on the bus in Florence," Amy put in.

"Later Amy," said George testily. "Now by Aviemore Ned, I want you to lay your hand on her knee, just casually, a gesture between friends——"

"Don't knead it Ned, just pop it there like this, see." Amy's hand dropped onto my thigh on the bunk beside her. George pushed it nearer my knee.

"That's where you go wrong Amy," he scolded her, "you've no patience that's your trouble. I know she wears stockings because she told me she finds tights overheating, and you'd have put your hand far too high up for a girl in stockings. No wonder you can't seduce people. Now," he continued, wagging a finger at me, "don't let her get up from dinner until the train is standing in Perth station. This is most important. Buy port—she likes port—bribe the waiter, say you've got cramp, anything. Perth is vital to you, the very gateway to your romance on wheels."

"You haven't said about the man in the mac on the bus yet," Amy told him. "Ned Susie was on this bus in Florence and a man lifted——"

"Amy you're so subjective," George complained. "The man on the bus disgusted her, why should Ned drag that up? Not all girls are like you about wops," he added. "Now I've lost the thread. Oh yes: get her to walk up the platform at Perth, say 'A spot of fresh air'll do us good' she'll like that. Exactly half way between two lamps, take her arm. Remember, it's much easier to kiss on terra-firma, trains rock about and you bump your noses. You've got her arm, dialogue will suggest itself to you. But I don't think you'll go far wrong with 'Oh I say Susie, give us a kiss'."

"Now have you got all that Ned?" asked Amy as we followed George onto the platform.

George's gravity had conjured up a kind of reality. For a moment the situation he described held together like a picture he had made me see in a fire. What was so minutely described seemed true. Amy was peeping into other sleepers on tiptoe, bored now, so I suggested that they should leave me and go to the cinema. "Let me know when you come to London," I said.

"I don't know when that will be," George replied.

"Amy said you'd take a flat in the winter."

"Might," Amy put in, "I only said 'might' George."

We bade one another goodbye, George as always, impatient of my thanks, and they walked off down the platform. Fifty yards away George turned and called along the train.

"Now remember Ned. Findhorn, rubber knickers: Aviemore, hand on knee: Perth——" He held wide his arms and Amy, taking two steps, hopped into them, an extraordinarily neat and trusting trick.

He turned and carried her off, both of them laughing, against the current of people arriving for the train behind porters trundling their luggage. Although they hadn't fused into the conventional "we", yet there was something —maybe Amy's trustful leap into his arms made me see it—which recalled what the old crofting woman had muttered on the lawn at Killaneen: "Aye, they're sair in love, those two." I turned in to the train alone.

Susie was deposited on the train by Robbie just before it started. My reaction was to back into my sleeper and close the door. Later I saw her sitting alone at a table for two in the dining car, but I chose a table behind her where two men were seated already. Ordinarily I would have had dinner with her, had not George complicated the issue by suggesting that just to sit and talk, with no predatory intention, was to fail. Nor was I content to sit and read the *Economist*, or eavesdrop on the men opposite, for George had disquieted my passivity. Of course I knew that although George or Amy separately might have amused themselves with "adventures" on the train, together they would have sat discussing administration; still, as the train rumbled across the viaduct over the dry Findhorn, I wondered if a girl like Susie could really be propositioned on the night-sleeper south. Opposite me I heard the military-looking man say to his companion:

"You count yourself lucky you've only got your boys to worry about. Take our eldest, you know we sent her off to that place Billy's girls went to in Paris? Well I'll tell you in confidence . . ."

His voice dropped to a murmur. The *Economist* seemed as dry as the Findhorn's beach of white stones, and I had left *Playboy* in my sleeper. I looked out of the window as the train dashed south towards Aviemore and Perth. The line of the hills hung in the northern sky, fading, sustained even beyond sight as the plaint of the pipes, in the dusky garden at Killaneen, still lingered in my memory.

VI

ONE DAWN THAT December, in an iron frost under a
bitter sky, the hills emerging from night like ominous
drum beats from silence, I was once again upon the Ardnagour track. A taxi from Inverness had dropped me at
the gate where tarmac ended and the rough road up the
glen into George's kingdom began. There was a shepherd's
cottage by the gate, its window a yellow smudge of light,
and smoke drifting from its chimney into the sharp, blue
air; the shepherd's wife had called out that I might wait
in the warm if I wished, but I expected George to collect
me at any moment; besides, in the cold there was a knife-
sharp clarity after the fug of London and the train, and
in the dawn a magnificent barbarity.

After twenty minutes' waiting, when the intense wind-
less frost had seeped into the marrow of my bones and the
strengthening light had showed me snow on the peaks
beneath the hollowing dome of sky in which the stars had
paled, I wished I had left the dawn to its own devices and
sat by the cottage fire. But it is awkward to push one's
way into people's houses. I stamped to and fro on turf crusty
with frost, to and from my suitcase dumped on the track
and the gate whose iron bars froze to my gloves when I
touched them. The scene was utterly stilled by cold: each
tuft of marsh grass a stiffly-silvered fan, each birch as deli-
cate as filigree, in the cottage garden the cabbages stark
with rigor mortis, and beyond, under alders where the
night still ruled, the river trickled faint as life almost
extinct in frozen veins, for no water flowed from the
heart of the hill, locked in iron cold. I had set out to enjoy
a Highland dawn after a discontented autumn in London,
but so much vast and icy grandeur all at once was more

than I had bargained for. Like a long wait imposed upon a victim in an enormous chill anteroom, it had the effect of reducing myself and my business to a very inconsequential size. And still George did not appear from the hills where he was rumoured to exist.

It wasn't George who had asked me to come up—he never came forward as the principal in any negotiation until you had committed yourself—it was Amy who had rung me at the office, her voice very faint and far off, and had entreated me to travel up this weekend. On reflection, that's to say when her voice was no longer persuading me, I regretted accepting; but I couldn't get an answer from the Ardnagour number so I had caught the Friday sleeper and come. There was nothing to keep me in London. A diplomat posted at home is thrown back on his own resources—both financially, for he isn't paid allowances, and socially because he has neither the entrée nor the rank which are his, *ex officio*, abroad—and my social resources had proved meagre. Visiting London for ten days a year I could dig up enough people I had known a long time for the seam of "Auld Lang Syne" never quite to be mined out before I went abroad again, and there, not expecting "old friends", I was prepared to make do with colleagues; but living in London month after month made evident how far apart I now was from these nominal old friends with their wives and children and jobs in cement. George was right, I really hadn't any friends, only business colleagues. And in London any of one's colleagues worth knowing have social lives of their own. Lonelier in London than in Rome I recognized that I had grown dependent upon the stockaded circle or cage, the Britain-abroad which Her Britannic Majesty's Embassies provide. Like an old rubber hand who is happier with his planters' club in the East than he would be in St James's Street, I preferred the Embassy shop to what it imitated.

All in all, once I couldn't get out of coming to Scotland, I had looked forward to it. Amy had said that there would be another guest on the train, she wouldn't say who, just that it would be "a nice surprise", but on the sleeper-lists I saw no name that I knew. Nor was Amy herself in the Station Hotel where she had promised to meet me for breakfast. I ate alone, expecting her with increasing disappointment. It was the first hotel in which as children we had made ourselves at home, thinking it the very apogee of cosmopolitanism to swagger about the foyer in our first long flannels, talking loudly and irritating everyone within earshot no doubt—as I've been irritated myself, since then, by the kind of children who collide with you in their games played in and out of the pillars of the Danieli in Venice—yet putting down roots in that solemn edifice which made any return to it like a homecoming. As a child of course I hadn't thought of the hotel as "home": with Saradon and Ardnagour I hadn't needed to. Nowadays the waitresses bringing me porridge and the hall porter remembering my name made it as homely as anywhere else I ever went.

For all that, by the time I had got George's message (that I would be met at the Ardnagour gate) and had travelled forty miles by taxi and had almost frozen to death in the dawn glen, any idea of home-coming or of welcome had diminished to nil. I could not go back. Even on a yacht I have never felt so completely at the mercy of a host as I did stranded with my suitcase under the snowy hills. There was no escape from the mountains, as there is none from the sea.

As I paced past the cottage for the twentieth time I saw a little girl, almost spherical in her jerseys, with merry red cheeks, gnawing a hunk of bread on the doorstep and watching me. I called good morning and she was encouraged to jump down amongst the frozen cabbages.

"Would you like to see the car?" she asked.

"Yours?"

"No!" she cried, contemptuous that I knew so little. "The other man's."

"I'd love to see it," I said. "Which other man? Mr George?"

120

"No!" This time she laughed out loud, a clear note that rang in the frost, as she ran with tottery steps, waving her crust, towards a tumbledown black shed against the cottage. I went round the garden paling and looked in. The paint of a Ferrari with Rome number-plates gleamed in the dark. Evidently the little girl had been told not to touch it, for when she did she looked at me sideways—so exactly as Amy looked, when she wanted to involve you in mischief, that it might have been Amy fingering the forbidden car. "It's the other man's up at Duncan's, it is," she told me wistfully. "It's a foreign one and so's he m'dad says."

That Leonardo del Traffo should be staying at Ardnagour seemed improbable and rash even by Amy's standards. Besides, "Duncan's" was the local people's name for Drumnakeel, the ruined croft high in the hills. Anyone staying there in December would be certifiable. I would have questioned the little girl, but evidently she thought I had feasted my eyes on the car long enough, for she had dragged the door shut and scampered back to the cottage. I looked up at the bleakness which day had now made clear on the hills. Cold and discomfort there would certainly be up there, but I feared something worse.

Then I saw descending the track far off at great speed a travelling speck which became a Land Rover hurtling nearer, the racket of its approach resounding off the steeps until it hit the flat and bowled towards me. With extraordinary accuracy it ran slap over my suitcase. Amy tumbled out of the driving seat helpless with laughter.

"Oh my love your poor luggage," she cried, running back to look.

I followed. Perhaps it was frost and clear air which made her laughter sound unnaturally loud, ringing out uncertain and ragged, like a burst of song from a bird in winter. The Land Rover had spilled my clothes across the track and Amy held up a pair of underpants.

"I think your knickers are more frightened than hurt," she said.

She looked twice her usual size, and for a moment I thought she was pregnant; but when she kissed me I found that the bulk was sheepskin and sweaters. I don't know why I was relieved. We bundled everything into my case and I opened the rear door of the Land Rover. A sticky puddle on the floor made me hesitate. I asked what it was.

"Blood," she said. "Everything's soaked in blood. Put your case on the seat I should."

When we were rattling up the track side by side the constraint which can succeed greeting lay between us. From my autumn in London I was familiar with this, the slack waters between two ships which ought to pass in the night, but don't; I'd never known Amy becalmed by it though. The silence and cold of the wilderness through which we climbed encroached upon us. To loosen their hold I said, "You told me there'd be someone else coming up on the train."

"Lennie came by car in the end," she said. "He's aching to see you."

I doubted that. She sounded defensive. "I wouldn't have thought the Highlands in December were quite Leonardo del Traffo's handwriting," I said.

She shifted her gloves irritably on the wheel. "George kept saying that. Maybe he came for the company. I don't know why he came. George and you," she went on, "I mean people like you, are always saying things like, 'Afraid I haven't arranged anything old sport' as if people had to play some game or something all day or they'd perish of boredom. You know?"

"Doesn't sound like George," I said. It had been the refrain with which my father had greeted guests, repeated every morning of their stay: "Afraid we've arranged nothing for you." Nothing makes people so ill at ease, as George knew, and if he was using this trick I guessed it was not in straightforward apology. I had never heard him use it, nor had I ever heard Amy use the phrase "people like you", which implied a recognition of differences which it had been one of her charms to ignore. "Not at all like George," I repeated. "It's been Liberty Hall at Saradon since my father went."

"Oh, Saradon!" It sounded like a curse.

"Have you been down there?"

"George has lost his driving licence," she said in the exasperated tone of George himself. "He says if he's got to be stuck anywhere it had better be here where he can drive about on his own roads."

"Why did they take it away?"

"Some silly accident in London."

I looked at her. The frost pinched her face and the hard light made it mean. She concealed something furtive. The cold anaesthetized my nostrils and extinguished her scent, and her thick clothes shut away the presence of her body from me, so that my antennae could not probe her.

We passed above the pool where we had picnicked in August, black water sliding between ice-skirted rocks. It seemed in another life that I had spied on her swimming there. So winter changes the world. Then we turned up the pony-track which was as rough as a dry water-course and led to Drumnakeel.

"So you're not living at Ardnagour?" I said.

"When Mrs Winder left George said it was too big to heat."

"Why did Mrs Winder leave?"

"Stupid old cow."

"Has she gone south?"

Amy smiled to herself. "Gone west more like. Oh I must tell you"—she turned her lighted face on me—"no I can't," she decided.

"Tell me what?"

"Well I will but—anyway George and I were having— we'd been down to Killaneen for dinner see, and when we got back feeling a bit, you know, we were having—oh I can't go on." The Land Rover slowed or accelerated with her indecision. "Yes I will, you'll laugh: we were having sex on the mat you see, in front of the fire and everything,

I made George, and in the middle Mrs Winder popped that frightful visage round the door. 'Did you call, Mr George?' " She laughed guiltily. "Anyway George got into a frightful pickle, furious. With me which was so mean. I know that's why the old bag went. Crazed with jealousy is what she was. Not that she need have worried about a repeat performance," added Amy peevishly, bashing the truck onward over the stones.

I stared out at the bitter stony faces of the hills. We turned a corner and a narrow strath climbed ahead of us. Under the snow peaks it opened dark as a fissure in the earth's crust. In its midst rose a gloomy rock in whose shelter crouched Drumnakeel, a colossal rock and a stone cottage, and around them tumbledown birches mostly dead where they had fallen, like slain soldiers round a keep. Innumerable assaults from the mountains had almost stormed the place, and now the powdering of frost, skirmishers from the snow above, threatened it again.

"My God it's bleak," I said aghast.

"Liberty Hall," Amy replied.

From the burn-course threading through the strath there appeared a figure striding towards us, his footsteps blackening the frosty marsh. George had grown a rough black beard and moustache, and he wore a sweater with the sleeves pushed up and plus-fours without stockings. His bare arms and legs were bone-thin and bloodless with cold, and his eyes under his cap gleamed very brightly in through the window of the Land Rover. He acknowledged my arrival and then said to Amy, "I think I've got the water to flow through the hose again."

"It'll only freeze tonight my love."

"Then it'll have to be unfrozen again. You say you have to have water."

"And you look so cold," Amy told him without pity, driving slowly whilst he kept pace with us. Her face sunk in the fur of her sheepskin was cold too. "It's not only me who needs water you know," she added. "You use it as well."

"There's a distinction between use and waste. Leaving the tap running whilst you clean your teeth is waste. That's just the kind of thing which has lowered the water-table throughout the entire world," he told her.

When we stopped at the cottage door George opened the back of the Land Rover for my luggage. Jumping about for warmth Amy told him how she had run over my suitcase.

"What an amusing prank," he said.

My unfortunate case had fallen into the blood on the floor. "I wish we didn't have to live in this sea of blood George," Amy complained. "And I'm sick of driving these corpses all over Scotland."

But George had dumped my bag on the step and disappeared into a shed from which came the rattle of shovelled coke. Amy opened the cottage door and we went in.

It was quiet and warm and dark in the kitchen, like a lair in the earth, the early light a glimmer through the frost-rimed pane. In the growing flame of the candle Amy lit I saw a table and some bentwood chairs, and their wavery shadows on a matchboarded ceiling. Coats and caps and gun-sleeves crowded pegs on the walls. It was extraordinarily still—until the door catch rattled and George tramped in lugging the hod. Opening the Rayburn door to chuck in the coke he continued his conversation with Amy. One felt that he had been brooding on his injuries in the coalshed.

"If I hadn't lost my driving licence I'd drive the carcasses——"

"Ned knows all that," Amy said, banging shut the outside door behind him.

"Knows you snatched the wheel and ran us into a Belisha beacon?" he persisted. The coals in the fire glared on his bearded face.

"Only because you wouldn't go back to the party. Ned," she appealed to me, "Terry gave this party and specially asked this agent who could have helped George, and George wouldn't stay."

"What a curious and trying fellow I am to be sure," said George, tramping out again.

"So you snatched the wheel?" I asked.

"I did give it a tweak. Come my love and I'll show you your room. George," she asked, for he had entered again with an armful of birch logs, "is Lennie up?"

"Could you open the sitting room door?"

"You're not going to light the fire in there surely?"

"Your friends can hardly all sit in the kitchen." In trying to open the door for himself George spilled a log off his load. Pettishly he let the rest fall, as if even the law of gravity was an invention to vex him. Amy pushed past him and up the steep stairs, and I followed with my case. If George had welcomed me I would have helped him with his logs.

My bedroom—an iron bed, a table and a chair on a deal floor—was unimaginably cold. Into the air my breath feathered out like a critical comment. There was a banana and an orange on a plate on the table, a mockery of comfort but nonetheless touching, so I fixed upon that to thank Amy for. She replied from the door, which she swung to and fro, "I didn't know what to do to show Welcome's written on the mat. If you can read it through the snow. I mean thank you for bothering to come." She disappeared. Silence and cold immediately filled the room.

All the view from the window, which was tunnelled into an embrasure in the stone wall, was the bare hillside across the burn, and you had to stoop to see out at all. Cold as I was I leaned there pondering the eccentricity of a couple who could live at Saradon or Ardnagour, yet chose this retreat. Retreat came to mind because George gave the impression of defeat and withdrawal. Under the snow hills this strath yawned dark as the mouth of Tartarus. So this was where George had brought his bride at last, from the flowers of Sicily by way of Saradon and Ardnagour. With its comfort there was also complexity at Saradon, and I dare say at Ardnagour too, whereas here life was shorn of both, pared to the bone. Water and fire were all that counted now. Something had driven George up here. I wondered was he trying to rid himself of irritants by immersion in austerity as a fox in water to dislodge its fleas? Moving north from London and Saradon had dislodged the world that didn't belong to him; moving up from Ardnagour had shaken off Mrs Winder; now there was only Amy clinging on—Amy and "her friends", as he had described myself and Leonardo. He could retreat no higher: the snow line lay a few hundred feet above the croft. His parasites were internal, swarming in blood and brain. I looked up at the white fangs of the hills. Stalking hinds up there was a dangerous way of freezing the maggots out of his mind. If he took to blood sports again it would not be for the sake of sociability, it would be—for himself, as he had told us that morning at Saradon. "And woe betide the world if I do" he had warned us. I turned in from the window to unpack my clothes.

But the blood: it was smeared on my case, on my clothes, on the floor, on everything. Suspicious of bloodstains I couldn't bring myself to put on the sweaters I had brought, so I tapped down the dark stairs to the kitchen, stooping as you had to stoop everywhere, as if the cottage was a yoke on your neck to break your pride.

Daylight exposed the dinginess of the kitchen and the candle palely burning. In silence George and Amy were leaning on the Rayburn's rail side by side. "Now," said Amy, bustling a tin pot and a plate of biscuits from the stove to the table, "now we'll have some coffee. And I made some biscuits," she added shyly, offering the plate.

I took one and praised it liberally. Then silence returned, a silence which possessed the cottage as it possessed the hills at the door. I blew out the candle and said, "Jocund day stands tiptoe on the mountain tops."

George shook his head in puzzled fashion before opening the stove door to poke the coals.

"Why the beard George?" I asked. His lips in the beard were somehow obscene.

"My pompholyx."

'You only get that on the soles of your feet."

"Not in my case."

"Anyway in the summer I thought your rash had gone."

"Well it hadn't."

"How can you tell, George?" Amy asked. "No-one's seen your face for weeks, let alone your feet. Anyway the sun up here can't give you a rash. It's like talking to some-one hiding in a tree," she complained.

He brooded in the flare of the stove, poking the coals obsessively, his profile given an ugly jut by his beard. I thought that for the first time Amy was alarmed by him, a little unsure of her sunniness, like a puppy at a death-bed. *Du bouffon favori la grotesque ballade Ne distrait plus le front de ce cruel malade.* "Amy," I asked, "where's that puppy you had?"

She shifted her chin on her hand so that her stare passed George the question, which he answered without turning: "It chased the deer."

Amy's hands cupping her face were puffy and red with chilblains. Mine too were growing colder. "George," I said, "you couldn't lend me a jersey could you? And some old trousers of some sort?"

George turned on his haunches. "Ned surely you knew—I don't know!" He gave me up, and poked the fire again, grumbling, "Lennie brings two silk suits is all he brings, but you're an Englishman dammit, didn't you know it was cold in the winter?"

Startlingly loud, Amy sang, "Oh it's greatly to his cre-he-dit, that he is an Englishman!—do you remember, Ned? Remember the signal-box?"

I did. Very clearly I remembered the Italian in his signal-box playing Gilbert and Sullivan when Amy had managed to get herself carried away on the train with me to Rome from the sea. I thought she would have for-gotten it amongst her innumerable adventures.

"Lord when I think how hot it was," she mused at the kitchen table. "Remember? Lizards on the platform ... you think back, and all little things come..." Her voice failed into silence, and then revived: "Of course we'll lend you clothes my love. Come, we'll have to squeeze you into mine. George's would dwarf you," she added with a sort of pride, measuring me with her eye as I stood up.

I followed her upstairs to their bedroom. Flat and cold stared the wintry light into a room bare and comfortless as my own. Iron beds were separated by a table whose broken leg was propped on the only book I'd seen in the cottage. I believe it was Mary Baker Eddy's book which had sunk to this functional use. Whilst Amy rummaged in a chest of drawers I noticed that on her side of the bed-table was a photograph of her puppy in her brother's arms. On George's side stood only a candle stuck in a tin dish.

"Choose," Amy said, laying an armful of jewel-coloured cashmeres on her bed.

"Cashmere's too good," I said.

"Lennie's borrowed masses."

"Why do you call him Lennie?"

"George did. The awful thing is it suits him up here, as if he'd shrunk. Or would you like this sweater?" She bunched out a handful of the heavy blue jersey she was wearing.

"Something like that, yes."

I suppose I wanted her to take it off. To find that she had not forgotten our adventure in Italy had regenerated my own memories, cross-pollination giving memory fresh hope of fruiting. She pulled the sweater over her head with the eel-like wriggle I remembered. But instead of that sunned nakedness was now revealed a vest, sexless as a stuffed sack, and white arms which the cold stubbled into goose-pimples. Quickly she dragged a cashmere over her head and shook her hair free.

"How about pants?" she asked, hugging herself for warmth.

"I've got trousers." I was terrified that she might take off her own. I left her brushing her hair at a mirror on the deep windowsill and took her jersey to my own room. When I put it on there was the warmth and scent of her in it like the lusciousness of a carnation house entered in winter. That was what I remembered of Amy, the summer's heat. As I moved about my room the boards of the floor mewed like a lost kitten. Lonely and comfortless nights without number had made these bedrooms miserable.

In the kitchen I found George grinding a skinning-knife at the table whilst Leonardo talked and laughed. I had forgotten his laugh, like a pebble rattled in a tin can; indeed I had forgotten him altogether he was so insubstantial, one of a group rather than an individual, so that when he greeted me as an old friend I looked at him in surprise. His coxcomb of black curls I remembered, his high colour, his cupid's bow lips and his blow-away elegance, but I hadn't an idea what he was like; and he was so small, a dainty miniature sitting swinging his legs on the table and gossiping about the people he had stayed with—all unknown to me—between Rome and Inverness. Evidently he was a creature who needed the people he was with to be his friends, whoever they happened to be; it is a kind of flattery, and it made me warm to him.

"Where is Amy?" George presently asked through Leonardo's chatter.

"Doing her hair," I said.

"She has made up her face too you will notice," George remarked. "This is one of the many advantages of having you to stay. But if you want to go for a walk we must go now, I can't spare the time this afternoon. Shout at her, will you Lennie."

When he had gone upstairs I asked George, "What are you doing this afternoon?"

"What?" He examined the oily knife-blade and cleaned it on his plus-fours. "I must cull some more hinds."

He clattered into the lean-to scullery where I could see him trying the taps. A trickle of water tinkled into a saucepan. "Water must be a problem in this frost," I called to him.

"What?"

It *was* like shouting to someone hiding in a tree, as Amy said. But he had heard me. When the saucepan was full he carried it to the top of the Rayburn, complaining, "People are so wasteful. You need far less than you think, but everyone wastes it." Then he went out through the back door. He was obsessed and secretive in manner.

I waited in the kitchen, where the only sound was the sizzle of droplets spilt from the pan onto the stove-top. I wondered if he had seen in the autumn the burns white on the hill and the river running full with rain. It seemed to me unbalanced, this obsession with water.

Presently I heard a door unlatch upstairs and Amy and Leonardo descending. Should I discuss George's state of mind with Amy—was that why she had asked me here, because he was going mad?

"You can wear pastel colours now you're so pale and peaky," she was telling Leonardo as they entered, he in a powder-blue sweater whose sleeve he examined critically. The effect of their entry was to make the idea of madness absurd, a chimera of my own imagining. All Amy was trying to do was to throw a house-party in a shieling on the snow line. That was folly, and maybe George was only reacting against her folly, making a labour of providing water just as Mrs Winder made a labour of providing breakfast eggs for guests at Saradon.

Before long, equipped with gumboots and coats, the three of us issued from the cottage door into the glory of the morning. In the upper air all was brilliance, the blue empyrean above the peaks, sunlight on snowy flanks, sunshafts even lighting the rowans on the great crag which sheltered the cottage; whilst the floor of the strath and Drumnakeel itself were sunless still, in violet shadow and frost. "Where's George?" Amy asked. "George! George?"

Her cry seemed to reach no further than the feather of her breath. Nor did George answer. He had gone.

"Did he take a rifle?" she asked me.

"I didn't see him go."

She looked doubtfully round. "I think we'd be safe walking over there so we could get where the sun is," she said.

As we started off Leonardo said, "It is possible he won't shoot all the three of us. Anyway I will wave a white flag."

"Don't!" Amy told him, reaching out to catch his hand waving a handkerchief, but staying her own hand before she touched his.

He clasped her wrist. "You mean don't surrender?"

"Just don't," she said earnestly, pulling her hand away from him.

We tramped on over the creaking frost, both Leonardo and I weltering in boots borrowed from George, without speaking, until presently Amy thrust an arm through each of ours. She did it almost with bravado, as if she too had been thinking of her reluctance to touch Leonardo's hand. It made our silence companionable. When suddenly our three shadows sprang out, long and spidery across the sparkling frost, she wheeled with a happy cry.

"Look!"

On the rim of the snow ridge burned the sun, a red fireball colouring our faces and lighting our eyes. It was heatless, but Amy didn't seem to mind that. "Every day I have to come a bit further to see it," she said. "When we first came sun used to come in the windows, now you have to walk miles. You see it only just trundles along that ridge like a penny in a slot then it's gone."

"Soon you'll have to climb the hill to see it at all," I said.

She looked up at the steeps behind us. "The sun can't get much lower can it?"

"We're not at the longest night yet."

"Don't depress me my love."

Already the sunshaft began to fade, and the shades of the strath, its Tartarian chill, lengthened its reach to engulf her. She didn't take the step which would have

132

kept her in its rays. Leonardo, last of us to lose the light on his face, waved to the departing sun and called, *"Arrividerci sole! Ci vedremo in Italia."* The liquid language was like a Roman's prayer to Mithras. "Is impossible to believe it is our same sun," he said as we started back towards the cottage after our pilgrimage to the sunlight, "our same Italian sun."

"You should see the sea," rejoined Amy. "I had my holidays one day and I went to the north coast. Pale pale blue the sea was—like your friend Malvina's eyes. How is she by the way?"

She walked cheerfully between us, teasing Leonardo who bridled and preened, recovering his dapper style as he gossiped about his clique in Rome. One remembered the existence of cities behind the mountains. *Fumum et opes strepitumque Romae.* I wondered what quest had brought Leonardo to the far north. Amy was the obvious answer, for apart from Amy there was nothing for him here. But I did not think Leonardo was large-souled enough to make the journey for love. Amy herself might be in quest of love or faith—I remembered George comparing her to Malory's knights seeking what adventures might befall— but not Leonardo. He was a poor unknightly stick, and if she depended upon him she would fail. I suspected that he travelled because he was idle, that he had come so that his winter should appear busy. He was in search of nothing. He had found it here: as the Roman invaders had said of Scotland 2,000 years ago, here at the ends of the earth was *nihil—nisi fluctus et saxa.* A waste land. "If there were rock And also water ... But there is no water. What is the city over the mountains ... Unreal."

"George, George!" Amy ran ahead as we approached the cottage, calling George with infinite optimism that he would be the lover she wished him to be.

When I entered the kitchen he was sitting at the table, which was laid for a meal, rolling a cigarette.

"You shouldn't have laid lunch my love," Amy said

133

from the scullery where she was clattering pans, "and you needn't have washed up breakfast."

"Shouldn't, needn't," George grumbled, licking the cigarette paper at his bearded lips. "You hadn't done it."

"I might have though," she called.

"We cannot live on the widow's mite." He scratched alight a match on the stone floor.

"And you, where did you go to?" asked Leonardo from the door, shaking off George's boots.

"Over the hill."

"You met McLeod," supposed Amy, irritated.

George smoked in silence. I asked him why he'd started rolling his own cigarettes.

Amy answered, carrying in a saucepan of soup, "Same reason he spits all over the place and won't wear enough clothes, to be like Willy McLeod."

"That's an extremely silly thing to say," George told her.

"No sillier than thinking puir wee Wully McLeod is the cat's pyjamas," said Amy. "There's nothing to drink I suppose George?"

"There's whisky."

"I mean proper wine. Haven't had a taste of wine since we had dinner at Killaneen months ago." She went out again.

"And it didn't suit you then," George commented tartly.

I thought of the scene Mrs Winder had discovered on the hearth at Ardnagour after that dinner at Killaneen. I watched George brooding at the table, his hands laid in front of him with the dingy cigarette smouldering between fingers which shook very slightly. Blood was caked in the corners of his nails just as it was in McLeod's nails always. From his pose of ox-like patience you might have thought George was a labouring man sitting waiting for his dinner. But there was tension; the trembling of the smoke from his cigarette and the tautness of his neck muscles made me think of an actor on a stage rather than of a stalker in his cottage home.

Before we had finished lunch George started collecting up his rifle and the knife he had been sharpening and his spy-glass in its leather case. Pulling on a peat-stained jacket and dropping ammunition into his pockets he said, "I'll be back by dark."

"Can't we come?" asked Leonardo from his tipped-back chair.

George's eye measured him. "If you want. It'll be rough mind."

"Let's all go. Can we George? Ned you'll come?" Enthusiasm bubbled from Amy. She was trying to give a party.

When the four of us set out from the cottage so pure was the air, so crisp the frozen ground, that you thought you would never tire. I easily kept pace with George's steady stride whilst Amy and Leonardo walked chattering behind, and our spirits rose as we mounted into the marvellous clarity. The snowy hills above swelled like wind-filled sails. After a mile Amy, who had run out onto a crag above the glen, called to us:

"George look, you can still see Drumnakeel. You must look, you wouldn't believe anyone could be living there it's so tiny."

I expected George to tell her to keep quiet, but he didn't, he strode on, faster now that the ground was steeper, or seemed steeper to me. Part of the mystification of stalking is that the stalker never does what you expect, or tells you what he plans. On we climbed, up and up, George pressing over peat hag or rock at his unbroken pace whilst I had begun to stumble and sweat. From the cottage I had thought that the snow line was close, but it was still as far above us as ever. I couldn't spare the energy to look round for Amy and Leonardo. Still we climbed. I gasped to George, "Shouldn't we let them catch up?"

He stopped. We saw Amy plodding up the slope with dangling arms, Leonardo trailing, and behind them the immense lines of mountain and glen. When they panted up to us George said, "Why don't you two go back?"

"I'm coming as far as you go," Amy told him.

"I think I'll go back," Leonardo said. "I am completely whacked."

"What about you Ned," asked George ironically, "are you 'whacked'?"

I couldn't admit it as Leonardo had—typical of an Italian, I thought, to express an un-English surrender in English slang. Turning, he raised his hand and spread his fingers wide. *"Ciao,"* he said, and began to saunter downwards. It looked so enviably easy to go back.

"Make some tea for us Lennie," Amy called, and again he raised a slender arm as he sank down the hillside. Amy said, "I wish he knew how to make muffins."

For a moment or two she and I watched him descend, and when we turned we found that George had climbed away from us and was setting off into the desolation above. We followed. Relentlessly he seemed to increase the distance however hard I tried to catch him. There was time neither to look into the glens below nor to talk to Amy; my only focus was that steady back receding, the rifle slung on his shoulder, striding over a crest, gone then seen again surmounting the further slope of a gully as we came over its ridge. I knew it was only the values of the Highlands that made endurance a virtue, but they were values which had been implanted in me summer after summer in these hills, walking to brown-trout lochs or stalking, and they arose in me now sure as the hills stood in their places, the virtue of strength immanent in savagery. It was a fight against the mountains and against the untiring figure always ahead, "larger than human on the frozen hill".

"Leonardo's lucky," I gasped to Amy, "he can just give up."

Instead of replying she called upon some extraordinary reserve of strength and forged ahead of me. Beaten, I slowed. Frost sharpened each breath to saw my lungs. Before me opened a gully strewn with granite into which Amy plunged. George, ascending the scree on its further slope suddenly dropped and crept towards the ridge. See-ing my chance to catch up I hurried, and was stumbling through peat hags in the bottom when Amy, who had caught George and was lying beside him while he spied, waved her hand at me to be still. I crouched by a boulder. Presently I saw George shut his glass. Evidently there was an argument between the two of them lying flat in the scree, for Amy first sloughed her sheepskin and then, when George still shook his head, she pulled off her light-coloured sweater. Then George must have agreed to take her on with him in whatever she wore underneath, for in another moment they both crawled over the crest and were gone.

Since I did not know where the hinds were, or whether George counted on me stopping still in order to flank them, I could only stay where I was. The utterly silent crater enclosed me as a trough between shale-grey waves encloses a swimmer, the toppling scree crests shutting off any view of shore or ship or rescue. The cold soaked into me bitter as sea water. I could only wait whilst somewhere out of my sight, perhaps close, the stalk went forward. I felt the tension. I strained to hear, but there was only silence—no clamour of hounds, no beaters' shouts, no roaring river —only ominous silence, and the tension of death creeping closer to the quarry.

The crash of the shot struck the hills and broke into echoes. Its peals hit crags and fell. I hurried to the ridge. There on the stones lay Amy's relics, her sheepskin and sweater which I gathered up and looked over the crest. "The rent earth opened wide a dreary gulf disclosed." There was no reason for believing that something terrible had happened, unless imagination and my view of George was reasonable. From the depths of the corrie rang Amy's clear joyful voice calling my name. My fears were imaginary.

By the time I came up with them they were standing over the dead hind which had fallen by a burn course. George had stripped off his jacket and was pushing up the sleeves of his shirt for the butchery. Amy told me excitedly about the stalk.

"Do you want your coat?" I interrupted her, holding it out. She was filthy and flushed. I didn't like her heated exultant voice.

"You have it, you look frozen. And George shot it stone dead, look you can see where the bullet hit, see?" she said, touching the oozy rent where the bullet had smashed into the creature.

"Help me pull her out of the burn," George asked, and the three of us dragged the carcass onto level ground. Its hooves were chilly to touch, its weight pathetically slack, its wide dark eye full of sorrow. From the desolate steeps a raven croaked. George looked up. "He's on cue," he said.

I watched George stand testing the blade of his knife above his victim. There was the flare in his eye which you see in someone who screws up courage for an out-of-character performance—the word "cue" made me think of acting. Then he set to work on the ritual, the knife ripping and slitting. Amy watched fascinated. "Is that thing its heart George?" she asked, or "Where's its liver?" Entrails steamed, blood weltered and slopped.

I had sat down out of range of the worst of the stench. As George splashed an armful of guts onto the stones he looked across at me. "It has to be done you know," he said.

"I know that," I replied. "There's no need to watch it done though."

"Yes there is, there are no non-combatants Ned. There's only the hunter and the hunted." Wearily he drew the back of his bloody hand across his forehead. "You ought at least to watch. You must face facts Ned."

"It's your fact, not mine. I won't eat it."

"It's a fact of life. You'll be telling me next there's no need to keep the light on when you're having sex. It's the facts of life you have to face."

"I don't see the connection," I said.

"You mean you won't look at the connection. That's

your problem—your vegetarian problem," he added, setting to work with his knife again. *"Quant à moi, je mange ce que je foute et cela m'évite la peine d'avoir un boucher."*

It made me laugh. From within the ogreish blood-dabbled performer it was the real George, surely, who quoted de Sade. I didn't believe in the Grand Guignol exterior, I believed in the George who had talked that morning at Saradon about the fragility of flesh-and-blood which protected life and was not to be smashed; but—it occurred to me as I heard him tugging and sawing inside the hind's broken body—did I only believe in the reality of the George I agreed with, the George I made up, like the Red King dreaming, different from moment to moment according to my needs? He had after all killed his brother, and half an hour earlier I had dreaded some terrible outcome of the stalk. In which direction did you have to look in order to face the facts? I shivered.

George, who had at last finished the gralloch and gone to clean himself in the burn, called to me, "If you're cold you can always do what the French did."

"George!" Amy expostulated.

"Not that," he said, "or not directly. I'll tell you what they did, they dipped their feet in a freshly-killed corpse when they were cold. One peasant per foot was the rule I believe." He dashed water on his face.

Amy laughed, but I said, "Rubbish George, you know that can't ever possibly have been true."

"You evidently haven't studied the twelfth-century annalist Villehardouin."

"Just because it's written down it isn't a fact George. De Sade is written down but you don't believe that do you?"

"Have you read Villehardouin or not? Because if you haven't," he said, putting on his jacket, "I fear we have no basis for discussion."

Amy too was putting on her coat. "I hope Lennie's made us a good tea," she said.

"You're going back are you?" George asked her.

"Aren't you?"

"Oh no. While the light lasts I must go on. I'd have killed two or three out of that herd if you hadn't been in my way."

I said that I had had enough. Amy said, "So have I then. Enough walking I mean."

George's eye gleamed as if he had raised the stake and won the hand, and he splashed away through the burn. As Amy and I walked in the other direction she evidently regretted that she had not gone with him, for she kept turning to look back until his gaunt figure at last topped the further crest and was gone. "I know what he'll say," she said, "he'll say I haven't been stalking properly because I didn't go on to the very end."

"One is plenty," I said.

"George has to go on and on. Like with something you think you believe, he makes you go on and on till there's nothing left. Except doubting." We walked in silence until she asked, "Does the blood and that turn you up, stalking?"

"I thought you didn't like blood everywhere."

"In the Land Rover I get sick of it true. But I got a sort of odd feel, like, I don't know, hungry, when we were stalking the hind. Do you get that?" she asked curiously, looking into my face as we walked. "I never know what you feel. I mean in Italy I didn't either. Not that night we stayed with Lennie even." She waited, still looking into my face. I said nothing. "In bed I mean I didn't know what you felt," she added. Then she gave up trying to read my face.

That night with her had been so bizarre that I had tried not to think about it, like a story read in childhood which it is no use trying to understand. I said, "All I felt was the bolster you put between us, that's all I felt."

"But I only put it there because you wouldn't let me know what you felt," she broke out. "That's all that worried me, that I didn't know. And it was only a pillow," she added, "you could have come over it."

140

"You drew the line," I replied. Until that night I had never known that the moral line, which I had always before recognized as obvious and clear-cut, could be drawn down the middle of a double bed; but apparently it was so.

"What's a pillow between friends? Trouble is it's all too important to you, these lines and things. I mean if all you felt was the pillow."

"I can't make out what you think either," I admitted. Truly I couldn't understand her, or even make her up into a consistent person as I went along.

She laughed. "Oh me, I think everything," she said simply. Her cheeks glowed and her eyes shone: flapping her gloves together she began to run ahead. She ran and waited, and I walked; she even hid behind a boulder and pounced out with an alarming cry. "Oh," she cried breathlessly, "I wish Rover was here. He so loved a scamper."

"What happened to him?" I asked.

Her face clouded. She turned to look over her shoulder. It was an exceedingly strange reaction, to look for an eavesdropper in that wilderness of mountains. "He died," was all she said, but softly, as if she had indeed seen a listener behind us.

"Poison probably," I said. "They put it out for the foxes and the crows."

She shook her head. "It wasn't poison. He'd—he'd been smashed to pieces. His head was all in bits," she added, fixing me with her large eyes, a stare which thrilled the hairs upright on my flesh. Before I could speak she said, "Anyway my love you must be weary from your ramble so I'm going to hurry you home for tea. Doesn't the thought of a crumpet put the spring back into your step?"

Though almost the shortest day of the year, to me it had seemed one of the longest since I had waited at the iron gate. Then dawn had hollowed the sky and now, as we dropped down towards Drumnakeel, stars already twinkled sharply in the luminous blue of dusk. Not far from the cottage a piece of driftwood white as bone lay in our path. Amy picked it up.

"I dropped that here yesterday," she said, "and I thought, Next time when I find it they'll be gone and I'll be on my own again."

She showed me loneliness like the spaces between the stars. Even her dog was dead, poor girl. At last to push away the pillow between us I took her hand. She jumped as if I had struck her. Sickened by my belatedness, and by my awkwardness, I dropped that cold, cold hand.

Tea without George was extraordinarily cosy in the white-painted little sitting room. Leonardo had lit a fire in whose light the three of us ate toast and honey and drank tea. Blood and brain unfroze in the cheerful blaze of birch logs. The cottage, which had seemed at first a lit stage-set in the darkened amphitheatre of hills, became with warmth and company reality, our home. The frost and night at the window was another world, unreal.

After tea I took one of the candles to inspect a canvas on an easel in a corner of the room. The easel was new, most of the brushes unused, the tubes of colour in the new painting box hardly squeezed, and charcoal strokes on the canvas had been rubbed out. When Amy saw me examining it she came over and took it off the easel. "I've given up," she said; "can't do it."

"I thought you drew rather well in Rome."

"Not now I know how difficult it's supposed to be I can't." She stacked the canvas with some others behind the sofa. "Now I'm lumbered with all this paraphernalia I can't begin."

In Rome she had drawn with a Biro on a letter-pad. "Why did you get it then?" I asked.

"George gave it me. Books as well; I mean great big books telling you like about tonal values."

"Throw them away," I suggested.

"You can't go back," she said. "Not once you know better you can't."

"True."

"And this he gave me." She picked up a wooden lay-figure. "You're supposed to practise drawing it. I mean picture the ennui."

I could see that the sexless, faceless wooden figure was not her idea of what people are like. She sat down by the hearth twisting it in her hands and chatting. As the tortured joints broke she threw it limb by limb into the fire.

There was a little buff book on the sofa beside me, its cover decorated with an austere classic arch across which was written "Thinker's Library", which I drew closer and leafed through. Entitled *Our New Religion*, it was a polemic ridiculing Christian Science, and Mary Baker Eddy, from the rationalist viewpoint of H. A. L. Fisher. "George makes you go on and on till there's nothing left except doubting," she had said. The painting equipment and Fisher's logic were all of a piece. They showed Amy no light, only how difficult, to George's mind, were the things that she had supposed to be easy. I grew sleepy by the fire. Scenes Leonardo and Amy talked of, Italian scenes, threw images of sun and colour against my eyelids. Time passed. If I slept, I awoke when the curtains suddenly backed, sail-like against the windows: a draught moaned, the house filled with wind, smoke puffed from the fire. George had come back. Calling "George, George!" Amy ran out to greet him.

" 'Ome is the 'unter, 'ome from the 'ill," said Leonardo to me.

"Yes," I replied. Far from it making him "English", he made the rhyme (as he made the British tweeds he wore in Rome) outlandishly foreign; un-English, un-Italian, unnatural. Nothing was natural to him. No plot of earth fed the sap of life to him. He was rootless, a cross-bred graft that had failed, a twig you could stick in the ground anywhere; and because it lived nowhere, anywhere was home. Such is cosmopolitanism. What Amy expected from him God knows. "Yes," I repeated. George would no doubt have told him that he had misquoted Stevenson's verse, but I didn't think it was worth it.

At first when we sat down to supper in the kitchen George, who had been labouring in and out with fuel for the fires, and who had filled many buckets with water before the taps froze, spoke little, eating soup and bread in the hungry, discontented way he always ate. I asked Leonardo how the yacht he was having built was coming along.

"Yes tell, Lennie," Amy begged. "Can we all come for a spin when it's finished?"

"Next winter you know what?" Leonardo replied. "I am going to make a trip to the Caribbean. Quite an idea, no? *Allora*, who do you think we should ask?"

At once Amy boarded his imaginary ship and sailed away on the adventure. Leonardo had the sort of nature that is attracted, and aggrandized, by the total power over other people which a ship's captain has, and he was full of plans for asking people onto the boat in order to revenge himself on them, or so it seemed. Presently he said to George in his English accent, "You'll come for a spot of sailing old boy, what?"

"I doubt it," scratched George's voice. "The Odyssey, it seems to me, is the prototype of all yachting holidays."

Leonardo laughed at him. "The Mediterranean is not so *mouvementé* any more. You know I sailed one time this summer where was Scylla and Charybdis and I couldn't see them at all?"

"It took Homer to see them," George replied. "And Odysseus to avoid them," he added.

"Anyway my love"—Amy preferred the fantasy voyage to the mythic—"anyway we're not going to the Mediterranean we're going to the tropics."

"The sun's no good to me any more."

144

"Oh George!" She mimicked, or had picked up, his prim moan.

"You can go," he told her. "You can go where you want. Tell me Lennie," he said, turning from her, "are you going to be the sort of skipper who plans to get away from it all, or the sort who plans to take it all with you? All the rubbish of civilization?"

It was interesting to watch George kindle in the warmth and the candlelight. Even if it was set in a kitchen on the snow line he couldn't resist a dinner table. Soon he dominated it, and we listened; we watched him as he sat rolling himself a shabby cigarette at the end of the meal, when he had fetched us each a whisky and water, and we listened to him complaining about pollution. "Smoke, filth in the atmosphere; no-one even realizes the balance between the spheres, no-one cares, yet."

"But George, you're always telling us how you love Liverpool and the soot," I said.

"I've changed my mind," he said. "Why do you think I'm living up here?"

"For the fresh air?" I said. "That's hypochondria on a very impressive scale."

"I am a surrogate hypochondriac for the ills of the world," he assured us. "And a much needed one. Let me tell you that the Promethean myth is about to manifest itself again, and in a very much more alarming way."

"So many myths you know," mocked Leonardo. "Tell us something true for a change."

"Evidently you don't understand mythology," George told him, "which is why you can't see Scylla and Charybdis I suppose, and would giggle at them if you could. Giggle at your peril. Far from being false, myth is truer than fact, it conveys the truths that are too deep for words. From history all you learn is what's over and who's dead. From mythology you learn what is ever-living. Prometheus is alive and well—and I'll tell you where he's living, he's living in nuclear reactors all over the world."

He drew on his cigarette, got to his feet and opened the

Rayburn door to throw the butt onto the coals. "For heisting this little pennyworth of fire in here," he said, "Prometheus was chained to a rock. The fire we've stolen now is the fire of the sun itself. Nuclear fission. The implacable eye of God. What, do you suppose, is the penalty for stealing that?"

He rose from the fire and turned and confronted us, his shadow scrawled on the wall by wavering candlelight like the writing at Belshazzar's feast. We waited for him to decipher it.

"I'll tell you. The whole of mankind is chained to a dying, irradiated planet. The figure of death," he added, a gloomy finger upraised, "is a skeleton with a scythe, and we'll live to see the reason for that—even those of us who can't see Charybdis will see this—when we see skeletons go out to reap, in deserts where nothing will grow."

He sat down, and in the silence succeeding his impressive voice one hardly knew whether to tremble like Belshazzar or to applaud like a playgoer. I wondered. I let Amy and Leonardo set upon him with a hubbub of objections. Was it entertainment, or was he serious? Did he himself know the difference? Because his own taps had frozen, did he think there was no water anywhere? I wondered if he still knew what his own face was like under the beard. His appearance was certainly oracular, minatory, Noah in this ark in the wilderness prophesying disaster—indeed insisting on disaster, as if private despair was only bearable if the whole planet was laid waste by his curse, the earth scorched behind him as he retreated. In the candlelight, bearded and blood-spattered, conjuring the mythic names, he certainly made one think of those large old legendary figures reeking of doom: Giant Despair, or the Fisher King.

Though Leonardo's beaky voice pecked at him, and Amy teased, he had spoken his piece and would add only Sibylline smiles. It seemed to me he was more interested in the effect of the whisky he fed them.

146

"No more George," Amy said, covering her glass with a lurch of her hand. "I mustn't make a fool of myself again, must I my love."

"Did you make a fool of yourself?" Leonardo asked.

"George said I did. I must get another candle."

George filled Leonardo's glass and Amy's whilst she rummaged in a drawer. "Now you've abandoned Mrs Eddy it isn't illogical to get drunk," he said.

"You've given up Christian Science?" I asked.

"George said I didn't believe in it anyway."

"I pointed out that you didn't understand it," George corrected her. "There is a good deal in the doctrine of Error," he added.

"Oh Lennie look"—in the drawer Amy had found a photograph which she dropped on the table in front of Leonardo—"do look at this." She leaned over his shoulder.

"What have you done with your hands, *poverina*?" he exclaimed, catching at her chilblained fingers to examine them.

She jumped. I noticed the little start, though she quickly hid it with another movement and said, "It's the cold and the washing up."

Leonardo had kept hold of her hand. "See George," he said, "*cosi screpolati* her poor hands."

"She should wear rubber gloves," replied George, who was riddling the Rayburn. "Mrs Winder always does."

The analogy seemed grotesque. It certainly irritated Amy. "You buy Mrs Winder washing-up machines. You buy her whatever she asks for."

"What a parsimonious fellow I am," said George from the door. "You coming to bed Ned?"

He wanted Amy and Leonardo left together. I was tired, and followed him. In passing the table I saw the photograph Amy had found, the one she had taken in the summer at Ardnagour, George with stag's antlers apparently sprouting from his head. In Amy's large round writing underneath I read "The Monarcuckold Of The

Glen". I followed the gloomy monarch up to bed.

I don't know quite why I allowed myself to be railroaded
into an expedition with George next day, which was
Sunday, but at half past three in the afternoon we were
walking through snow on a path over the shoulder of the
highest hill of the forest—at least, George had assured me
we were on a path: to me the white wastes were trackless,
and I was afraid that he was lost. I had stopped saying so
because it irritated him, and because I couldn't think of
anything else we had stopped talking. Our boots squeaked
on the frozen snow, George's breaking through the virgin
crust and mine following in his track. Though I was sweat-
ing, the cold hurt my lungs. Dusk wreathed the corries
below like smoke from infernal fires, ascending towards us
as alarm ascended from the pit of my stomach. I was
certainly lost.

When George had suggested a walk I had thought he
wanted to talk to me alone. The four of us had laboured
away all morning to provision the cottage, filling the
water butt with buckets carried from the burn (for the
hose supplying the tap had finally frozen solid in the night)
and carrying coke and wood for Rayburn and fire. The
hills rang with the clank of buckets and the whack of an
axe splitting logs. After lunch George asked me if I'd stroll
up the hill with him. Amy, flaked out on a sofa beside
Leonardo in front of the fire, opened her eyes and said,
"So you're off my loves. Take care of each other."

And George *was* taking care of me; he wasn't trying to
outwalk me, that evidently wasn't his plan. What his plan
might be I had no idea.

"George we'll never get back before dark," I called after
him.

"Anything wrong with the dark?" He walked on, adding presently, "Anyway we're nearer Ardnagour; haven't
you recognized where we are? Fortunate you've got a
cicerone."

148

"I'd hardly be here on my own."

"You wouldn't would you. It's the guided tour for you. Not that you see the point up here unless you're on your own," he added.

"The point of what?"

He didn't reply for a few minutes. Then he said, "Did you ever look at the plaster cast of this forest they've got at Killaneen?"

"Why?"

"Oh—'what, why'—you really do need a cicerone," he told me impatiently.

Tramping on in silence I tried to see the connection. White as the snow around us, the plaster cast had seemed like a carving expressing in miniature a purpose which the mountains themselves wrote in hieroglyphs too enormous to read. But what purpose? I looked around me. In the snow wastes at dusk the light was uncertain. In winter the most ancient of days was at hand. I was glad that I was not alone. I had fixed my eyes on George's back, shutting out the brink of understanding, which was imminent as the brink of a precipice, when my boots grated on rock. We were descending. From the opalescence of snow we soon gained a definite landscape of frost and crag, and close horizons etched against the dusk.

"Are you planning to go to Ardnagour?" I called ahead.

"If you'd rather not walk back in the dark."

"What about Amy and Leonardo?" Only when I'd asked the question did I realize its implication. "I don't mind going back," I said.

He didn't reply, striding ever more steeply downhill. I guessed that he had always planned to spend the night away from Drumnakeel. I think Amy had known too. I was the excuse. Down we tramped, down into the dusk until at last our boots rang on the road, and the floor of the Ardnagour glen stretched ahead. We turned along the glimmer of road towards the lodge's welcome bulk amongst its trees.

The house was cheerless inside, the damp chill of big brown rooms, and cold dead hearths, and black windows reflecting the glitter of electric light harsh after the candles at Drumnakeel. George had disappeared. I followed stone passages to the kitchen. To my surprise he was taking sea-trout, and bread and potatoes, out of the deep freeze. "One shouldn't thaw them in hot water," he said, "but it can't be helped."

"You leave the electricity on all winter?"

"I sometimes come here if I'm stalking on this side. I did it the other way to begin with, I spent the odd night at Duncan's till Amy came up there."

"That was when Mrs Winder had gone south was it?"

"It was foolish of Amy to quarrel with Mrs Winder," he said. "When people are not used to having servants they will treat them like waiters in restaurants, as Lea warned me."

"They had a quarrel did they?"

"Anything that interferes with Amy's illusion of centrality has to go."

"Mrs Winder interfered?"

"Or Amy interfered. Will you get some wood for the fire, please Ned."

I fetched wood whilst he prepared supper and brought up hock from the cellar. There seemed to be several interpretations of Mrs Winder's departure. Which was the objective truth I didn't know. One never does, and what does it matter? Then we made up a bed for me into which I insisted on putting hot water bottles. He watched me boiling the kettle. "Might as well make one for my bed," he said, "you forget about bachelor comforts when you're married."

"Does Amy not mind being up there on her own?"

"She isn't on her own, she's got her *cicisbeo*."

I wasn't sure what that was. "Usually I mean."

He turned away and paced about the large uneven flagstones. "Nothing scares Amy," he said. It was not a compliment. "In a hurricane in a rowing boat do you know what she'd say?"

"It's a bit blowy," I suggested, filling a bottle for him.

"Yes and that's what she'd actually think. She actually thinks in those terms," he said with exasperated vehemence. "It's impossible to scare her. All she minds about me coming down here is that I'm independent of her."

"So is she independent, left up there I mean."

"Yes, but we already know how independent she is, with her illusion of centrality," he said, taking his bottle and stamping away up the back stairs.

Loquacious and sociable as Amy was, it was true that her heart was her own, as I'd guessed watching her dance at Killaneen. Within her was a core of untouched independence. Only with her brother Terry had I seen her heart-to-heart: they were the fused-together "we" which George and she were not. "Love consists in two solitudes which greet and touch." So cold, cold as the iron beds in those freezing rooms at Drumnakeel, cold as Amy's hand when I had taken it. She had jumped, I suppose, because in the loneliness of two solitudes to be touched is a shock. I went into the sitting room and stood on the hearth rug. The fire was beginning to thaw out the room's spaces, glinting on the glass of the big engravings, liberating warmth to flow through the house and melt the stagnant cold. You could picture George and Amy making love by the fire: whether they had or whether they hadn't, Amy's story was feasible.

We ate supper on a card table near the fire. Sea-trout and hock tasted of summer, and the large room full of firelight became tranquil, a sanctuary. The winter hills were remote from us; no draught could stir the heavy curtains, no frost creep under the doors. The size of the house isolated us, as the spaciousness of a church isolates you from the town at its door and frees your thoughts. The world beyond the mountains came once more into existence. I asked George if he had seen anything of Leonora.

"In London on that disastrous trip I stayed there," he said. "Her courtier friends crawling out of the walls, each richer and more famous and more effortlessly successful than the last—what's the point? I give Lea up. I mean anyone who's grown so unlike, what's the point of bother-ing—caring. Hostages to fortune. 'Caring too much is just for children at scho-o-ol'," he sang. He thought for a while, possibly about the song. Then he added, "Caring for any-one is handing over hostages to the enemy."

"Fortune the enemy? I wouldn't have thought it was yours."

"Anything you can't control is the enemy," he replied.

I laughed. "And you accuse Amy of the illusion of cen-trality! George you're used to living in your own houses on your own land, you've got used to controlling the con-ditions of your life. Maybe too used to it. Most people can't. Most people would call you fortunate. I do."

"As well as dragging in 'most people', which is a phan-tom army which doesn't frighten me," he said, "you're confusing Luck and Fortune."

"But they're synonyms George."

"Not the way I use them," he said, like Humpty Dumpty. "Luck is what you have to start with. What you want would be Fortune. What I have, I've got by Luck—luck, chance, accident, what you will. It's what I want that's withheld. By malignant Fortune. You must see the dis-tinction."

It was true that his possessions had come by accident—the "accident" of his brother's death. I could see that guilt prevented him from calling that accident "Fortune". "Well I don't know what more you want," I said, for he possessed everything I had ever wanted. "The world works its life away to get somewhere near where you started."

"Oh money!" he retorted, rubbing his bearded face wearily. "You don't work for money Ned. You only think you do because you won't face facts. The fact is you actually want to be just what you are, but you won't admit it. I bet you," he went on, "bet you when your old dad dies and leaves you a cool million you'll hide it and go on clocking in at the Foreign Orifice. I know you will. God that depresses me. How're they treating you back at the FO by the way? What does the PPS to HBMA reckon to your Pin-Insertion Plan, or PIP as we now call it?"

I smiled. "They may send me to Mexico after Christmas," I replied, hoping that it might suggest a life of more worth and adventure to him than it did to me. Exotic postings often impress people outside the Service. "But tell me George, what is it you want that Fortune withholds?" He was silent, turning his hock glass in his hands. "Not this song writing," I said, "you can't mean that?"

"Why not? It's no sillier than wanting to be a fucking ambassador."

"I know it isn't sillier, it's just much harder and more improbable for us, people like us. Don't you see George, you've got to capitalize on your advantages, use your qualifications? I mean with our education we know what ambassadors are like before we start. But we've no idea what people who listen to pop songs are like. We can't——"

"Okay okay, stop 'us-ing' and 'we-ing' and lumping me in with you will you? I know I could be a diplomat if I wanted and spend my life worrying about pins—dead easy, that's why there's no point. I want to do something hard." He pondered his wine. "Like be content," he added gloomily.

The Earthly Paradise beyond the iron bars of temperament, unyielding. To the complex nothing, no life, not even Drumnakeel, is simple. He could stalk and gralloch deer like McLeod, but it was only "like", never real. It was all charades.

"Is that why you came up here?" I asked.

"It doesn't matter where I go. It's all so bloody easy for a moron like Robbie Afflick," he complained. "I'm like the Fisher King, where I'm not is where it is."

"Where what is?"

He looked at me with the full stare of his eyes. Out of them, out of his bearded face, floated a look so gentle, so

153

full of longing, that it was like a dove flying out of a briar. I looked away. "Anyway," I said, "the song writing's come to nothing has it?"

"Come to nothing! Christ you are irritating!" His defences were up again.

"But at Terry's party you wouldn't meet whoever it was."

He put his hands behind his shaggy head and laughed up at the ceiling. "They're such frightful bloody oiks," he said delightedly. "And snobs to boot, you should hear them: 'You de guy wid de big like a mansion in the country or someplace?' is the sort of greeting I get when I try and be fantastically humble. Oh God. They're as unlike as Leonora. Unlike as Robbie Afflick. Everyone's unlike," he concluded, slumping his elbows on the card table. "And I hate London now—hate it. What I can't stand is all those godawful parasitic non-industries like advertising and the Stock Exchange polluting the atmosphere."

"You've got rather a bee in your bonnet about pollution at the moment," I said. It always seems to me that individuals who forecast doom and destruction, be it from atomic fall-out or the exhaustion of the world's resources, would in the middle ages have ascended mountains and there awaited the Last Trump. It is withdrawal from reality. "Yesterday you were complaining about the Midlands, today it's London."

"At least in the Midlands all that smoke and muck comes from making real things," he said. "But in London you get all those stockbrokers we were at school with making paper money out of paper money and filling your ears with rubbish. Even worse is advertising, those bloody hoardings polluting the air with sex. I mean soot's on the skin, but that muck blackens the soul."

"Sex blackens the soul?"

"Selling it—using it—that's the smut. Christ, it's okay for us, we've screwed models so it doesn't hurt us. But what about the poor bloody janitor? You come home between the hoardings and the ads on the Underground and you have to climb into bed with some old charlady. That's tough enough without the bill-boards leaning on you. That's what blackens people's souls."

"Songs sell sex," I pointed out.

"Mine won't."

"The ones you hear do." I watched him throw a log on the fire. Only when there is a market for acrostic verse chanted to lute music could I foresee George as a song writer. He didn't realize that it is never a favourable sign to think that your successful competitors are no good at their job; it's a sign that you don't know the market. In my own profession I had spent a year or more criticizing the prose style in which my seniors wrote dispatches; only when my own drafts had been invariably returned to me for rewriting did I learn to copy my masters' style. This lesson, that what is acceptable should be copied, is not taught at the universities, where teachers—themselves often disqualified from the real world by eccentricity— encourage any tuppenny-ha'penny quirks of "originality" in their pupils. George hadn't needed to learn pragmatism : at least he hadn't until perversity, or Amy, had led him into Tin Pan Alley. "It's the ones you hear that count," I repeated.

He soused himself down in an armchair with another glass of hock. "Anyway the whole thing's impossible, like everything else I've ever wanted to do," he said. Presently, even more gloomily, he announced, "It seems I will have to accustom myself to being a failure."

I laughed, telling him, "When you had your broken ankle you said you'd have to accustom yourself to being an invalid, remember? That's healed hasn't it."

"For the moment. It still errs. Failure and sickness"— he held up two fingers of each hand to show that he was quoting—"sickness and failure are a state of subjective error contrary to truth. Those who wickedly insist upon being ill failures end up in the wilderness without love. The sun burns them and the rain never falls. Witness if you will the waste land 'where no-one comes or hath come since the making of the world'."

His voice sank almost to a whisper, and he stared into the fire. The line of Tennyson conjured up the hills at our door. They strode closer. I have never understood mythography, in which figures and symbols are so large and vague, and I couldn't remember the legend of the Waste Land. I asked him across the fire, "Tell me George, what was the crime of the Fisher King that laid waste his kingdom?"

"If I knew that," he sighed, "I'd know everything." He began to poke the fire again, hunched in front of it, coaxing flame from the wood. He said thoughtfully, "Perhaps it wasn't so much a crime as a ghastly error."

"An error of what? Oh I see"—I made the connection—"you mean like Christian-Science sin, error against the true spirit of love. Hate you mean. Do you?" I wondered.

"In a way. You see supposing—suppose that pagan girl he married only pretended she was converted to his faith. Pretended because she fancied him."

"Or fancied being queen," I suggested.

He turned on me. "No that's irrelevant Ned. Will you never understand that ambition is irrelevant? No—suppose the king found out that secretly, secretly," he repeated, tapping sparks from the fire for emphasis, "she went on being a pagan. What he'd hate was, that his judgement had erred and let her con him. And why he'd been so easily blinded, the reason he didn't listen to his inner judgement, was because he fancied a spot of the other. *Son desir eust aveuglé sa raison.* Then it's the archetypal error you see, mistaking sex for Love. The error of the ad-man."

I said, "Doesn't seem enough of an error to call down all that drought and famine and barrenness."

"Oh but you see you have to understand about the freeing of the waters," he replied. "The sin is against love, and it's love that makes the land fruitful. Rain is the divine ejaculation. Mushrooms and all that. It's hate which locks up the springs and wells. I thought you'd know all this if you're going to Mexico. Haven't you read any Indian mythology?"

I ignored the enfilading fire he was so fond of. "And doesn't self-hate lock up the springs? Isn't self-hate a sin?" I asked.

"You know the Greek for sin also means missing the mark, as at archery?" he said, turning from the fire with the energy he was always prepared to expend upon defining words. "Of course you do. Well the most difficult mark of all to hit is exactly the amount you should hate or love yourself. What I mean is for example, did the pilgrim Christian hate himself enough to fall into the sin of self-hate, or only enough to qualify as a broken and contrite heart? Answer me that if you are able, and pass the hock."

When I had filled his glass I said, "Self-criticism isn't self-hate, and Bunyan——"

"What I mean is," he interrupted me, "you're supposed to say 'There is no health in me' but you're not supposed quite to believe it or you'd loathe yourself body and soul."

"George the General Confession is an incantation, as most prayers are. There's no point worrying about each word."

This maddened him. "God!" he expostulated, "sages and scholars argue for centuries, often sitting up all night no doubt, whole armies fight wars—and you say the words don't matter. You're just like Amy—reads Mary Baker Eddy, picks up one or two things as if she was shopping around the supermarket, and just leaves the rest of the entire system on the shelf. But you—you've been educated for God's sake."

"Faith doesn't depend on semantics and logic George."

"If it doesn't it's not worth having. It hasn't got proper foundations."

"That's your opinion," I said. "It isn't Amy's presumably. Or wasn't."

"My opinion is rational and happens to be the truth."

"Not the truth to me."

"Well I hope you don't wake up," he said.

157

"Wake up?"

"Yes, if you do, your idea of reality will go out bang! just like a candle."

I didn't tell him what I thought, which was that he had self-hate without humility, because he would surely have told me that humility didn't mean what I thought it meant, and he would have redefined it, citing sources, to describe himself exactly. He broke words into such small pieces that they had no meaning and couldn't function: he was like a boy taking the wings off a fly to see how they worked, and when he found they didn't work any more, he concluded that flies couldn't really fly at all. All arguments with George ended at last, as this one did, with the hair-splitting of semantics and epistemology. The trees interested him more than the wood.

We drank the three bottles of hock, and it was late by the time the last of the wood I had carried in had burned away to embers. "Shall we fetch more?" he suggested, holding out his hands to the dying fire.

He was like a boy, or an intelligent adolescent, and in arguing semantics and epistemology with him (as we had done that night years before when Leonora had told us to stop our childish shouting and go to bed) I felt that he had got out his old toys and asked me to play. It was a retreat into the toy cupboard from things-as-they-are. Now that there was no Leonora to tell him to go to bed, I had to play her part. "It's late George, I must go to bed," I said, getting to my feet. "Is the water frozen here too?"

"Fire and water," he muttered dreamily into the ashes, "water and fire, these be hard task masters my friend. Tell me Ned, and tell me true——"

"Yes?" I was stacking the dirty plates.

"Oh God leave that!" he said angrily. "Why must people fuss about and do boring things interminably!"

"It's got to be done."

"Mrs McLeod comes and does all that, what are servants for?" He rose from his haunches and strode out of the room.

His independence, I thought as I cleared the table onto a tray, didn't take him very far, only away from Amy into the care of other women. Impersonate as he might the craggy self-sufficiency of a stalker in the winter hills, the stalker's wife was still paid to look after him just as the stalker brought down from the hill the carcasses he had shot. I followed him out of the house into the sudden clutch of frost under the stars. He stood peeing on the frozen gravel. "Tell me Ned," he said, "what's your opinion of our visiting Cupid?"

"Cupid?"

"Doesn't Lennie remind you of the baby-faced godling?"

I laughed. "A sort of pantomime Cupid, yes he does."

"But she lives in a world of panto. Do you think he's up to it?"

"Up to what?"

"Up to the responsibility. I mean can he—I don't know, maybe Cupid is a pantomime figure," he said resignedly. He gazed up at the black rim of hills which hid the far high strath of Drumnakeel, then turned back towards the lighted door.

As I mounted the stairs behind him I asked him a question which I thought he mightn't answer in a less open mood in the morning. "What happened to Amy's dog, George?"

His step didn't falter. "Rover? He's in London with Terry. Why?"

"I just wondered."

"She got sick of him as soon as he grew up. Lovebirds and rabbits in cages are Amy's idea of nature's place. A world of panto," he repeated.

"How's Terry's garage business gone?"

"Fantastic. He's a genius," George told me morosely. "He said all he needed was some pathetic amount of capital, and it's absolutely bloody true."

"So you're making money out of it?"

George was at his bedroom door, and I was across the landing at mine. "I gave my share to Amy," he said.

159

"The only thing they've got between them which I don't want is their fucking money." He slammed his door.

I shut my own and began to undress. I closed my mind against Amy's insidious scent lingering in the sweaters she had lent me. She had cheated sympathy out of me for her dog's death, cheated me into taking her hand, cheated me into thinking that only the pillow came between myself and her that night on the Italian coast. No doubt she laughed.

If, that is, Rover was really with Terry in London. The shiver in her voice saying, "His head was all smashed to bits" was like dramatic truth. If Amy lived in a world of panto, George lived in a world of Grand Guignol where the disappearance of any living creature had sinister under-tones, and his explanations had the logic of Machiavelli. The only truth of the matter was that I was deceived into believing whichever one of them I was with.

In the morning George's mood was changed, as was the weather, a lightless dawn threatening snow. He had already eaten breakfast by the time I came down, and he tramped heavily and impatiently in and out of the kitchen whilst I ate mine. I noticed that he had washed up our dinner. He was playing the taciturn, self-sufficient man of the hills again.

"Have you finished?" he asked, coming into the harshly-lit kitchen once again. He had a rifle in his hand which I suppose he kept at Ardnagour. "Look if you're going to Inverness this afternoon for the train Ned, there's no point your trailing all the way back to Duncan's, you'd better walk down the track and someone'll pick you up at the iron gate okay?"

"But what——"

"The thing is I'm going to shoot on the way back to Duncan's. You'd be out of the way on the track."

"What about my luggage?"

"Don't fuss Ned, someone can easily pack it and bring

it down to meet you," he explained as if to a child.

"And I'm wearing Amy's clothes."

"That you don't need to tell me," he said. "God, you and Lennie sitting around in Amy's clothes—it's like having three bloody principal boys in the pantomime. Take them with you, she won't need them. Anyway I've got to go now so goodbye. There's food for lunch here and someone'll pick you up at the iron gate about three-thirty. So goodbye."

Through the barred kitchen window I watched him climb into the wintry hills behind the house, a dark figure in the dawn ascending towards the snow, and towards Drumnakeel beyond, at the relentless, killing pace of the stalker.

My journey into the mountains ended where it had begun, waiting at the iron gate at dusk instead of dawn. The shepherd's wife had come out of the cottage when I arrived at three, and she had told me that Mr George had brought my suitcase down and had ordered a taxi to take me to Inverness. "It's a shame about the blood," she said, handing me my smeared and sticky bag, "he brought some carcasses down with him. Will you not come in to the fire while you wait?"

As I had done before, I refused; and once more I regretted it, pacing to and fro as darkness gathered. A dreary wind pushed clouds over the whale-grey humps of the mountains receding into night, and moaned in the black trees. Out of the cottage pane spilled warm yellow light, the peace of home. It overflowed like a cask of gold, riches beyond price.

Eventually my taxi came. By its headlights I saw into the shed where Leonardo's Ferrari had stood. The car had gone. If only I had entered the cottage and sat by the fire I would have learned who George had brought down with the carcasses, and who had left in the Ferrari. But as usual it was too late to know the truth. I could only speculate and imagine.

VII

Before travelling to Scotland I had known un-officially—official and unofficial knowledge are two of the many subdivisions of reality in the Service—that I was to be posted to Mexico City in the New Year, so that in the weeks before Christmas, which I planned to "celebrate" with my parents in Antigua, I was too busy reading up Mexican politics, and reactivating my Spanish, to take in anything but the headlines of the English newspapers. So if the press reported the accident, I missed the report.

My parents' house was a single-storey frame building under a red-tiled roof, sequestered by the jungle green of palms from identical neighbouring houses on the development, its cool rooms furnished with cane and cotton covers, its colonnaded veranda giving onto a lagoon under the round green hills. The beach washed by the lap of wave-lets was a couple of steps beyond. So near was the water that its reflection, a living membrane of light, trembled on the ceilings of the rooms. Amongst plastic holly, and a Christmas tree laden with cotton-wool snow, in great heat—and especially to an eye which still retained images of frost and real winter at Drumnakeel—this make-believe Christmas was extraordinarily false.

I had arrived late on Christmas Eve. On Christmas morning, in hats and suits, the three of us motored to church. Afterwards we stood chatting with neighbours under the brass sky before motoring home again through the cane fields, avoiding black children playing by their hen-coop houses, and drunks thumbing lifts by brandish-ing their machetes, to a heavy Christmas meal. It was whilst we were chewing the plum pudding, sweat starting from our brows, that my mother said in her aggrieved tone, "You haven't mentioned the accident Ned dear."

"What accident Mother?"

"Of course," she said, myopically dabbing at a spot of brandy butter on the table, "George is such a dear I'm sure he'll try and stop it making any difference. If poor Amy is disfigured."

Instantly I saw George's dark figure ascending the hill towards Drumnakeel. I heard the crash of a shot strike the hills and break into echoes. I saw Amy's clothes strewn on the scree. The welter and slop of the bloody gralloch filled my mind as the sticky pudding filled my mouth. All this in an instant whilst I heard my father saying:

"He's a good deal knocked up though, I gather. I wish you'd tell me if you're going to put money in the food dear, I might have broken my bridge."

From a great distance I watched him picking a sixpence off his tongue. Careful of my voice I asked, "What accident are you talking about?"

"You mean you haven't heard?" My mother's eyes lighted, with news to impart.

"I wouldn't ask if I'd heard."

But she would spin out the treat, tasting it with a moistening movement of her lips. "I boiled the money rather than wrapping it this year, it's so much more Christmassy somehow," she said. Then she added, "Oh yes, it was all in the papers. I don't know how you missed it."

The pressure in my head broke into unchosen words: "Just tell me what he's done to Amy will you?"

"Well!" She regarded me curiously. "I don't know that he's done anything to Amy. It was the time their friend was killed, and putting two and two——"

"We don't know it was the same accident dear. We don't know it was a motor smash at all come to that," my father added. He too was studying my face.

"I know we don't Jack dear, I've said we were putting two and two together," my mother conceded. "It's all one can do, hearing as little news as we do out here," she added, her mild wail returning to her own grievances after her moment of curiosity in what I had let slip.

"But have you heard something we haven't?" my father asked me.

"I've told you, I didn't even know there'd been an accident," I said. "Perhaps you'd tell me what did happen," I suggested, meeting his eye.

He looked away. His bony hands, which had been pottering about the table, picked up spoon and fork again. "Seems this friend of theirs, Italian chap, was motoring along the A832—he'd been stopping with them up at Ardnagour—motoring along to Contin Bridge, you know where the road turns sharp right there?"

"Not Contin Bridge Jack, Moy Bridge," my mother put in.

"Moy? No no dear, I know exactly the spot—driven that road often enough in my thoughts out here I can tell you—you're through Garve, right? Go on past the loch on your left, it's twisty mind..."

His curiosity in the accusation I had let slip was forgotten in recreating the Highland scenery he doted on. I recovered myself. I don't know why I had immediately blamed George for whatever had happened. Eventually he told how Leonardo's car had been found, by George apparently, upside down in a river, and my mother added details of how Leonardo's remains had only appeared several miles downstream, very much smashed by water and rock, and how Amy had been taken to hospital in Inverness. Those were the newspaper facts. Still I saw George's armed figure climbing the dawn hillside towards Drumnakeel: it was like a grim woodcut hung on the wall of my imagination, an illustration from the *danse macabre*. "Amy was in the car was she?" I asked.

"Well one assumes so. She was pretty badly knocked about."

"Have you got the newspaper?"

"Threw it out I'm afraid. Got a letter from old Bryce though," my father said through a mouthful of crystallized fruit. "You remember Teddy Bryce? Awfully good

164

of him, always writes about Christmas time, keeps in touch."

"You write to him dear," my mother said.

"I know I write to him. Goodness gracious. I've got nothing else on, he's got Glentornish to look to, big place that, fine shoot."

"Could I see the letter?" I asked loudly before the past closed completely over their heads.

"Not exactly a letter," my father admitted, getting to his feet, "more a card in fact. He's a busy chap. Here we are."

Having knocked a whole lot of Christmas cards over he handed me one of teal springing from a pool. I read, "Rotten luck poor Amy's smash-up, these plastic chaps can work wonders nowadays, all the best, Teddy". I dropped it on the table. My mother picked it up and began to fuss all the cards upright again on their shelf whilst my father unstoppered a decanter from which he filled his glass before shoving it towards me.

"I'm afraid we've nothing much arranged for you to do," he said. "But give yourself a glass of port and tell us your news. Didn't you write us you were going up to Ardnagour in the back end?"

"I was hoping to," I said, "but I was too busy to get away."

The subject was too complex to embark upon. As well expect Santa Claus to tether his reindeer to a manchineel tree as to adumbrate the misty, hyperborean menace which hung round Drumnakeel. In that tropic heat the snow figures melted. My father would have laughed at my fears, and my mother would have said comfortably, "I'm sure it's only your imagination dear". It had been her refrain ever since my breakdown.

When my parents had taken themselves off for their customary nap, after a show of trying to keep awake on my account, I went through their Christmas cards to learn anything I could about this "accident". All I found were a few words in Lea's spiky hand: "They are keeping G very quiet, but I went up to Chester to see him and he sends his love." Then I took some personality reports on the Mexican government out to the veranda, where I sat in a long chair and tried to concentrate my mind upon them, and upon my future in Mexico. But continually, more real than the heat or the tropic scene, I saw again the streaky dawn sky threatening snow above Ardnagour, the wintry hill and George ascending to fade from my view. In the next frame, so to say, I saw the shepherd's wife handing me my blood-wet suitcase and telling me that George had brought some carcasses down with him. What had happened in between these frames, up at Drumnakeel, was as my mother would have said "only imagination". The figure of George splashed with blood, the gloomy king in Tartarus revered—only a Grand Guignol ogre? Perhaps. It had to be admitted that George's guilt for his brother's blood, which had in the past (so I had been told by the psychologist) filled a need in my own mind, was an invention of my imagination. It was I who had put the mark of Cain on him.

Boating with my father—not much fun because he sprang about his dinghy rapping out orders in a panicky falsetto as if we were aboard a foundering tea-clipper— or listening to my mother complain of their neighbours' wealth, I tried to forget Drumnakeel. It was pitiable how they and their neighbours pored over their English past, boasting of country houses which had once been their homes and of children who had dispossessed them. It is an effect of the tax laws, to dispossess a generation at an age when it most needs continuity with the past. I tried to forget Saradon, and tried to project my mind forward to Mexico, though there was little enough to attract it there. Nonetheless I couldn't help thinking back. Leonardo's car, for instance, had gone from the shed before my taxi driver and I set out for Inverness, so wouldn't we have seen signs of an accident if it had run off the road ahead of us? Like slivers of ice from the Scottish winter, thoughts circulated in my blood and occasionally, icily, needled my imagination.

Settling into a new post in a strange city is, compared to the hazards of ordinary travelling, a fairly painless business. Much is familiar—the routine work, the social round —and Admin. Section buffers you from the outward vicissitudes of local life by dealing with landlords and finding a servant and in general doing their best to make you hear Bow Bells through the hubbub of the bazaar. Familiar too, especially to a bachelor, is the lonely setting up of yet another flat which will never be a home: of seeing one's possessions attempting to be household gods against another impermanent alien background. It was a strange thing, in the first few days, how often there came back to me the memory of the cottage by the iron gate at Ardnagour, its window spilling warmth into the frost as if a cornucopia of homeliness overflowed.

I saw no particular reason to dislike Mexico City. Broad tree-shaded avenues connected squares in which colossal statues of revolutionaries struck heroic attitudes amongst the hydrangeas, and I learned their names, and the street names, with the palimpsest-like part of my mind which had learned and forgotten the names of the streets and public heroes in Belgrade and Rome. The winter light was extraordinarily rarefied. Such was its clarity that it singled out infinite tones of each colour; in the trees, for instance, with which the city was so freely planted, the eye distinguished a thousand shades of green. This intense light was the only effect of the altitude which I noticed, although the roneo'd bumph distributed to incoming staff threatened all manner of terrors consequent upon living at 8,000 feet: fluttering hearts, intoxication, ungovernable rages. I laughed at the idea of one's whole temperament being altered by living a fraction nearer the sun. The curiously-shaped volcanic mountain tops which brooded round the city looked more like stage-flats hung from the sky than threatening upheavals of the earth.

Only in retrospect can I see their menace, and feel through the clarity of the light the threat of the sun, Tezcatlipoca, the smoking mirror, who would if he wished, and wasn't propitiated by sacrifice, destroy the world.

It is necessary to explain that I had got into the way of seeing a good deal of a person who worked for the British Council. A girl? A woman? At first I had thought of her as a lady, and had called her Miss Tozer. We had met when she came as the Council's representative to the meeting of a cultural committee whose chairmanship had been fobbed off on me. She was evidently suffering from what was known as Moctezuma's Revenge, for she kept rushing out of the meeting grey-faced and trailing back in again with uncertain steps and a resolute air, so that my impression was of a gallant spinster determined to carry on against whatever odds. Perhaps sickness made her look older than she was, because I got it into my head that she was a middle-aged woman, at that first meeting, and I suppose did not look at her very closely again. She had a smooth plain face, her hair scraped off it in a no-nonsense style, as if hair were best forgotten, and she wore loosish blouses and longish skirts. Under her arm wherever she went she carried a clip-board for note-taking. Only her eyes, when she took off her glasses, were vulnerable; they looked bruised, as if the resolute spirit that looked you in the face had suffered a secret hurt.

Our committee meetings, which were to do with exchange exhibitions of folk-art, were lengthy and repeated. Although I was in the chair I had no views of my own and adopted hers, relying on her insistent, rather toneless voice to wear down opposition to our ideas. She was thoroughly in earnest, humourless unless a joke was well signalled, and relentless in her pursuit of improved understanding between different cultures. But she was a kindly person. The first instance she gave me of her kindness was when she said, as we left a meeting together, "Sliced bread is so much easier for us single folk: shall I try and get you a loaf?" In the Amazonian jungles she would have been on the trail of sliced Hovis, and I thought it kind of her to share the tip-off.

Over the next few days she telephoned several times with news of my loaf, and at last we arranged a lunch-time handover at the archaeological museum in Chapultapec park which she knew I had not yet visited. In the following weeks other outings, always cultural, were made together, and if she accepted my offer of a meal it was only as a makeweight squeezed into our programme. "Yes I think we've time for a bite," she would say, and we would gobble an omelette between rooms at the museum, or a sandwich at the bus station on our way to Teotihuacán. Only once was the meal an object in itself, and then it was a failure; a lecture she had taken tickets for was cancelled, and I took her to dine instead at a restaurant off the Calle Londres, which she rather spoiled for me by comparing the prices on the menu with the annual incomes of families living on the city's outskirts. For the first time she revealed a guilt-inducing, accusatory sharpness of manner.

I knew of this restaurant because I had had lunch there a few days earlier with Leonora, who had rung me up from Acapulco and suggested that we lunched together before she caught her plane to New York. Of course she knew the best restaurant, and there we met, she sweeping rapidly in to find me waiting, time as usual short before a friend's chauffeur would call to take her to the airport. She settled her bag on a spare chair, chose food, surveyed the restaurant with her cool grey eyes and only then brought them to rest with their quizzical glint upon myself.

"Well Ned," she said, "tell me about yourself." Nothing to interest her came to mind. She would not have arranged our meeting without a purpose. I waited, smiling. "Christmas with the old folk?" she supposed. "And a trip to Scotland I hear."

"George told you I'd been up?"

169

"It was the talk of the Station Hotel. Pity you didn't stay for the drama though. Someone sane was sorely needed," she said, looking about for a waiter from whom she ordered mineral water. "Not that sanity appears to be our long suit as a family," she resumed.

"What do you mean?"

"Well George is eccentric. I live on my nerves and you've visited the psychiatrist's parlour in your time. Still, you'd have been a help clearing up the mess if you'd bothered to come."

"I didn't even know there'd been a drama till I got to Antigua," I protested, "so it wasn't a question of bothering; I didn't know."

"Didn't you?" Her arched brows disbelieved me.

"I still don't know exactly what happened. Tell me."

"How much do you know?"

"Only that Leonardo was killed in his car and Amy was hurt somehow, presumably in the same crash was she?"

"Ah then, you know all anyone knows," she said. I had the impression that she was relieved, for her face relaxed. Too late I realized that I had played my cards whilst she had kept her own close to her chest.

"What else is there to know?" I asked, although I knew she wouldn't tell me.

She opened long nervous hands as if there was nothing to conceal. It was a tiresome thing to happen. Poor George."

"Where is he now?"

"He had to rest. Even *his* love of misfortune was rather glutted."

"Is he at Saradon?"

"Maybe by now." Sipping her mineral water she would dispense no further snippets of what she knew.

"What about Amy?" I asked.

"What about her?"

"Well I heard something about plastic surgery. I mean is she——" I didn't want to face the thought.

"Badly smashed?" Lea supplied. She touched her lips with her napkin. "To someone who didn't depend quite so much on looks," she said, "I don't believe the scar would matter. And they shaved her head of course."

"One scar?"

"One that shows."

"Where?"

In answer, Lea's shining nail traced a line from the corner of her right eye to the corner of her mouth. For a moment her nail left a white weal on her tanned cheek. Imagining the damage to Amy's face I turned away. Our food came, and Lea told me what had happened after the accident, when she had gone to Scotland—as in a novel by Henry James, I knew what events had led up to the drama, and now learned what had followed it, whilst the event itself, the moment of truth, was an abyss full of imaginings. "That poor Italian boy," she said, "no-one in the world wanted his wretched body. It was rather pathetic, in the end I had to dispose of it myself." She had buried him in Inverness, herself the only mourner. I thought of the north wind blowing over his grave. Her derisive tone, seemingly callous, achieved what perhaps she intended; it reduced the accident from disaster and mystery to bathos and muddle. Nothing was terrible: at worst things were irksome. She knew what had happened that day; at least I thought she did, just as I had always thought Lea knew exactly how George had killed his brother. But she wouldn't tell. She paid for lunch and flew to New York, taking her unruffled air of omniscience with her. Again I tried to forget George's figure ascending the dark hill to Drumnakeel.

To my mind the former civilizations of Mexico reiterate below their evident glories one theme, a sinister bass, a refrain of cruelty and blood. Hardly an obsidian blade which had not been sharpened for sacrifice, hardly a stony-staring god who was not girdled with skulls or cloaked in a flayed skin: there seemed to be no monument which wasn't built upon foundations of bone and blood, so that the sickening smell of so many myriad ritual deaths made the whole country reek like a slaughterhouse. I am aware that scholarly minds discover beautiful objects and marks of advanced scientific development in the pre-conquest civilization: my point is, that in order to see the beauty of a hollow-backed stone jaguar one must forget its purpose, which was to contain the hearts torn from living men; in order to marvel at the Mayan calendar-stone one must forget the hecatombs of victims sacrificed so that spring should follow winter. Perhaps my mind discovered under the stones only the sanguinary sermons that my imagination had already hidden there, for I could not forget.

Still, I was anxious to pick up some knowledge of meso-american history, if only to answer the endless questions of my Ambassador's guests, and Angela—Miss Tozer—was more than anxious to instruct me. She had the enthusiastic attitude towards archaeological remains which can reconstruct a human being from a handful of dust in a funerary urn. The people whom she constructed in this way turned out to be very like herself. She knew homey details of the Aztecs' domestic life: she would pore over a codex which showed women gardening or washing clothes, and if in another section of the same codex dreadful-faced gods were slavering over meals of flesh, she completely ignored them. In the National Museum one Sunday I interrupted her raptures to say, "I believe you would peep and botanize upon your mother's grave."

"Pardon?" Her kind face was already smiling as she looked up, expecting from my tone a pleasantry of some sort.

As I repeated my remark I realized the awful inappropriateness of Wordsworth's line.

"Poor Mummy," she said, bending over the glass case again.

For her mother was gallantly dying of unspecified

diseases. Brave letters told how puzzled the doctors were by her worsening symptoms—at least, Angela told me how brave the letters were, though to me they sounded like a list of complaints against everything from the weather to North Sea Gas. She read me the letters because I was mentioned in them, which had at first flattered me but more recently began to make me uneasy, for from generalization ("diplomats do such important work in these troubled times") her mother had moved to the particular, "I would like to hope that I might live to see your friend here one day," and there was now something spider-like in this correspondence spinning its toils around me. I walked softly away from Angela through the hushed rooms of the museum, passing Indians sweeping the marble floors with long-tailed mops, and emerged to find a seat on a stone bench in the courtyard where I often sat, weary long before Angela, and listened to water falling from the immense mushroom-shaped fountain.

The Mexicans have not lost their ancestors' skill at erecting monoliths. The fountain suggested Titanic vastness whose weight, like the weight of that colossal rock behind Drumnakeel, crushed the individual to nothing. The earth groaned under it. To me, from the dark-glazed rooms around the courtyard all those cruel artifacts cried out in their blood. The purpose which had shaped them, and had raised the pyramids at Teotihuacán, and had sculpted the mountain-top at Monte Alban, was the same grim purpose which had carved the hills and corries of Ardnagour. I could smell the shambles' stench of the hind George had gralloched. Here, as in Scotland, "mother earth" wasn't the maternal Ceres of the Mediterranean but a flesh-eating monster, India's Kali rattling her necklace of skulls. Regeneration by cannibalism: the eater eating is eaten. Through the sound of falling water I was glad to hear Angela Tozer's busy step approaching. She did not hear the shrieks of the implacable sun's victims. "If you want to break for a snack I don't mind," she said, rubbing her eyes behind her glasses.

I sat on for a moment. She was so brisk. I wanted to sound her imagination. "I wonder if the fountain is mushroom-shaped because of Tlaloc," I suggested. "To appease him I mean, like a lightning conductor."

She looked mystified. I explained the belief that mushrooms grow where lightning strikes. "That's only superstition." She said, "I'm sure the Aztecs didn't believe anything so silly, they were keen naturalists you know. But I'll look in the Council library." She made a note on her clip-board. At first I had been rather flattered that she wrote down my questions, but since she never brought me back any answers I began to suspect the notes she took. She might well have been marking me nought out of ten for silly questions. "Come," she said, "a quick bite and then I want to pop upstairs to the second century. Why do you laugh?"

I had laughed because George once pointed out to me the absurdity of the sign posts you see in museums, directing you to other centuries as if you were in a time machine. I didn't explain this because I had never mentioned George to Angela. As well describe colours to the blind. Besides, I didn't want to mix her up with what I had turned my back on. I stood up. "Let's go and have lunch," I said, picking up the handkerchief I had been sitting on.

She looked hurt that I hadn't explained my laughter. "A hanky won't stop you getting haemorrhoids," she sniffed, marching ahead. A shrewishness had begun to show its teeth through the deference she had at first shown me. She had cast sliced bread upon the water, and now I felt the hook.

In my bath that night I considered the pros and cons of Angela Tozer. Sharp as she sometimes was with me, she was sharper still with anyone who slighted me in the office politics which I told her about. She was ambitious for me, and that was an advantage because I was decreasingly ambitious for myself. She was equipped to handle the other end of a dull dinner table when in the course of time I became an Ambassador. And time was coursing. If you leave marriage until late in life you don't have, in old age, the pile of shared years stacked round you to keep out draughts. I would soon have to set about stacking up some shared years if ever I was to have a home so snug and warm that the superabundance of homeliness could overflow into the frosty night as it overflowed from the cottage window by the Ardnagour gate. It is true that these considerations were the pros of marriage rather than the pros of Angela, but I had drifted into comparative intimacy with no-one else, Amy excepted, for years and years. Amy I certainly excepted. Angela didn't attract me sexually, but this, like her deafness to the shrieks of the sun's victims, I found a relief. Like a plinth upon which to exhibit her head, her body was a functional device. When it went wrong she discussed its malfunction—in terms such as "costiveness" or "haemorrhoids"—like a plumber, and I no more worried whether I should hold her hand than one worries about holding a tap. Indeed once, using the bathroom in her cosy flat, when I had come face to face with a pair of blue pants drying on the towel rail I had looked instinctively away, rather shocked that she should sport anything so flighty. One pictured her in off-white. As I have said, I hadn't really thought about her age, but when I was with her I felt younger, which I liked. I also felt that my perceptions were quicker than hers, that I laughed when she didn't see the joke, that I was more sensitive than she was: in fact I felt more nearly the person I would have liked to be. More like George perhaps.

How old was she, I wondered as I lay in my bath? Then my condescension received a jolt. For the very first time in my life I felt through my hair the cold touch of the bath-enamel on my scalp. I was almost bald. It was a shock. It was a chill reminder of my own age, and of my true appearance, however I might picture myself in Angela's company. In the steam as I lay there I saw the two of us tramping into the future, a middle-aged couple, myself seedily bald on the heels of an earnest wife whose tireless stream of trivia reduced history to dust and drove the terror and splendour of the old gods off each mountain temple we ascended. I thought of hill temples because in a month's time I had a week's leave due, as Angela knew, and already she had begun to feed me bumph about Monte Alban and Oaxaca, her own leave planned to coincide with mine. If we went to Oaxaca together I was scuppered. To avoid going I would have to take action. I knew I wouldn't take action. Like an image from a lost life I saw Amy dancing that reel on the grass at Killaneen under the oak and the evening star, and I heard her say "It was only a pillow between us, you could have come over it". But it wasn't only a pillow: it was the bars of my temperament, fixed and unyielding.

One Sunday in midsummer Angela and I made an expedition to a village called Tepotzlan, which entailed catching an early bus to Cuernavaca and crossing the town to catch another into the mountains. In the bus station the noise and confusion were like pandemonium—loudspeakers raining music on our heads, Indians swarming, flies everywhere—and my temper suddenly rose against the dreary misery of always behaving as if one had no money. I knew that this expedition was a dry-run for our trip to Oaxaca, which grew inevitably closer as each day passed. I shouted through the uproar to Angela, "Come on, we'll take a taxi if you want to go to this bloody village."

"Typical!" she replied with a peck of her head, tight-faced, trying her best to queue in the disorderly mob, jabbing her elbows at the Indians.

"What's typical Angela?"

"Your reaction dear."

"Typical of what?"

She tossed her head. "Privilege. People like you."

We went by bus. Tepotzlan proved delightful, a cluster of adobe round a large tumbledown monastery in whose

176

neglected walls flowers, even trees, had taken root, so that it seemed like a great earthy hummock thrown up by nature; contrarily, the rock faces of the mountains themselves were columned by vertical strata which looked like the piers of a Norman cathedral, so that the impression was of a monastery built by nature amongst hills decorated by man, an ambiguous landscape. The bus had left us by a bandstand in the cobbled square, deserted in the heat and peace of noon. Angela was puzzled. I don't know what she had expected, a museum perhaps, even folk-dancing, but I left her interrogating her guide-book and walked into the monastery alone.

A sonorous bell sounded from the gate-tower as I passed under its rust-coloured tufa. Inside, the sun struck through the arches of an ambulatory from which I mounted by shallow stone stairs to the passages above. Cell after cell had a vaulted roof, and a window cut in the thickness of stone which framed a view of towering, pine-prickled crags. The cells preserved the cool of caves, and were utterly quiet. It was as though I had plunged into the peaceful pool of monasticism. But thoughts of Angela soon caught up with me. I had become almost obsessively aware of her clean, square nails, with which she had a habit of scratching the skin of her arms, a disagreeable dry rasp like a rat gnawing in the wall. In the bus it had nearly driven me mad. I sat on a window ledge in one of the cells trying over in my mind various ways I could stop her doing this without insulting her. Before long I heard her footsteps searching me out, and I went down to join her.

"Oh dear we've wasted a precious Sunday," she said as we walked back towards the square. "Apparently there's nothing to see."

"There's the place itself."

She looked round the plaza dismissively. "But if we're quick," she said, "we can have a snack at the posada, I found out where it is when you mooned off—then if we're quick we can catch the early bus. There's plenty to see at Cuernavaca."

We walked up a steep lane across which trickled dubious liquid from the adobe huts. "...red sullen faces sneer and snarl from doors of mud-cracked houses." Again *The Waste Land*. I said, "You were so keen to come I thought you must have looked it up in your guide-book."

"You know I looked it up Ned dear," she said archly, tapping my arm with her clip-board. "I made a mistake, I'm sorry, need I say more?"

"I like it," I replied. "I like somewhere real rather than a site sometimes, don't you?"

"Real? Don't you find the olden times real enough?"

"Not bits of pottery in glass cases, no I don't."

"I should say Mexico's rather wasted on you if you don't," she sniffed.

"But Angela, the world's wasted on you if you do," I said. "And if you've been bitten by mosquitoes or something, shouldn't you put stuff on the bites rather than scratching your arms all the time?"

"What you need dear is something to eat," she informed me.

So as not to miss our bus we ate quickly in the cool tiled dining room of the posada. I would have liked to have walked in the garden beyond the Moorish windows, under pines and cypresses shading the bougainvillaea-covered walls and brilliant flowers, but there was no time. The prospect reminded me of Italy, of the garden of Leonardo's farmhouse above the Tyrrhenian sea, which I had so precipitously, and stupidly, left after only one night when I might have stayed another, in the same bed as Amy. But we had our bus to catch. When the bill came Angela insisted on paying half, which she had never done before. "Fair do's," she said, "if we're going on holiday together we'd best start sharing now." My heart sank to new depths.

It was probably in reaction to her stolidness that I admired the gaiety and wilfulness of the Mexicans more than I would have done if I'd been alone. They were so carefree. As they swarmed on and off our bus to Cuernavaca, regardless of stops or queues, I said, "It's nice to see people en-

178

joying themselves without inspectors in peaked caps bossing them around."

"I wonder if you've really thought that one out?" she enquired. "Remember there is no-one in a peaked cap to stop them starving to death."

The trouble was, I saw her point of view only too clearly; I took her points before she made them because, in many ways, we were alike: I was capable of having made any one of her remarks, from a part of myself I was heartily sick of. She fostered in me what I no longer wanted to become. I stared out of the bus window at the burnt wastes passing.

She was not always so severe. Because I was busy at the office—the Residence drains were causing trouble, and I was involved in endless discussions about sewage—Angela was convenient at the end of the day, ready with tickets for this and that, tirelessly informative, like a textbook I could take down or leave on the shelf. But the threat of our holiday approached. Poring over leaflets giving the prices of accommodation in Oaxaca Angela had alarmed me by saying, "Of course a double room is better value."

As I sat at my office desk the morning after she had made this remark, drinking tea and thinking that if ever I did spend a night with a girl it wouldn't be to economize on the hotel bill, my outside telephone rang. "Yes?" I said, expecting Angela and prepared to be brisk.

"South of the border, down Mexico way," sang Amy's voice in my ear. "Admit you're surprised."

Though my heart turned over I was immediately on my guard. "Where are you Amy?"

She laughed. "Not in your flat. That's what you thought, isn't it? You thought I'd picked up a few of the spouse's tricks. But I'm safe in a hotel so don't worry."

"Shall we have lunch?"

"Can't," said she with complacent promptness.

"Dinner then? Is George with you?" I remembered to ask.

There was a silence. When she spoke again she said, "Ned? You know in Rome when I phoned, you got me to meet you on Via Veneto? Well I know why. It was to see what I looked like, wasn't it? Before you asked me to anything smart. Well I look different now. So we'd better meet at a café again."

"Oh Amy don't be so silly. I know you've got a scar, I don't care if you've got fifty, it doesn't make any difference."

"People only think that," she replied. "People only think they don't mind."

"Anyway we'll have dinner," I assured her. "Is George in Mexico?"

"Terry's with me, you remember my brother? He could come couldn't he, you wouldn't mind?"

"Oh God——"

"Okay then don't bother, I'm having dinner with Terry anyway."

"No Amy, I didn't mean Oh God about Terry"—I explained that I'd remembered that Angela and I were supposed to go to the opera that evening. We arranged that all four of us should meet at Leonora's restaurant, early enough for Angela and myself still to make the opera if I chose. In this way I avoided choosing, avoided annoying anyone, and avoided the issue.

As is not unusual in Mexico the electricity had been jittery in my flat for some days, and when a man arrived that evening to set it to rights he managed to plunge about a quarter of the city into darkness. Consequently I was late at the restaurant. In the entrance Angela was waiting unhappily. I don't usually notice what people wear, but that evening Angela had got herself up in a cheap red dress, short and low-cut, which to my mind neither fitted nor suited her. A rebozo was hung round her scrawny collar-bones, and the prim look on her face disclaimed responsibility for the legs and cleavage displayed below, like a woman leading a dog which has misbehaved. In the bar I saw Terry and Amy. Making the introductions I avoided looking at Amy's face for fear of the scar, as you fear to look at the wound when a knife has slipped in your hand, and I fastened my eyes on the new, brassy, sheen of her hair. Then I let my glance fall on her face. Relief: there was a scar, a stitched seam which fractionally drew down the corner of her eye and lifted the corner of her mouth, like a frozen wink, no more than the riveted crack which prevents porcelain ringing true. Instead of kissing me she had hovered, but when I chose her scarred cheek to kiss, her hand tightened responsively in mine. All this was quick, whilst Terry played the host.

"I've ordered you margaritas," he told us, bustling up a chair for Angela; "come along, sit ye down and we'll choose the grub, and by the by Ned this is on me, all taken care of—not a word old boy, my pleasure. Here's to you Angela—it is Angela isn't it? yes that's salt on the rim of the glass, clever beggars, one of these mixtures makes you want another, as I'm sure a pretty girl like you's found out to your cost, eh?"

Whilst he talked, which he did continuously, I appreciated the change in him. Though he was fatter, expensive clothes and a certain sleekness of manner had made him prosperous rather than gross, jovial instead of vulgar, dynamic where before he had seemed pushing. He had come up in the world. Like a sentry faced with a besieger who has succeeded in scaling fortress walls thought to be impregnable, I had to readjust my view of him. Still, I was glad that he talked, for it gave me time to quieten the nervous flutter of being with Amy again. When he led us to our table Angela excused herself and disappeared towards the cloakroom. Amy lent forward and put her hand on my arm.

"Is she your girl-friend my love?"

"Heavens no."

Terry said, "Really no? Say the word if it's hands off." This didn't amount to quite the same thing. His fleshy

181

rapacious lips were parted. I suppose I looked uncertain, for Amy laughed. Her face moved crookedly, the scar whitening, and though the sound was her lovely throaty chuckle, it looked an ugly laugh. What people look like does alter them, or the way you construe their meaning, which is the same thing. When Angela had sat down I asked, "What news of George?"

"Poor old George," Terry boomed, "you can't help feeling sorry for the mutt. I told him, but he would do it."

"Do what?" I asked.

"Why, hand over his share in my company to Amy."

"I doubt if he's short of money," I said coldly.

"Well he needn't come crying to me when he is. Dull for you I'm afraid," he went on to Angela; "this chap George is Ned's cousin, married to Amy, had a stake in my business."

"Not a very adequate description of George," I protested. "Would you say Amy?"

"You describe him then," she replied neutrally.

"What business are you in?" asked Angela, who was more interested in Terry. I listened to his account of his rise to riches. From cars he had diversified into scrap metal and other ventures. He and Amy, his only partner, were in Mexico "on business", selling agricultural machinery. Angela hung upon his words, drinking in every exaggeration and looking, I thought, more ridiculous with every simper.

"And all this prosperity," I finally broke in to put the record straight, "was built on the money George lent you wasn't it?"

Terry parted his hands. "Could have borrowed it from the bank just as easy," he said. "Gave old George the chance since he was one of the family, that's all."

I looked at Amy; still her neutral expression seemed to accept this version of the facts. Perhaps it was the true one. I knew perfectly well that George's loan had been meant as a hand-out, but Terry had accepted it as an investment, unaware that people like ourselves, removed by a

182

generation from the business world, regarded money lent as money given away. On the financial face of it, which is one kind of truth, it was George who had been offered the benefit, and Terry scorned him for giving it away. It doesn't particularly surprise me that Terry's brand of brashness makes money, but it does surprise me to see it making conquests. Angela, silly fool, was magnetized. She wriggled in her seat, giggling and throwing coquettish looks over the rim of her wine glass. I had never seen her behave so ridiculously. Of course I had never seen her react to a sexual approach, and Terry's eyes were like paws on her. I suppose energy is the voracious force which in one guise or another—like the various avatars of a single god—makes money, conquests and everything else. Amy, who seemed to me rather exasperated by her brother, eventually caught his wrist and pushed up the silk cuff to look at his watch.

"Shouldn't you be getting along to the opera Ned?" she said.

"If I may make a suggestion," Terry said, "shoot me down if you want, but how about me taking Angie to the show?"

Amy said hotly, "No Terry you bloody well——"

But he smoothly ignored her: "That suit, Ned? No hard feelings?"

"Ask Angela."

All the stupid girl did was make sheep's eyes at him. He patted her hand. "Grand, that's settled," he said. "I know you and Amy want a good natter Ned. Jolly good. Now I'm paying the tab don't forget, no Ned, not a word will I hear."

"Oh shut up Terry, Ned hasn't even offered to pay the bill," said Amy angrily. "Pay the bloody thing and let's get out."

Imperturbably, from a wallet stuffed with money, Terry paid lavishly and led the party out into the street. A taxi appeared as if by magic, and as he held its door open for Angela he said, "We'll be a bit late I'm afraid."

183

"Better late than never," replied Angela recklessly, scrambling in.

They drove off and left Amy and me alone in the silent street.

"Is your flat handy?" she asked.

"There's a café you'd like near here," I said quickly.

"Okay if you'd rather. I did offer to meet you in a café."

We walked towards it without speaking. Our feet clipped the pavement loudly. Feeling that I owed her an explanation about my flat I said, "Amy you remember when you picked up that stick outside Drumnakeel? You said you didn't want to find it again when you were alone. My flat's the same."

"You mean it'd be lonelier when I'd gone?"

I realized that I had said more than I had intended. She was looking narrowly into my face though the street was dark. "Maybe I won't be gone," she said lightly, looking away into a shop window we passed. "Funny how they just dump stuff in the windows here, have you noticed? No tempting displays."

"People here aren't rich enough to be tempted into buying stuff they don't need," I said, sounding like Angela, falling into my character-with-Amy.

She skipped a couple of steps. "I love being tempted now I'm rich."

"You're rich are you?"

"Well you and George wouldn't think so," she said, "but I do."

"I'm not rich, good heavens."

"That's what I mean," she rejoined irritably: "George doesn't think he is either, and you know why, because he's got less than his grandfather had. Well fuck Grandad, what's he got to do with it?"

"I'll tell you what he's got to do with it," I said with asperity, "he made the money which George gave Terry for one thing, which you and your brother don't seem very grateful for."

"Money isn't this fantastic heirloom or something

184

darling. There's money everywhere just as valuable as your grandfather's—oh you'll never understand, you're just like George," she broke off impatiently, tossing hair which glittered like metal in the lamplight. Her voice too had a new metallic edge. She began again, "It's like the trees at Saradon, just because Grandfather planted them George thinks they're irreplaceable."

"Sentiment is value of one sort," I said.

"Only if you can't do anything yourself. Only if you're incapable of planting more. It's impotence, that's what being sentimental is, just impotence."

"What nonsense Amy."

"Well it is in George's case."

I didn't take this literally. I said nothing until we had sat down outside the café in its cobbled square amongst tubs of greenery. The chiaroscuro threw Amy's scar into relief; though she could easily have arranged her hair to hide it, she had not, she wore it like a duelling honour. "Now tell me about George," I said.

"You tell me about Angela," she countered, sipping her drink.

"What do you think of her?"

"She's just like Mrs Winder isn't she."

"Like Mrs Winder?" I said in astonishment.

"Oh I don't mean to look at, I mean—no it's a horrid thing to say, I don't know what I mean. Secretly I love her little red frock. What I really think is ... do you know," she finished with surprise, "I simply can't be bothered to think anything about her at all? Not one single notion about Angela burdens my brain. Poor Terry, stuck with her."

"But about Mrs Winder," I said, "what did you mean? How old do you think Angela is?"

"Thirty-five?" she wondered.

"Thirty-five? She's far more than that. Surely?" I wondered in my turn.

"Well Mrs Winder's only about forty."

"Mrs Winder forty? She's over fifty," I said.

185

Since neither of us knew the facts our opinions were subjective. It occurred to me that Amy's outlook (as usual playing ducks and drakes with the truth) reduced Mrs Winder's age because she saw the woman as a rival. And possibly my outlook required Angela to be older, safer, than she really was. "Anyway Terry seems rather taken by Angela, whatever age she is," I said.

"Oh I told him to take her off so we could talk," said Amy. "You don't mind do you?"

The trouble was that Amy couldn't look innocent now. The scar suggested duplicity. It had seemed to me that she had been angry with Terry. "So we could talk about what?" I asked coldly.

"Don't you want to hear the story of my heart?" she asked; adding, when I said nothing, "And about George?"

I looked at her coldly still. Like a cracked pane which diffuses the sun's strength, her scar had diminished the heat of her rays. I could take her or leave her. "All right, tell me about George," I said. "Where is he?"

"In the loony bin." With satisfaction she watched my shock. "They don't call it that of course, but it's the booby-hatch all right. You know that place in Chester? He's shut up there."

"But—why?"

"Darling he had to be shut up. I mean no-one minds the odd family scrap but darling admit, George has decimated his relations."

"What do you mean by that?"

"Well we all know he murdered his brother for a kick-off and——"

"Rubbish Amy, that's entirely imagination."

"Well whose imagination? It was you told me."

"I told you no such thing, all I——"

"Well," she interrupted, "you made a great mystery of it, whatever you did do. Anyway you can't get round it, he did kill Tim, and that killed his mother and I was next. Or next but one."

"You believe George tried to kill you? Aren't you being a bit melodramatic?"

A sudden twist of the muscles, which she must have practised, made her scar really frightening. "Maybe melodrama to you sitting here," she said. "You should have seen the sea and the rocks where he pushed me."

"But I thought—I thought you were in Leonardo's car when he——" Then her meaning struck me. "What do you mean, you were next but one? Are you implying he killed Leonardo?"

She didn't answer. She didn't need to, having made her insinuation. There was enough fuel in my mind for a spark to set it blazing. Not only what fuel I had imagined in the abyss between George ascending the wintry hill and the appearance of my blood-soaked suitcase at the iron gate; the whole sanguinary atmosphere of Mexico had fuelled my subconscious. I trod down the flames and said as levelly as I could, "So George attacked you did he?"

"Darling I was in hospital for weeks, I'm covered in scars, I'm wearing a wig—do you want to see? Do you?"

"No!" It was her very looks, that crooked smile, which made it hard to believe her. Yet they were the evidence of her speaking the truth. In my mistrust I remembered something concrete: "And what about your dog Rover?" I asked. She was playing with a button on her shirt cuff.

Her eyes left my face. "What about him?"

"You told me you'd found him with his head all smashed to pieces, and he turned out to be with Terry in London."

"George told you that? Why don't you ask Terry?"

"Because he'd say whatever suited the pair of you."

"And you'd believe anything George said," she replied. "Your trouble is you're infatuated with George, you always were, there's no point in expecting you to be whatever the word is, impartial."

"Do you promise me that your dog was mysteriously killed in Scotland?" I persisted.

"Yes." She lost patience with the loose button, ripped

187

it off. "All right no, he wasn't, what does that prove?"

"It proves you lie."

She leaned towards me. "Little bits of fact Ned are much less true than whole general feelings. I didn't lie really. You felt what it was like on that bloody mountain. George kept saying he was going to shoot Rover. That's the real truth, it's much truer than whether he did or didn't."

The reason I didn't reply was that I knew she was justified. But she must have interpreted my silence the other way, for she pushed back her chair and rose, preparing to leave.

"George mesmerizes you," she said, "that glittering eye, I've watched him do it to people. And now what can I do against him, in this state he's left me in?"

I made no move to leave the café with her. "George mesmerized you once," I said. "You married him."

"I did indeed," she replied. "And now I've divorced him."

"You haven't!"

"My love what do you think I came to Mexico for?" She was standing looking down at me. "Or do you believe that stuff about selling tractors?"

"A Mexican divorce doesn't hold much water."

She smiled. "If it comes to things holding water," she said, "George's story about how he happened to find Lennie's car upside down in a river and me covered in blood, that story's got a few leaks in it. Goodbye and remember," she added bitterly, "remember it's true what I told you."

"What have you ever told me that's true?"

"People only think it doesn't make any difference what you look like. When I was beautiful you believed me. Goodbye Ned."

I sat on alone when she had gone from the cobbled square. There were profounder reasons than her scarred face for letting her go. I could marshal such reasons; but uppermost in my mind, before I left the café, was the worry that I didn't know the name of her hotel, and the fear that I would never see her again. Damaged porcelain may be rejected from the connoisseur's collection, but its flaws bring it within a poorer man's reach.

In the office next morning my Ambassador's drains did not prove as absorbing as they had done when I only had Angela to worry about. I tried to interest myself in the technique of negotiation, no different whether drains or world peace are at stake, but once I had admitted that drains are dull work I was done for, like a lawyer who admits to himself that his client's injury is trivial. Few people can afford to view their day-to-day work objectively. When my telephone rang I hoped to hear Amy's voice, but it was Angela. "Yes?" I snapped, pencil poised as though work had been interrupted.

"You haven't got the tickets I suppose?"

"What tickets Angela?"

"For the train to Oaxaca of course."

"It's quicker to fly down," I temporized. I had put off getting tickets for the dreaded holiday.

"We've been through all that Ned. So you haven't got them?"

"Not yet, why?"

"Though I asked you—anyway for once it's just as well you haven't bothered because I may not be able to get away."

"Why on earth not?" Even though I didn't want to go, it was extremely irritating to be let down. One counts on the future, even if it is distasteful.

She huffed and puffed about crises in her office whilst I wondered how to extract Amy and Terry's address from her without waking her suspicion. "How was the opera?" I asked.

"The opera? Oh the opera, we didn't go, no, it was too late. We went dancing."

"Did you." I digested this. "What did you think of Terry and his sister?"

"One feels for that poor girl, married to a psychotic."

I was so irritated that I broke the connection, and lost my only chance of tracing Amy. Maybe the height of Mexico City had affected my temperament without my knowing it, that I acted so touchily.

Fortunately Terry rang up later in the day and asked me to get him an interview with the Minister of Agriculture. I had him transferred to the Commercial Section as soon as I had taken down the address of their hotel. Ringing back, I left a message for Amy, asking if she would like to see the *luz y sonida* at Teotihuacán next evening. She in turn left a message with my secretary, agreeing to come, so I rented a car and a driver and was waiting at the appropriate hour in the foyer of a small hotel on the Calle Puebla. The moment I had given Amy's name to the desk clerk his walnut face had cracked into smiles: chuckling to himself—he was an old man—he rang her room, then popped out of his cubby-hole, despatched the lift to her floor and stood awaiting its descent, as if the punch-line of a favourite joke were about to unfold for my amusement. Used to Angela, who carried over rancour from one meeting to the next, I wasn't so optimistic. But no yesterday existed for Amy. She stepped out of the lift as if she had been created on the way down. Watching her talk to the desk clerk, when she had kissed me and we were walking to the door, I realized that this newly-minted look of hers was partly *maquillage*; it must have been, or how else could she have hidden the scar on her cheek which I looked for but couldn't see? The clerk took a worn book from his desk and offered it to her.

"You leave this in the dining room after lunch," he said.

"Keep it for me will you?"

"I give it to your husband to take up," he said.

I registered this mistake, but had no time to consider it because Amy did such an extraordinary thing; she lifted the clerk's hair, a toupée, off his head and let it flop crookedly back, where it sagged like a burnt pancake. We left him on the steps, his hands pressed between his thighs as he dipped and creaked with laughter, and went out to the car.

"Do you let him take your wig off sometimes?" I asked.

"What wig? My postiche you mean? My oh my!" she exclaimed at the waiting chauffeur, "you get a car and a driver out of them now do you? You know I suppose," she told me as she got into the car, "you know George tried to go into the Foreign Office?"

"George did! When?"

"Do get in my love, don't stand and stare. "Yes," she continued when we were sitting side by side, "he tried last year. Of course he failed, I mean can you imagine?"

I didn't believe her. I didn't say so for fear of resurrecting our last quarrel. "How surprising," I said.

She looked at me. "You'll never understand that George isn't God Almighty," she said, "so let's forget him. Aren't you fascinated by these bumps?" she asked as our car slowed to negotiate an axle-cracking ridge set into the road at the approach to an intersection.

"I hadn't thought about them."

"It tells you more about Mexicans, that you've got to break their cars in half to slow them down, it tells you more than all the guide-books tell."

I thought about it as she talked. She was right. Amy picked her way towards understanding by way of details as trivial as the broken twigs a tracker follows. But she got there; she understood.

Mile-high billboards she didn't read, or couldn't: that was why the spectacular at Teotihuacán, which spelled things out for Angela, told Amy nothing she wanted to know; all it did, the rioting coloured lights and the gods' voices wrangling over tannoy, was make her laugh. At a point in the programme where human sacrifice was supposed to ensure the sun's return she said, "For two dollar tickets they might sacrifice somebody."

I laughed. "It might work too."

"My God that'd be good value. Think if we could have

sacrificed somebody to get the sun back at Drumnakeel. Some handsome youth."

It was a relief to be with someone who treated the myths as a comedy; the dark and awful nature of the old gods lost its oppressiveness with Amy beside me. As we drove back to the city she said, "Any more jokes as good as that up your sleeve my love?"

I wondered where else I could take her. I only knew what Angela had shown me, sites and museums. "There's the National Museum in——"

"Boring boring. Don't want to go there. Try again."

And I did try again. I told her about Tepotzlan, the one place I knew that Angela had considered a waste of time.

"What's it famous for?" she asked suspiciously.

"It isn't famous. It's just a village in the sun."

"Then I'll come."

Only when I had dropped her at her hotel, where she disappeared into a world peopled with bewigged desk clerks and other oddities, did the inconsistencies of the evening, and of Amy in general, even her appearance, come to mind like the holes in a pantomime's plot. Why were they staying in that shabby hotel, for instance, so unlike Terry's vulgar grandeur? And did the clerk speaking of her "husband" mean that they shared a room? And what about Amy's scar, and her wig? None of it mattered when I was with her; somehow the broad strokes of her brush painted out the cracks and painted in a living self-portrait. The only assertion I could check was whether George had sat the Foreign Office examination: I found that he had, in September last year, and having passed the written tests with distinction had failed the interviews. Amy had spoken the truth. I wasn't surprised that he had failed—he would have made every effort to despise the examiners in order to protect his sense of superiority against the risk of failure—nor was I surprised that he hadn't told me: he feared that I would think less of him for having failed. I did, too. It altered our relationship to find that I had one thing at least which he coveted, when I had always thought that he had everything I wanted, Saradon and Scotland and money and attraction—and Amy too, I suppose.

When Sunday came I collected Amy in the car. She gave me a parcel. "Open it up," she said excitedly, "it's a gift."

The moment I'd untied the string she snatched the paper herself and took out her present, a fine suède shirt, beautiful, but the sort of garment I'd never wear. However, she made me put it on as we bowled along in the car. Even over my own shirt it was far too big; it would just have fitted George, and suited him too. The idea that she might have bought it with him in mind took the gilt off the gingerbread. I thanked her, and said it must have cost a great deal.

"It was costly indeed," she agreed with pleasure, settling back in her seat, "and what's even better it won't wear a bit well. There's the beauty of riches in a nutshell."

We drove south across a landscape exhausted by the sun. Drystone walls divided fields of maize from fields of dust where tractors trailed dust-plumes like a steamer's smoke, and dust blew in with the heat through the open windows of the car. "I'm sorry I didn't get an air-conditioned car," I said.

She took her eyes from the landscape and looked at the car. "I hadn't noticed. I don't care."

"I thought you liked the rich life nowadays."

The chuckle flooded her throat. "That's not what you're rich for you booby," she told me, "you're not rich so you can go the same distance poor people can, only shutting everything out—I mean shutting out sun and dust and stuff."

"What are you rich for then?"

"For going twice as far as poor people, whatever the weather. See those tractors?" she asked, whilst I wondered how far she planned to go. "Terry and I sell them those you know."

"With no thought for the harm they do," I replied, unspecifically jealous of her and Terry.

"Harm? It does good my love, handing tractors out."

"They're pounding the topsoil to dust," I told her. (Ecology was one of Angela's hobby-horses: a cover, in the case of machinery, for her yearning for "the olden days".) "The topsoil compacts under heavy machines, or blows away, and it won't be a generation till they're through to the rock."

"You're like George and the dying planet. Remember? And all the time it's only people like George who are dying. I bet dodos thought the end of the world was nigh before they snuffed it."

"It is true about the planet dying though," I said.

"Oh it may be true in facts and figures and graphs and things," she replied impatiently, "but you know perfectly well you don't really feel it's going to happen. Admit. No-one does, except I mean George, who's determined to blow the last trump on his very own trumpet."

When we reached Tepotzlan, and climbed out of the car into the cobbled square I had remembered, by the rusting bandstand, I felt that I had brought her somewhere pointless. Perhaps Angela had thought the same when she had brought me here. It was still and hot. Around the venerable monastery the grass lay spent and white. Between roofs and rickety posts festoons of cables webbed one's view of cruel toothy mountains soaring above their forests. In a hard blue sky the sun glittered and burned above all. Angela had been right: "There's nothing much to see," I apologized.

"There's the place itself," she replied, just as I had done to Angela, and set off under the bell-tower alone, as I had done.

Burning on my scalp, the sun made me feel stout and bald. Amy walked rapidly, lightly, and disappeared; I heard her footsteps patter on the stone passages above the ambulatory, but when I plodded up the stairs she was in none of the cells, though their stillness was troubled like the water of a pool where someone has swum and gone. There was no peace where she had been. When I found her it was by the sound of laughter below, where she and the old custodian were leaning together over a well and dropping stones into its depths. When the pebbles ran out Amy dropped money instead.

"I wouldn't do that," I whispered to her, "he's probably very poor."

She looked at me with disdain. Then she gave a coin to the old man. He too dropped it delightedly down the well.

I knew that I must understand, and alter or eradicate my Quakerish nature which didn't. Never mind the poverty of the shacks lining the lane up to the posada, enjoy the bougainvillaea frothing over the walls. A small boy who was peeing against a wall, watching us pass, laughed when we both hopped over the trickle in the dust: I hopped in the air and didn't come down, but floated on beside Amy, kept aloft by the child's laugh, into the posada and through it to a table looking out upon flowers and cypress-shaded lawn. But I did come down when Amy said, "My love, you look a complete mess."

I returned with a bump into my physical appearance. She came round the table and roughly turned up my shirt cuffs and opened another button at my neck. I sat like a lay figure whilst she twisted my limbs. "No it still won't do," she said, "you still look like people watching cricket at the Oval, put on my present, go on." Since the restaurant was empty I took off my shirt and put on her suède one to please her. She pulled it about to her satisfaction. Her touch was oddly undisturbing; indeed it was so natural that it was settling, it settled me in myself as preening settles a bird in its feathers. I had thought that the touch of her fingers would pull knots tighter but it didn't, it unpicked them, it unshackled me.

After lunch we strolled down the garden. To walk in the heat on watered grass, amongst the dark shafts of cypresses, was delightfully like Italy. The time we had been in Italy together seemed bridged to the present by a rainbow which over-arched the chasm between. Amy was sitting on the grass. "Let's stay," she suggested. "Shall we?"

Her eyes were mischievous, like the child who had touched the forbidden paint of Leonardo's car. It seemed possible. But I temporized. "Here you mean? We could see. Only I doubt if they'd have room at the weekend like this."

"Oh my love, the doubts you doubt," she mocked, holding out a hand for me to pull her to her feet. She floated off in the sunlight between the flowers.

"Where are you going?" I called after her.

"To have a pee," she called back.

When she had gone I followed, and went to the reception desk.

"A room?" replied the clerk to my enquiry. He was a sleek Spaniard running a fateful finger down his ledger. "Twin beds or matrimonial?"

Before I could explain his mistake an English voice made me turn. Down the stairs came Terry. Behind him I saw Angela. Terry spoke. "Small world," he said, and when I looked past him again, Angela (if it was Angela) had gone. Terry commandeered the clerk's attention by chucking his key on the desk. "Bill of number twelve if you please, and get our luggage down pronto will you."

"One moment, I am assisting this gentleman," the clerk told him. "Now sir, we have a double room for one night only."

The gesture Terry made on hearing this—a fleshy finger laid by his unpleasant nose—included me in a world so sleazy that I could only back away from it, with inchoate mumbles, and regain the sunlit garden. My mind flooded. I hadn't known that Angela had counted as a fixed point in the landscape until now, when the flood swept her away head over heels. It was from the brink of a cataclysm that I stepped back into the peace of the Italian garden. I found Amy on the grass, chivvying an ant along her arm with a twig. "I don't want to stay I've decided," she said.

"That ant will bite you eventually," I said. When she continued to tease it, and it scrambled desperately through the down on her arms, I found my nerves screwed taut for the creature's nip as if her flesh were mine. "Do knock it off Amy," I asked her.

"And do you know why I don't want to stay here?" she said.

"No why?"

Taking her eye off the ant she let the slow upcurve of her mouth smile knowingly at me. "Because—ow! Oh!" she cried, hopping up in a flurry and slapping at the ant in her shirt. She opened a button, caught it on her stomach and crushed it between two fingers. "Little brute!"

Though she buttoned her shirt quickly I had seen the scars on her stomach. They had writhed when she moved. It was as though I had seen the lid lifted on a basket of snakes, which crawled into my mind.

It wasn't rational to ask Amy to fly down to Oaxaca with me for my week's leave. At sea level I might never have suggested it. At sea level Miss Tozer mightn't have spent the weekend with a machinery salesman. "Close to the sun in lonely lands" I asked Amy to come, unsure that she would comply until she appeared at the airport, taking large comic strides in the midst of a billowy cotton safari-suit, like someone upon whom a parachute has fallen, and smiling at everyone from under a floppy hat. Soon we were airborne in a small friendly plane, up in the sunlight above the volcanoes whose lava lips bearded in forest passed below, like the snoring mouths of giants the plane sneaked over without awakening, and was free.

The immense continent to the south unfolded. Over wild and barren uplands cut by gorges we flew, over deserts of ochre sandhills, over mountain ranges pleated with shadow, until at last, nearer the equator than I had ever been, we came dropping down towards a green plain squared into fields, skimmed great stands of eucalyptus and landed at Oaxaca. Amy put away the cloth-bound Victorian book that she had kept on her lap throughout the flight from the north and explained to me, as we got off the plane, her system for selecting a hotel in a strange city. "The only way is," she said, "you find the nicest taxi driver you can and let him take you where he thinks best."

"That's how you found that place in Mexico City is it? I thought it didn't look the sort of hotel Terry would have chosen."

"Fuck Terry and his bloody awful taste," she said venomously.

The taxi driver she chose took us to a hotel on the central plaza. Around its inner glass-roofed courtyard ran three tiers of balconies, all tiled, which echoed to the clatter of feet and the clash of keys in locks.

"It's the penitentiary!" Amy exclaimed, "we've got a week's porridge by the look of things."

We separated to unpack, but Amy soon tapped at my door to come in and compare my view with hers, to look in my bathroom, to criticize my toothpaste, to take things out of my chest of drawers as fast as I put them in. In the first hour I doubted whether I could stand the strain of such togetherness.

But the effect of continual proximity was different from what I had expected: its effect was that after a couple of days Amy had become an indivisible part of my own self. I found that isolation with one person you know, in a strange town, increases their importance to you until life-in-a-strange-town, and therefore actuality, is unimaginable without them. Wherever I looked, Amy was there; she became as much a part of my outlook as contact lenses, tinting or distorting or magnifying what I saw, but a lens I had to look through, in contact with my retina. Liking or disliking were transcended by dependence. Probably

198

prisoners have this same sense of interdependence with their fellows.

We breakfasted together under the arcades of the plaza, we walked together in the town, we sat at café tables and dined together at night. We looked into churches, if we happened to pass them on our way to the market, which fascinated Amy, and we only separated for the night at the doors of our rooms. Still, in the dark, my mind was full of her, as it is of a book you are reading when the lights go out. And just as a book can compress lives into a few hours, so the few hours of our first two days seemed like a lifetime's experiences together. "Before" didn't exist, nor did "after", or London or Mexico City; only us, here, now, suspended.

On Tuesday afternoon we took a car up Monte Alban, leaving the green and watered orchards to fall away below whilst our road climbed into windswept regions of scrub and whin. Like the Sicilian temples abandoned by the Greeks to bees and flowers, the hill-top seemed empty of its builder's purpose. Sculpted it was, but for a transient epoch; not carved once and for all like the wild hills, whose corries and glens are instinct with an ever-living purpose. Huge and hushed, Monte Alban was an empty ruin. The gods had gone. Amy too had wandered away.

I found her on the further slope of the hill, seated on a stony patch of earth with her back to what was famous, and her face towards the eternal prospect of valley and mountain, eating the toffees she kept in her handbag. I thought of the day she had preferred tea in a Liverpool café to the pictures in the Walker Gallery, and had pulled George after her.

"Want a toffee?" she asked. "I'm glad we came, you get a nice view."

"You should paint it," I said, sitting down beside her and taking a toffee.

"Painting it wouldn't make any difference."

"Not to the view, but to you maybe."

"Don't need it any more. I am the view," she said simply.

She gazed out across the landscape, the far tumbled ranges, valleys in violet shadow, the grandeur of mountains. Then she added, " 'I spoke to the earth and the sun and the air. I am the view.' "

I didn't recognize it as a quotation until the next morning.

I was sitting after breakfast under the arcade outside our hotel (Amy had run upstairs for something she had forgotten) and I picked up the book she carried everywhere, curious to see its title on the decorated cloth cover. It was Richard Jefferies' *Story Of My Heart*. Inside was the Saradon bookplate. I sat with the book in my hand. Earlier the pavements had been watered so that the air smelt wet as it does near fountains, and across the street a sprinkler pattered spray on the green foliage of the garden, the sound redolent of summer rain on the magnolia leaves at open windows at Saradon. I turned through the book's pages reading a sentence here and there: "The sun is stronger than science, the hills more than philosophy", I read; and "I am in the midst of eternity now, as the butterfly floats in the light-laden air. Now is the immortal life. If the clock had never been set going, what would have been the difference?"

I sat with the book open, thinking of a line of Young's *Night Thoughts* which expressed an opposite view of time, hitherto to me the true one: "We take no note of time but from its loss; to give time then a tongue is wise in man." In Oaxaca no clocks struck. Nor did time have a tongue where Amy had sat on the bare hillside, though it had tolled the ruin of the Aztec temple behind her.

I found Amy's quotation in the early pages of the book in which Jefferies describes the downs where he had first understood his heart: "I spoke in my soul to the earth, the sun, the air and the distant sea far beyond sight. In becoming the object is the fusion which brings tranquillity."

"Snooping in my book?" Amy's shadow fell across the page.

I closed it and pushed it across the table. "Richard Jef-feries has taken over from Mary Baker Eddy has he?" I said, looking up at her.

Her hand touched the scar on her cheek, either so fami-liar to me that I usually didn't notice it, or less disguised with make-up that morning. "I gave up science fiction," she told me.

"And took to animism?"

"Annie what? Funny the way I found this book"—she laughed—"you know how there aren't any books at Sara-don practically?"

"What about that flat George built over the stables? It's full of books."

"Only dictionaries and rubbish. Anyway I wasn't going in there. No, in the house I mean there aren't any. I was poking about in the servants' hall place, and I found *Story Of My Heart* and thought it would be like one of those weepy romances Mrs Winder cries over with her feet in the Aga for a comfort."

"I can't picture Mrs Winder reading romances."

"Mrs Winder's head is a turmoil of sex. If you knew!"

"I think you've got Mrs Winder wrong Amy. I think——"

"Oh you and George are so innocent you're like children," she berated me. "In fact that's exactly what it is, I mean George about Mrs Winder is like a child about his mother or something—you know, I mean the idea of her having sex or anything—well it's just like you about that rotten Angela creature. And they do," she added earnestly.

Again the linking of Mrs Winder and Angela. "And they do what? Have sex?" I asked.

But her mind had gone off at a tangent. "Guess who Mrs Winder insures herself with? The Scottish Widows Provident Fund, isn't it ideal?"

I forgot what I had wanted to ask. Amy put her book in her bag. "It's a strange book that," I said. "If Jefferies had lived to read D. H. Lawrence it would have interested him."

201

She looked at me, and re-opened the book. She found her place as rapidly as a Methodist finds a text in the Bible, and she said, "Listen—I can't hardly read as you know, but listen: 'These were they'—he's telling about the Greeks—'These were they who would have stayed with me under the shadow of the oaks while the blackbirds fluted and the south air swung the cowslips.'" She closed the book.

I should have known that a remark such as mine about Lawrence was meaningless to Amy, annoyed her indeed. My silence acknowledged it.

"Do you know what George said when I read him that bit?" she asked. Imitating George's slightly bent head and scratchy voice she said, "South wind would be more euphonic than south air I should say."

"So you divorced him."

"Lea and Mrs Winder between them turned me out of Saradon you know, when George was coming back. Out in the cold."

"You mean they thought it would upset him?"

"I don't know what they thought. Come on, let's go and look in the market," she said, putting the remains of our breakfast bread into her bag in case she saw a hungry bird. I followed her across the street under the shadow of the trees.

I followed her along the streets beyond the square. She never got out of anyone's way, she walked straight ahead whilst the crowd pushed me into the roadway or made me walk behind. I was hot and cross. Trailing along behind I saw men continually turning to watch Amy pass, and I resented their eyes on her; now that she filled the lens of my mind—now that she *was* the view—I was jealous, jealous of the smiles she strewed like flowers on men passing, jealous of the kindled look in their animal eyes. What more could I do to own her mind—what more could I do, hamstrung by chastity? "In becoming the object is the fusion which brings tranquillity." But there was still between us that hard and fast line like the sword in a mediaeval bed between the unmarried, the hard and fast line of my temperament. That I had once been proud of it—had treasured it like a morality—was ignominious. I was like someone in a street fight who only knows the rules of boxing. Ahead of me Amy stopped at the window of a hardware store.

"Wow!" she exclaimed, "look at those machetes. Just what George would like, shall we nip in and get him one?"

"Oh for heaven's sake!" Jealousy welled in my throat bitter as vomit. "Do you never stop thinking about George?"

"He is my husband darling."

"I thought you'd divorced him."

"Only a Mexican divorce, you told me that wasn't any good. Anyway I have to take him a present."

"Then take him a bloody great chopper and see who he chops up with it next," I shouted, and marched away.

If only rage didn't, like all my emotions, cool so quickly; I had gone into a nearby church in order to hide, and soon I felt merely ridiculous. Anger and desire would not put out the eye of reason. In the calm grand gloom of the building my unwelcome cautious self caught up with me and resoldered the bars of my temperament around me, a leaden lattice set in stone like the glazing-bars which cramp the doings of the saints in their stained-glass windows. What reparation could I make?

An Indian peon and his wife had crept past my chair and now stood like two children in the aisle, market baskets on their arms, their hands straying into each other's for courage as they gazed about with wonder and humility. I never saw two souls so meek. Their faith burned above their heads like the flame above a candle.

"Wherever you're going that's the only way," whispered Amy's voice from the chair behind mine. I didn't turn for a moment, but watched the Indians humbly approach the sanctuary. Simply, meekly, to whatever altar; without love of self or hate.

"Amy I'm sorry," I said leaning back in my chair but still not turning to face her.

"Why be sorry? Look at me."

"But Amy what about George?" I asked.

"Look at me! You must face the way you're going."

I turned towards the glowing oval of her face in the gloom. "Have you divorced him? You have haven't you?"

She smiled. "Whispering in church makes you so intense darling."

"And if you haven't you will, properly in England? Will you——?"

She scraped her chair on the stone and let her liquid chuckle gush like a fountain into the spacious vault. "Are you about to pop the question my love?" she said. "Come and I'll buy you a Coke to wet your whistle."

VIII

THREE DAYS LATER I was in a taxi on my way towards
Saradon from the station. Like a man recovering consciousness after an accident I wasn't sure how much of myself
was left. I had discarded pieces of myself as if I had been
exploded. I had dropped my work in Mexico and Amy in
London; even flakes of my skin burnt by the Mexican
sun kept dropping off on the floor of the taxi. Amy had
lit a touchpaper which had rocketed me to Mexico City and
to London, but the rocket's rush fizzled out as I fell towards
these familiar fields. And the rain; I wasn't sure what sur-
vived from the heat of Oaxaca. On my knee was a toy hind
made of plaited reeds which Amy had bought for George
and made me bring him, and this I stared at like an object
I'd seen in a dream, which hadn't dissolved as the dream
had, now that I was awake, on a wet Sunday, approaching
Saradon.

We passed the curved railings which marked journey's
end, and I saw the fond face of the house looking out for
its children through rainy trees.

But the door of the porch was shut, which I had never
seen it before. I knew George was there because I had
rung up Mrs Winder from London. I got out of the taxi
onto the sad wet drive and wondered how to get into the
house. Presently a rattle at the library window drew my
eye through the reflecting pane to a long pale face glim-
mering behind it like a fish in an aquarium.

"Hello Mrs Winder," I said appeasingly when she had
unlocked and pushed up the sash.

"We didn't know just when to expect you, with the
Sunday trains," she said, unappeased. "There'll be baggage
if you've a mind to stay. Hand it in, it'll make less com-
motion."

I put my case into the big impatient hand reached through the window. "Where's Mr George?"

"Away down to the graveyard scything. The taxi'll take you on."

As she began to close the window I asked, "How is he?"

"Well enough—why would he not be?"

I saw that the room behind her was under dust sheets, before the opaque glass rattling shut eclipsed it. A wind shook rain off the yew and holly clustering against the house. I turned away from the impenetrable blank stare of its windows and climbed into the taxi, telling the driver to drop me in the village.

I still held in my hand the reed toy Amy had bought in Oaxaca from a barefoot Indian child at the café to which we had gone from the church. "Wouldn't you like a little hind?" she had asked me persuasively, herself on the child's side against the adult world which shoo'd the swarms of Indian children away from their tables. She had bought it for me I had thought, but she put it in her bag and said, "Did you know George couldn't have children? It's why there didn't seem any point going on, when I knew." I had needed to believe every reason she gave for leaving George, every assertion she made which diminished his potency, so I had believed her. It nurtured the contempt I needed to have for his inadequacy.

But that was far away in the heat of Mexico. When the taxi dropped me at the lychgate in the village, and I knew that George was at hand in his own setting, contempt evaporated. It was I who felt inadequate.

I walked up the church path empty handed, for I had left the reed hind in the taxi. Amy had not produced it again until this morning, when she had pushed it into my hand at the last moment to give George. "But you bought it for me," I protested. "No, I secretly bought it for George, he must have it," she insisted. "He'll understand why." I didn't want George to understand her sign, which I had worked out on the way to the village. The hind had no horns, and nor as yet had George.

I walked round the church's sandstone walls to a sloping graveyard where tombstones were lost in the decaying grass of autumn. Under the yew worked a back bent by the stoop and plod of scything. Pigeons fled out of oaks like townsfolk scattering before a street duel, but George laboured on, a shuffling step, a rhythmic stroke, another step, the grass going down before the blade. That the grim reaper knew of my presence I felt sure. The pigeons, his familiars, had warned him. The impetus which had propelled me from Oaxaca finally petered out in a feeble cough as I cleared my throat and spoke his name.

He completed his stroke before wearily upending his scythe and leaning on the curved ash haft. His beard had gone, leaving the skin unweathered except around sunken, glittering eyes. Rain dewed his rough black hair. I had forgotten how tall he was. "We didn't know when to expect you," he said in echo of Mrs Winder, "what with the Sunday trains."

"I caught the eleven o'clock," I said.

"Amy thought you would."

I swallowed. "Amy thought? What, did she ring up?"

"Oh yes. She rang up all right." With his thumb he tested the edge of the blade. I waited for him to reveal how much Amy had told him on the telephone. Instead he pulled a whetstone from the hip pocket of his cords and began to sharpen the scythe stridently. "I cannot learn to put a proper edge on a blade," he confessed as he rasped the stone on the steel, "I get what they call a wire edge, sharp as you please but doesn't last. You feel that."

The edge was so keen it prickled the skin of my thumb. "Deadly," I said.

"Oh it feels sharp," he complained, "but it won't last you see Ned."

"No," I agreed. One could not discuss the subject indefinitely.

"But this is dull stuff," he cried, as if noting my preoccupation for the first time, "just when you want to tell me all about Mexico no doubt." When I hesitated, uncer-

207

tain how informed he was, he continued, "The most interesting part of the country is the Yucatan isn't it?" He set himself to mow again.

"I don't know, I haven't been down there," I said. I took a deep breath and began, "I've been in Oaxaca George——"

"Haven't been to the Yucatan? But it's much the most interesting province, in fact I should say it's the only part of Mexico worth seeing. I'm amazed you haven't been there."

This was George at his most irritating. "You can't go everywhere in five minutes," I said, keeping pace with his shuffling steps as he reaped. "We'll probably go there next leave."

"Oh so you're going back are you?"

"Yes, next week." My courage was leaking away. "George I only came over to see you. Amy made me—I mean she suggested it."

"To see me? Well well. To see me, upon my soul!" He plodded on, the blade whispering amongst the graves. "People have rarely come so far."

He wouldn't accept my challenge. He was like a killer who won't draw on a tenderfoot. Or was he mad? "I heard you hadn't been well," I said, wondering if it was perhaps unwise to upset him—was his pose a defence mechanism? The scythe was a fearful weapon.

He straightened from his labours and coughed hollowly, tapping his chest. "No I wasn't well," he admitted. "You don't want to fool around with pneumonia. The patch on my lung's clearing up though, if the medical men are to be believed." He tested the scythe-blade on a thumb. "Blunt you see. Yes," he went on, plying stone on steel again with its ringing, dangerous music, "if I'd been able to get out to Mexico with Amy the climate there'd have fixed me up a treat by all accounts. But Terry went. The inseparable Terry." He pondered the blade for a moment, and I thought he was going to tell me something. But he only said, "So you've been in Oaxaca. Looked rather pretty on Amy's postcard I thought."

It was pig-in-the-middle. I'd intercepted the toy hind

but not the postcards nor the telephone call lobbed over my head. But surely there hadn't been time for a postcard from Oaxaca to have reached England? "What did Amy say in her card?"

"Wish you were here?" he suggested. "Would that have been about the size of it?"

At that moment, from the church tower, a single bell began to toll.

"My God!" cried George, aghast and gloomy as Dracula in the sun's first rays, "quick, run, or we'll be caught up in the bloody Evensong."

He leaped a grave and ran towards the church with his scythe wildly outstretched. I followed, and joined him in the shelter of a buttress which hid us from the road. Above, the bell tolled urgently. His run for cover convinced me that he was not mad at all—it was so typical of him—but playing some waiting game with me. When a car drew up at the lychgate he peeped round the buttress and reported, "It's the dear vicar and his lady. Then we can make a dash for it." To share a hiding place with George took me back many years along the road we had come together.

"Why have you taken to cutting the grass here George? I thought Pusey did it," I said.

"Damn, here's Mrs Brewer all eager for the treat. What? Oh Pusey's past it, I said I'd do it because—oh various reasons. Instead of going to church for one. Run along, Mrs Brewer," he urged a parishioner.

I knew George's religious views. I knew why he worked in the churchyard. Works absolved him from making the act of faith, for which he was too stiff-necked; though he would paint or caulk the ark, he wouldn't put to sea in it. As we waited in the shelter of the buttress I thought of the two Indians in the church at Oaxaca, their simple acceptance "the only way", so Amy thought. She and George didn't share a way, and if they shared an objective it was beyond my sight. "Can we go to the car now?" I asked.

"No car, I walked across the footpath," he replied. "I have to drop the scythe in on Pusey."

The fabric of the church had begun to shudder with organ music, and the jangling tongue in the belfry ceased. We crossed the laid swathes of the graveyard and started out on the path towards the cottages, the farm and Saradon. Embrowned woods filled the hollows. Drifts of rusty leaves had blown against the stiles. The light was moist though the rain had passed, a wide wet sky above the stubbles. It was hard to recall the fierceness of the sun. This was the landscape of reality, to me as to the humble cows peering mildly over the hedge. The Welsh hills were the edge of the world.

George asked, "What was that nanny called we had who was so jumpy about cows?"

"Margery Hursey." The name came up from the depths with circumstances clinging to it. "She hated this path. 'Nasty beasts!'—she used to open her umbrella in the cows' faces."

"Marge Hursey, yes. Lea said margarine was called after her. Typical of Lea—omniscient, and completely wrong."

I laughed. George and I had shared a way through the world. It seemed I could leave all of Oaxaca behind as simply as I'd left the toy hind in the taxi. It was only a dream. The figure of George I had constructed in Mexico wasn't the real George walking the real landscape beside me. Imagine him impotent—imagine him trying to kill Amy! I couldn't. I was awake. So that our conversation should be commonplace whilst I tiptoed out of my dream I asked, "Is this stubble undersown with grass George?"

"What? Oh, pooh, who cares, I'm not farming it any more. Ned——"

"You haven't sold the farm?" Reality quaked underfoot.

"It's let. I've got other fish to fry. Ned," he began again, pausing on top of the stile into the cottage lane, "Ned, you know Amy's scars?"

He conjured back the dream. "The one on her face. It's not bad."

"Do you know how she got them? Did she tell you?"

"Only that she——" I looked away. "No, not really."

"She tried to kill herself."

"In Leonardo's accident?" I wondered.

"Nothing to do with Lennie, not directly," he said. "Though on the *post hoc, ergo propter hoc* fallacy she may run the two things together."

"Then why?"

He rocked thoughtfully to and fro on the stile. "I think because she discovered she can't have children."

"But she said——" I looked up at him. No, he couldn't be impotent. "Can't she," I concluded.

"The doctor says not. Or advises not. Anyway she jumped in the sea at Killaneen." He leaped off the stile and continued along the lane with the scythe bobbing above the hedgerow. A phrase of Amy's came back to me: "There didn't seem any point going on when I knew." Not "going on" with marriage, but going on living. I caught up with George at the gate into Pusey's garden. "Dragging her out over the rocks cut her badly," he said, opening it. "Nearly killed me with pneumonia too. I thought you ought to know the truth about the scars and the wig and everything, that's all. It has to be faced."

I had once glimpsed the wounds snaking across her stomach. To remove her wig, if she wore one, was unimaginable, like scalping her. George's horrific image of her didn't coalesce with mine. Like two Red Kings we dreamed separate Amys. "That isn't her story," I said reluctantly.

He paused among Pusey's zinnias. "What is her story—at the moment?"

I realized that Amy had never told me step by step what had happened. She had conveyed an impression. "George," I said, "George, tell me exactly what happened."

He let the scythe down off his shoulder. "There's no mystery." He rubbed his brow as though it ached, and began to talk rapidly in a level, controlled voice: "I got to Duncan's about midday after I left you. Lennie was packed. We all came down to the gate, picked up Lennie's car and went to the shore at Killaneen—I'd got some carcasses to drop off and Lennie wanted to see the sea. It was bloody cold on the beach. He took off after a bit. Amy and I walked out to the point. She'd got herself into a state about, I don't know, living at Duncan's and everything. And Lennie not—I don't know." The scythe blade grated on the concrete. He contemplated its point.

"You said just now it was because she couldn't have children," I reminded him.

He looked up, blankly for a moment. "Yes, there was that too. She fixed on that to shout about, accusing me. She was out on the rocks with the sea breaking, shouting and yelling. It was Lennie leaving too, the failure. She was yelling about it not being worth going on. I finally went out to pull her off the rocks and she fell in. It was extremely difficult to get her out." He was silent for a minute, scratching at a weed with the scythe. "Eventually I did, God knows how. She was streaming blood—pouring blood. I got her to the Land Rover and started for Inverness hospital. On the way I saw the car in the river. Lennie's. I rang the police from a house. Of course they couldn't find Leonardo. They thought we'd been involved. I hadn't got a driving licence." His voice rose and broke. He banged the scythe on the concrete and swallowed. "Anyway the ambulance finally took me and Amy to hospital and Lea came up and sorted things out. Until Terry arrived," he added with a sigh, as if opening another issue. He walked round to the back door of the cottage without continuing it.

Amy had conveyed an impression, George narrated a story. I heard her insinuations whilst I watched George's pictures unreel. Like the wrong soundtrack, her voice put very different constructions on the actions. When I caught up with George at the cottage door he said without rancour, lifting the latch, "Amy is a pathological liar as you know."

Pusey's whitened old head might not have moved in the two years since George had introduced Amy as his future wife. He sat against the window stony as an idol to whom offerings are brought. "What you been doing with yourself this time then?" he asked me, as he used to ask when we came back from school.

"Oh—nothing much," I replied, now as then. In his kitchen, so still and changeless, it seemed true. If one hadn't brought him cuttings from someone's garden one might as well have stayed at home.

George hooked the scythe on a peg. "Thanks Pusey," he said.

"You been trying mowing then?" The old man pushed himself to his feet and shuffled across the kitchen to feel the blade. He puffed out his lips contemptuously. "You can't sharp that yet can you? You got that stone I'll show you how."

He held out his hand but George dropped the stone on the table. "Never mind now Pusey. Come on Ned." He lifted the door latch again.

Cheated, Pusey still tried to detain him. "A hang of a mess you'll make in that churchyard you will. I'll sharp that up for you proper for next time," he conceded, almost whining for George to stay.

George didn't, or wouldn't, see how important he was to the old man. "Come on Ned, I'm tired," he said, opening the door.

"You think you know what that's like to get tired," the croaky voice railed, bitter now he saw George wouldn't stay, "you don't know what that's like to get tired ten o'clock then go on along dinner time, go keeping on all day flat tired like I done. An acre a day I cut with one of they, many's the time."

I followed George. Through the closing door I saw Pusey crumple into his windsor chair at the window and spread big vacant hands on the bare table. Night would come upon him there.

In the lane George quavered in Pusey's voice, "A half

213

a crown looked big as a cartwheel in they days." It was the general favourite from a treasury of Pusey's sayings.

"You ought to have stayed, he's lonely," I said.

George flared as if I'd put a match to tinder. "Don't try and teach me how to run Saradon Ned. I know how it's going to be run from now on. God," he went on less vehemently, "it's all very well for you and Lea and your parents going round the cottages once in a blue moon. I have to live with the relics. Anyway Pusey was never anything but a tyrant. We encouraged him, we let him be a tyrant—pretending he was this remarkable old character. I mean like you saying just now you'd done nothing much. You don't believe it, why say so?"

"What I do seems nothing much in his kitchen."

"You never get anywhere if you believe different things in different places."

"I do though," I admitted. "Everyone does."

"Not me any more," George said. "I'm sick of kowtowing to gardeners and stalkers and ghillies because I'm not as good at my amusements as they are at their professions. The idea of the amateur who's as good as the professional is class-guilt for having no profession. So get a profession is the answer. Of course Pusey can scythe better than I can, who cares? But he'd make a very poor Secretary to Her Britannic Majesty's Embassy at Mexico, and so you ought to tell him."

"He used to be rather a favourite of yours though," I said, "and he probably doesn't know why the favour has been withdrawn."

"Such I fear is the universal fate of tyrants, not to understand why they've been deposed," George said as we crossed the road by a cottage where another pensioner, the old chauffeur of my grandfather's day, lived alone. As we continued towards the farm he said, "And tyrants are deposed because people come to their senses. You know Pusey was there when Tim got killed?"

It was a direction my mind would not look in. "Was he," I temporized.

"Yes, hanging about with a wheelbarrow, doing bugger all as usual except croak away about how we wouldn't have been allowed to play golf on the lawn 'in your dad's time'," said George, thereby to me painting a vignette so vivid that I saw it against my will. But it wasn't golf surely?

"I thought it was cricket you were playing George?"

"Cricket?" He shook his head. "No, it was a golf-club. Anyway just because Pusey was there I felt—I don't know —in his power. So long as I had a hang-up about it."

The scene I had imagined for so many years was irreconcilable with golf substituted for cricket, unreal. "Now you haven't?" I asked. "Haven't got a hang-up I mean."

"No I haven't," said George simply as we walked through the farmyard. "Tim can haunt the man I've let the farm to, and Ardnagour now Robbie's taken it. They won't notice him anyway. I thought I could lay him by facing it out but you can't. You can only face facts. The spectres are always behind you."

"And you," I asked as we crossed the park towards the white blind stare of shuttered windows in the florid, towered, yellow, ornamented birthday-cake of a house, "what are you going to do?"

"Cure people's hang-ups," he replied instantly, turning his glittering eyes on me. "Teach them to face facts not fantasies."

Saradon shocked me. We had entered by kitchen and back stairs, and I had gone to unpack in the nursery where I had been put to sleep, given a stranger's viewpoint from a small spare room; now I came out to look for George. On the long dim landing and in the hall below lay a stillness so dense it entombed me; and in room after room, looking for George I found dimness and silence undisturbed, and the sheeted coffin-shapes of furniture discerned by the crannies around shutters: pictures stacked, rugs rolled, rooms dismantled, a hushed dereliction. The rest and

215

quietness of Saradon had settled into the sleep of death. Order, that arrangement of objects which creates atmosphere as arranged notes create harmony, had disintegrated: this dereliction no more conveyed what I meant by the word Saradon than Daranos, though the same letters, spelled its name. If it was reality, it wasn't the truth I believed. Like a shattered temple—like Monte Alban—it was empty of purpose.

Eventually, in the old servants' hall next to the kitchen I found George writing in an exercise book under an overhead light at the table. He put his book on the television, which faced two chairs, and rubbed his sinuous hands. "Rather chilly," he said. "Better light the fire."

I watched him pull an electric fire from under the table and plug it in. When the bars began to glow wanly he emptied his ashtray into the grate as though this was the touch that would make comfort complete, and sat down.

"You've shut the house up," I said.

"Have you never seen it like this? No of course you haven't. It's too much for us all the time."

"Us?"

"Well—for Annie Winder," he said.

I looked round the dreadful cheerless room. "I wouldn't have thought it was worth giving up everything to keep Mrs Winder."

"I've only given up the fantasy," he said, "I haven't given up anything I need. What's shut up mattered to all of you coming once a year, not me. All I was doing—you know what I was doing? Running a Tilton museum. Annie's quite right."

"So you did it for Amy." Had he said Amy or Annie? "Or for Mrs Winder?"

He looked at me with his fingers steepled under his chin. "Time did it," he said succinctly. "Old Father Time with his scythe. Blame him for taking the past away from you."

I sat down in silence on the other chair, facing, like George's, the milky blind eye of the television.

"Shall we just watch the news?" George suggested. "Annie'll be back from church and get our supper soon."

He switched on the set. It remained on loudly, like a boring host on his own hearthrug, throughout the evening. Before long Mrs Winder appeared, unpinning her hat and examining George from the door as a nurse might look through the spy-hole of a ward door on her rounds. Or so I thought. It had never occurred to me that Mrs Winder, who Lea had engaged and imposed upon George, might be a nurse. It did now. It would explain not only her class-lessness, the way she stood outside the domestic hierarchy, but also the ambiguity of her age, the starchiness and firmness of manner (if she were a trained nurse) overlaying a woman who might be no more than forty, as Amy had suggested. As a nurse, too, her grip upon George would be much more limpet-like, and therefore the threat to Amy more real. He had certainly become a great deal more eccentric out of her care, at Drumnakeel. She came in and out several times, laying the table, more nurse-like to my mind each time, before carrying in a cottage pie and cabbage which she set on the table in front of her own place, and sat down. She dished portions onto the white plates and handed them to us; I thought she had for-gotten that I didn't eat meat but no, there was only potato and cabbage on my plate, and a slab of cheese which she pushed silently towards me. There was no conversa-tion. Mrs Winder frowned at the television, forking pie into a pursed mouth, and George seemed to shelter behind the successive programmes, so I judged from his abstracted gaze, rather than to attend to them. Watching the flow caused a kind of vacuum in my head, rather pleasant, like watching clouds passing. Recovering objectivity during a commercial break I said, "That was a pretty silly programme."

"The thing about TV," responded George sleepily, "is that the shortcomings of the medium dictate the content of the programmes."

"Aye they do," agreed Mrs Winder comfortingly, her eyes on the screen.

"What do you mean George?" I asked.

"I mean"—he looked startled at being questioned—"What indeed do I mean? Ah, I have it: in a medium where one programme follows immediately on another there is no interval in which the audience can think. So there's no use putting on programmes you have to think about. I mean as soon as you think 'that was interesting' you have to stop and attend to the next programme. Look at the way——"

"Will we turn off the set while you have your discussion?" Mrs Winder suggested sourly.

"No need," said George, "my point is proved by the need to turn the thing off in order to comment on it."

After a survey of George her flat eyes refastened themselves on the screen. After supper, in an upright chair which she insisted silently upon taking, she began to knit. Side by side, yet separated as if upon islands in a flood, George and I sat watching the entertainment pour by. A play succeeded a travelogue, and a film about voles followed the play. The knitting needles clicked and a tiny bootee grew from them. Sinking deeper and deeper into the hypnotism of the screen, my sense of reality—whether of the servants' hall or of the play or the voles—blurred until I accepted fact and fiction like two flavours in the same spoonful.

The kitchen was deserted when I came down about ten the next morning. What is bizarre one day becomes on the next, if you sleep heavily, the accepted fact. I accepted that this was breakfast at Saradon nowadays, stewed tea from a brown pot on the Aga, and the wherewithal to boil yourself an egg. Maybe it had been the fact for a long time—I remembered George's tip for preventing tarnish on egg-spoons. Maybe the graduated row of copper meat covers hung on the wall, polished I had thought for use, had been museum relics a long while.

What sleep and Saradon had overlaid with layer upon layer of insulation was the actuality of those three days in Oaxaca. They seemed irrelevant to everything except themselves, a rift in the continuum. Unfortunately, irreversibly, they had happened, and not in my head or on the television screen (remote as they seemed, like the doings of the voles) but where action has its consequences. Footsteps approached across the cobbled yard. Now I would tell George. But it was Mrs Winder who entered with a wet rustle of plastic to dump on the table a secretive black hold-all such as widows take shopping in Scotland.

"We didn't know if you'd be wanting to be away off early," she replied to my apology for oversleeping.

"Where's Mr George?" I asked.

"Away to his teaching," she said, unwrapping packets taken from her bag. "Mondays and Wednesdays are his days at the hospital."

In an Embassy one is frequently told things by a junior which one ought to have been told by one's senior. I don't like it. I ignored Mrs Winder's information and walked to the door.

"You'll be going this morning will you?" she asked.

"When will Mr George be back?"

"Not before he has his tea."

"Then I'd like some lunch please. Thank you Mrs Winder." If no-one told me she was a nurse, I would treat her as a housekeeper.

I went out and walked in the wet garden, to and fro under mist-pearled trees. In Mexico I had imagined my interview with George. But I had imagined George—had imagined an impotent diminished George rejected by the Foreign Office and left by Amy, left behind by events to his outdated life at Saradon. And guilty: on the grass in front of me, as I sat in the summerhouse amongst the clutter of croquet mallets and ancient wicker chairs, George had killed his brother. All that guilt and failure was the position I had imagined myself storming, to carry off Amy.

But George no longer defended it. My maps were out of date. The picture Amy had drawn of him was false. So was mine. I didn't even know whether he'd killed Tim at cricket or golf. As always George commanded a height, a picked position with the dazzling sun behind him.

Yet I was bound to the consequences of the action I had taken in Oaxaca. The chain of causality was a necklace of skulls. Admirably as the Mexican divorce laws suit the indigenes, who require that their licentiousness be licensed, they seemed from the summerhouse at Saradon —whence one glimpses the slate steeple of the Church of England—outlandish and unreal; as irrelevant to actuality as would be the sacrifice of live hearts to the sun in northern climes. *Autres climats, autres mœurs.* But frontiers and climates mean nothing to chickens coming home to roost. Where the implacable sun ruled I had promised my heart, and come rain or shine I had to sacrifice it. I had to tell George that I was engaged to marry his wife.

Perhaps he knew. Amy might have told him on the telephone or even, since her indiscretion knew no bounds, on a picture postcard. In any event something had to happen, and I expected to be the victim.

Something did happen, almost in the nature of an earthquake which cants open the prisoner's door at the eleventh hour.

I heard Mrs Winder calling from the front of the house, her shout decipherable, when I crossed the rose garden towards her, as "They want you on the phone." In the morning room I picked up an extension of the telephone. It was Leonora, from London, and she told me that my father had died in Antigua. My mother in trying to trace me had called Lea early that morning.

"Is Amy with you?" I asked. We had stayed in Lea's flat on arrival from Mexico—Lea was away, and had not been expected back.

"Isn't she at Saradon?" asked Lea's voice.

"No."

"She said she was going down when she left here last night."

I told Lea that I would come up to London at once. Just before I rang off I heard the click of another extension being replaced somewhere else in the house. It could have been Mrs Winder eavesdropping.

Or was Amy hidden somewhere in the house? The silent dismantled rooms, the ambiguously-sheeted humps in the shadows, the listening stillness, seemed all ears and eyes. Besides the house itself, there was the apartment I had forgotten, the secret room over the coach house. She might have been there all the time.

It would be wrong to say that my father's death was a heaven-sent chance to escape from Saradon. But duty and inclination did not conflict.

I believe that children go through the bitterest of the pain of their parents' death years before the actual event when, at an age of dependence, they imagine the small realm of childhood shattered, bereft of its king and queen. Later, the landscape is wide enough to include shadow without the whole being utterly overcast; or, in my case, shadow which was a cool shade from the sun I had escaped. In the grey chill of lawyers' offices sympathy was formally expressed, and drily accepted, before deed boxes were unlocked, the will read and matter-of-fact arrangements discussed. Staying in an hotel with my mother I was kept busy for three or four days. The other reality did not impinge and so receded. Unfortunately my father had stated that he wished to be buried at Saradon. I rather hoped that George would make some objection when I telephoned him but he didn't, he said, "Of course, we'll expect you all."

So, without knowing quite whom he meant by "we" or "you all", my mother and I and my father's coffin travelled down by train within a week of my leaving Saradon. In the taxi from the station I warned my mother that George had closed the house. "God knows where we'll be put to sleep," I said.

"Of course we'll only stay a few days," she replied.

"We can't stay a few days mother. The house is shut up," I repeated. "Anyway I'll have to start back for Mexico by Tuesday."

"I'm sure we'll find Amy expecting us to stop on a few days," she assured herself. "The young nowadays are so good at coping without staff you know. Dear me there are our railings. How you all used to look forward to seeing those."

"Did we?" I looked away from the curved iron rails which for the first time in my life, far from dispelling homesickness, made my stomach turn over with apprehension. "Now mother," I went on, "Amy may not be at Saradon, she may be away."

"Away?" My mother was gazing at the house through the trees. "Oh no I think you're mistaken dear. I don't think Amy goes away much now, not with the scars. You often find that misfortunes bring people together, the way it's done with George and Amy. Besides she'd want to be there. She was fond of Daddy in her funny way, you could tell. Of course everyone was."

"Well I don't know about that," I said, "but she's been in Mexico without George."

"Yes so Lea tells me. With that brother who's turned out so well after all. It was kind of him."

Wherever she looked she saw in events the proofs of platitudes, and ordinariness. There was no use disabusing her, for our taxi had stopped at the porch. I would let the facts speak for themselves.

They spoke, if they were facts, in a way I did not expect. George and Amy stepped out through the front door arm in arm.

They were solicitous to my mother, they were charming, they led her into the drawing room where a fresh-fuelled fire threw its cheerful light on pictures, furniture, chairs strewn with the papers and magazines of a comfortable afternoon's occupation and, asleep on the hearth, either Rover or a mongrel just like him.

I returned to the hall. I looked into the other rooms. The remains of a fire glowed in the grate of the recreated morning room, and in the dining room the table was laid for dinner. The so-called library, in which there were no books and where no-one ever went, had exactly its old air of dark-panelled mustiness. I went to the hall table under the stairs, upon which had always stood a thermos of water and two tumblers, to catch out the deception by finding the thermos dry. It was full of fresh water. It was then no surprise, when I carried the cases upstairs, to find the south spare room prepared for my mother and my own old room beyond the tiger-skin ready for myself. The illusion of continuity was complete. The jumbled letters were in order, and spelled Saradon. Illusion? You have to believe the evidence of your eyes. Had I in reality come to Saradon the week before? A faint tremor of the supernatural passed through the house.

I only re-entered the drawing room after listening at the door to make sure that my mother was there as insulation against George or Amy. I found them seated round the fire, Amy on the sofa with her feet drawn under her tweed skirt and George beside her, the pair of them the very picture of a young married couple who listen politely to an aunt whilst their thoughts stray to such subjects as finding a good pony for the children. Presently my mother broke off her recital of my father's death, which I had heard her repeat, and perfect, perhaps twenty times in four days, and said, "But I'm sure you were busy when we arrived, don't let us interrupt. Or can I do anything?" she wondered dubiously.

Amy left a margin of silence, which framed my mother's words like the black band around mourning paper, before assuring her, "There's really nothing to do Aunt."

"Good Mrs Winder's coping, I'm sure. Such a comfort."

Another margin of silence. Then George said deliberately, "Mrs Winder had to go and see her sister. But Mrs Crouch has come in—you remember her?"

Mrs Crouch was recalled in every detail by my mother. George and Amy listened, George pitching his cigarette end into the fire with the precision of someone who knew to an inch the range from his accustomed seat. I ventured to look at Amy; her eyes had slid sideways to a pack of cards on a stool, so I studied her appearance unobserved. Her scar—like everything else at Saradon—was just what my mother expected, a cruel weal you pitied in a fresh-complexioned cheek without make-up, and the brassiness of her wig, if it was a wig, was at odds with her quiet clothes and folded hands. Stifling a yawn she looked quickly full at me. She winked. Then she said smoothly, "George and I *were* playing sludge, but..."

My mother's eye lighted on the cards and gleamed. "Since we are four," she suggested, smiling bravely, "maybe we should play Bridge?"

"You're sure you'd like to?" said George, staying his leap up from the sofa.

"It would occupy our minds, wouldn't it? And I'm quite sure," she added, making a way for George carrying the card table, "quite sure Uncle Jack would have wanted us to."

So levels of artificiality were layered one upon the other as we arranged the formal square for Bridge. It was the first time I had heard my mother try out that phrase— "I'm sure Uncle Jack would have wanted us to"—which was to become her skeleton key opening all doors to freedom. Whether she proposed moving to London, or taking up needlework, or buying a cat or going out to dinner, she forced my father's shade to approve. It was a curious revenge for a life of total dependence upon his orders.

At dinner awkwardness returned, reality at one level emerging when the four of us re-gathered round the dining-room table at which, without the conventionalized intimacy and jargon of Bridge, it was necessary to begin again from the premiss—a convention of another sort—that we were too woe-begone to speak of ordinary matters. And suddenly in the silence sorrow came. Suddenly I missed my father. The wills and deed boxes and lawyers' condolences, far from being the reality of death, occlude it; the reality was a missing figure, a stilled voice, in the dining room at Saradon. One figure less, particularly one who believed absolutely in Saradon, and the house itself perceptibly cracked, like the House of Usher before it slid under the waves, as if it were all part of his dream, and he was on the point of waking. The walls he had sustained trembled. This all came at me as we picked up our soup spoons. Too slippery to catch it was, but brutal as a stone flung hard and unexpected at your head. I ducked the stone. The candles burned calmly, the house stood firm. I listened to George's roundabout and decorous approach to a subject which interested him, the amount of money in my father's estate.

He wouldn't ask the question, and my mother wouldn't volunteer the answer; but her longing to name the sum, which had surprised her even more than me, made her reveal it in a dependent clause, always a less vulgar place for money than the main sentence: "Of course if I am to live in UK, as I know Uncle Jack wished, one doesn't get a large income from half a million pounds. And I can't touch the capital, that's all Ned's."

"Still," George said, evidently staggered. We had all treated my father as a comparative pauper. He looked at me calculatingly, though preserving the solemn tone suitable to recent wills: "I dare say this rather alters life for you Ned."

"Oh I don't see why," I replied blandly. I had already had a little practice, with the lawyers, at the insouciant pose of the rich.

"You remember I told you once you'd go on clocking in at the FO whatever happened?" He was irritated, and looking for superior ground. I hadn't thought that being richer than me was important to him. "You're like one of those dustmen who win the pools and carry on dusting," he said.

Amy began, "If I had anything to do with it you'd——"

"It's possible that Ned may not ask your advice Amy," George warned her. "You'll have to watch out for gold diggers, Ned," he continued. "Now this young lady you met in Mexico: nace tape is she? Not married or anything?"

"What girl is this?" my mother asked me.

I looked helplessly at George, who smiled.

"Angela Tozer she's called," Amy supplied, as if the name was for some reason an irritant to her.

George expressed a charade of surprise; "But didn't you tell me Amy that Terry had a girl-friend called Angela?" He looked from Amy to me. I probably reddened. "Oh I see," he said. "Well, there are as good fish in the sea Ned, as were ever caught by other anglers. It would be nice to feel he was settled, don't you agree Aunt? Lonely life as you get older, the diplomatic."

At the end of the table his head weaved to and fro, dark as a cobra's hood in the candlelight, his eye aglitter, his hands rubbed with the dry rustle of scales, the shadows of the big room behind him. I hated him. I said, "Quite a lot of people envy the diplomat's position you know. I'm always surprised when I see from the list how many people fail the examination."

He inclined his smile towards me. "Are you referring to the fact that I retired halfway through the ridiculous interviews? I almost came to blows with an absurd old person about regulation three, so I didn't bother to go back."

"Regulation three dear?" my mother enquired.

"Ned will tell you."

"I don't know it," I said.

"Don't you? I'm surprised. It's a regulation, Aunt," he went on, "about members of the Service who get involved in a matrimonial suit which may be thought to bring discredit upon them. You have to resign, no less. Very

Draconian I thought. Still I suppose diplomats accept what the penalties are if they get into muddles."

I said, "Of course if you've got money of your own resigning isn't such a blow. You can please yourself more." Since it seemed to be my inheritance which annoyed him, I hid behind it.

"Rather a *nouveau riche* view," he drawled. Then, brightening, he added to my mother, "Did you know that Amy and her brother have joined the new rich, Aunt? They travel about selling machinery and having all manner of adventures—don't you Amy?"

Amy's slow smile kindled, playing upon each of our faces in turn. "We did have an adventure or two," she admitted.

Her enjoyment was inward, for herself alone, as her dancing had been: that was what George resented. His mouth compressed angrily. I guessed that whatever he knew he distrusted, for his source was Amy whom he knew to lie. Whatever part of Amy he had, it was not the whole of her. Till I saw, in his anger, his impotence to control her as he controlled the rest of his environment, I had only wanted, and hoped, to tiptoe away from my commitment. Or perhaps her smile was one shaft of the sun's heat through the bars, tempting.

Meanwhile my mother's tongue had returned to the sore place. "One had always assumed," she complained, "that one's neighbours in Antigua were a good deal wealthier than we were."

Amy asked, "What's going to happen to your house there? Because if you thought of selling it I know someone who——"

"Terry's not that rich," George cut in. He was handing us vegetables, and the silver dish jerked irritably at my elbow.

"It's Ned's of course," my mother said, "and he's promised to pop out and clear up for me."

"When are you going?" Amy asked me.

"Next week, on my way to Mexico. Do you want to

227

come?" It was incredibly rash. It was to goad George, circulating powerless as a butler with the vegetables. There was also the thought of the heat in the Caribbean.

Amy only smiled, but the butler spoke, returning with his own plate from the sideboard. "Yes," he said, "why not Amy?"

I temporized, "No need to decide now."

"Yes we'll both come," said George. "I should like to do something to help."

"You'd be a great comfort to Ned," my mother agreed, "and the clearing up has to be faced I'm afraid."

"Yes I'm afraid facts have to be faced," said George sententiously, "and I think we can help Ned there."

"What about your teaching?" I asked desperately.

"Teaching?" echoed both Amy and George.

"What teaching George?" asked Amy, suspiciously as I thought.

"I shall teach as I go," George announced, his equilibrium quite recovered, sipping his claret with pleasure.

And I remembered his answer when I had asked what he was going to do: "Cure people's hang-ups—teach them to face facts." It was for me that the school bell tolled.

Before dinner was finished, Lea arrived. She entered the house with a clapping of doors, her sharp voice heard giving orders, feet on the stairs; at once the focus shifted from George to her, and when she swept into the dining room, pecked us with kisses, took a chair, picked at grapes, talked—at once Saradon was hers. George sat tapping his teeth with his thumb-nail until, peevishly rising, he snuffed out the candles and walked ahead of us to the drawing room, closing on his way, with a moan of exasperation, the inner front door which Lea had left ajar.

In the drawing room too, since we were five and couldn't play Bridge (and Happy Families had an inappropriate name) we listened to Lea. I gathered that she had not seen George for several weeks at least, although as a matter of course she assumed that she knew all about him, and all about every one of us. Lea always did: her omniscience depended upon appearing to learn nothing new from the people she was with. Because for once I knew a great deal more about the present circumstances than she did, I for the first time saw the truth of George's paradox, that she was "omniscient, and completely wrong". She didn't know, for instance, that Mrs Winder was not at Saradon; but when she was told, she continued to talk as if she had known all along:

"Will Mrs Winder have put a bottle in my bed George?"

"Mrs Winder isn't here. Mrs Crouch has gone by now."

"I mean will Mrs Crouch have put a bottle in my bed George?"

"I don't know Lea."

I wondered how much she had ever really known, behind that wonderfully unruffled air of knowing all. Her energy all went in preserving her balance. Nothing extraordinary ever happened. It lulled one—as my mother said, "You're such a comfort Lea dear." I had the impression that in talking of my father's death Lea's tongue painted out his image, painted out the reality of death, as you might smooth over a sparrow's grave in a flower bed. Perhaps that was what my mother meant by "comfort".

At about midnight, when Lea and my mother and I had retired upstairs an hour before, and I was on my way back from the bathroom, I heard laughter downstairs. I descended softly to the half-landing and looked (as we had done as children during dinner-parties) across the dark hall into the lighted dining room. I could see George's back bent over the table, which he was rubbing with a leather. "That Miss Lea," he said in flat Liverpool, "she's a proper mucky pup with her fingers on my table." "It's her nerves Mr George," replied Amy's voice, "she's jumpy as a cat." She crossed my field of vision carrying a tray of silver, laughing.

I crept upstairs. Imagine the two of them struggling by the sea's edge at Killaneen. I couldn't. It was the impression of ordinary high spirits that bewildered me. You would have thought they were perfectly happy, which I disbelieved, or resented. So they had seemed when my mother and I had arrived. Was Mexico only one of Amy's "adventures", as George had said? Perhaps that's what an adventure was: an action without consequences.

A further layer of artificial manners descended upon the house next morning in the form of cousins and old friends of my father arriving in mourning clothes from distant parts. Solemn faced, gravely they shook my hand; but evidently they were delighted to see one another. I saw them take each other's arms and walk off round the corner of the house saying, "Been meaning to get in touch, we wondered if you'd come down and shoot in November." Groups strolled round the garden eating grapes. No-one except the undertakers talked to me. I was quarantined by bereavement, emotion, the unknown: all of it like a volatile explosive, best left to the professionals, the undertakers whose glibness reminded me of the hundreds of letters of condolence I had written on behalf of Ambassadors to unknown widows. So much paraphernalia was placed between oneself and the fact of death—and one's own deportment in the complex figure became of such importance—that one could only face in the general direction of the facts. The earthcrack which had seemed to shake the walls of Saradon at dinner last night was now muffled and remote. Remote too, beneath so many layers of manners, ticked the other, unexploded, bomb: Amy. Like one of those terrible artifacts in the Mexican museum, hollowed to contain human hearts, the sacrificial altar was buried beneath the layers of succeeding civilizations; but not buried so deep, I feared, that George's interfering and scholarly curiosity would not unearth it.

In church there were other things to think of. Because for form's sake George, Amy, Lea, my mother and I had to squeeze into a front pew designed for four, and because I was on the outside with George's unhelpful elbow next to me, throughout the funeral service I was in danger of tumbling into the aisle, and I thought with considerable resentment about this.

IX

THE SMALL FRAME house on the Caribbean beach, where I went alone a few days later—neither George nor Amy had spoken again of coming with me—was more melancholy far than Saradon. Here loss was absolute, for all that remained was rubbish. The relics were touching. I rifled locked drawers and uncovered what my father had thought secret, or sacred: it was the smallness of his secrets (estate maps of Saradon and Ardnagour locked in his desk for instance) which touched the heart. From his notes about birds and weather I saw how bored he must have been, bored and homesick: "Saw a Red Tailed hawk—might have been a buzzard over the loch, light just like Scotland. Hot again. 87° at 10 a.m." Because his thoughts were so trivial I threw his diary away without reading it. I did not want to overhear, from his loneliness, the accusation that I had neglected him.

Yet I discovered signs of an indivisibility between my mother and father which I hadn't guessed at. Sorting their possessions one from another was like disentangling a clematis from a rose, I couldn't tell which tentacles belonged to which plant, or which supported and which clung. There were business letters in his drawers drafted in her hand, and a shopping list in the kitchen written by him. They had intertwined as George and Amy had not.

I thought frequently of George's account of that final day at Drumnakeel, and it seemed to me on reflection that their inability to have children together epitomized their divergence, not only from each other but from truth. Physically the truth probably was that they couldn't, or perhaps shouldn't, have children together—he couldn't father hers, and she couldn't bear his—and they were in this sense a flawed union, like a joint of metals magnetized but never welded. I guessed that Amy, who reconstructed facts so that they could not possibly prove her guilty, blamed George; and that George accepted guilt as his due. I thought about all this as I tried to extricate frail tendrils of my mother's life from the dead tentacles of my father's, though in the end I threw everything away, so intertwined they were.

There was nothing worth keeping. I have left more débris in moving from one office to another than my father had left after sixty-six years on the earth. The reason was that the move from Saradon had been his real death. The red-tiled bungalow under the palms was only a waiting room, just as Pusey's back kitchen was a waiting room, for those with a sentence to serve in limbo.

My own life too seemed a kind of limbo. I had a feeling that I would never go back to Saradon, and the empty years stretched ahead. When I had filled and burnt half a dozen waste-paper baskets there was nothing more to do. I swam, and cooked for myself, and sailed the blue lagoon under the toy green hills; even then only half the three days I had allowed myself, before flying on to Mexico, had dragged by. For hours I walked on the beach where the sea flooded.

Time did not so much pass, as recede over the horizon like the smoke of a ship I had missed. I could have been on it, but I had delayed until it was too late. If the clock had never been set going, what would have been the difference? Ah, but it had been set going: clock or time bomb, in Oaxaca Amy had wound the mainspring, wound the snake-coil tight. Now, evermore, I knew time's existence by its loss. Its tongue clamoured like hounds hunting, but hunting another quarry, away from me, over the hill. It is the tension between hunter and hunted which coils the mainspring of the clock, which is the impetus of the Mayan calendar, the force behind the seasons themselves. I had thought, awaiting the rifle shot in the hills above Drumnakeel or looking reluctantly at the blood-soaked calendar stone, that such tension meant only death. But it meant life too. It meant both indivisibly. The wheel of destruction is the wheel of creation. The hunter hunting is hunted. That was the truth I had delayed facing until it was too late; for now the clock had run down, and time hunted another quarry over the hill. "Where is that avarice of time the thought of death inspires as rumoured robberies endear our gold?"

A day or two more and I would have started collecting sea shells, as my mother had done. As it was I became, like my father, subjectively aware of the weather. It was hot, damp; the light wet, like the light in Venice, sun through vapour; the moist air was prickly except when one was naked; vegetation and fruits of the heat bloomed rank and fleshy round the house. Never was I in a place or a climate so suggestive of sensuality: it seemed that nature had surrounded me with genitalia, be they figs, cowries or humdrum bananas. I say this, if not to explain what happened, then at least to set the scene.

Or perhaps what happened doesn't need explanation. Perhaps such goings-on will be accepted as everyday events, like wife-swapping parties in towns one doesn't live in oneself. It depends so much upon what papers and books you read, your idea of an everyday event. Miss Tozer found them in the codices of the Aztecs. Under stones you find sermons you have already hidden there. You can only judge of reality by your own experience, there is no objective touchstone, no book, no newspaper, no codex or mythology which persuades you that actuality is different from your own preconception of it. The fiction you believe is the fiction which depicts the world as you already see it. One's belief shuts up shop in face of what seems improbable, or offensive, just as the bedroom door shuts in the face of the Victorian novel-reader: there reality ends and imagination, which tells you more about the reader than the writer, takes over behind closed doors. Anyway, my last twenty-four hours in Antigua were to me highly improbable and although, as George had often told me, I

233

wouldn't recognize an everyday event if it jumped out of the hedge and snapped at my garters, I can only record what seemed to happen. Probably my mother, if told, would have said comfortingly, "It's only your imagination dear." And perhaps it was.

On the day before my departure for Mexico I was lying on a bed in the heat of the afternoon reading my mother's copy of *Ten Thousand A Year*, that excellent novel which depicts a four-square copper-bottomed Victorian reality. Perhaps I fell asleep. The telephone rang. Half-waking I picked up the receiver and said, "Yes?"

"Hello my love, it's your relations come to stay like we promised. We're at the airport."

It seemed all the action in my life was to be sprung by telephone calls from Amy. The succulence of her voice brimmed with laughter as the island fruit spurted juice when you bit it. I pulled the sheet over myself and said, "I can't stop you coming I suppose."

"Yes you can," she mocked me, "I rang to give you time. You can get out if you like. There's still time, George is quarrelling with the nurse in Immigration."

Succulent, succubine, her voice teased. I thought of the ship gone over the horizon, the hounds hunting over the hill. "No, come," I said. "Amy tell me, how much does George know?"

"How much do any of us know?" she replied, and rang off laughing.

The clock or time bomb was rewound and began to tick.

There were three bedrooms in the house and I remade the bed in each from the "coffins" into which I had arranged the bedclothes the day before. Any fewer and I would certainly end up on the carpet, as I had nearly ended up in the aisle at my father's funeral. Musical Chairs is not my game. Then I walked up the path under the palms to the iron gate in the perimeter fence which enclosed my parents and their neighbours in what the developers called "a tropic paradise". Iron though it was, no gate nor setting could have been more different from the iron gate guarding the track to Ardnagour under snowy hills. A livid light had turned the bay to copper aglint under a heavy sky; egrets flopped snow-white across it, and dropped amongst others decorating the mangroves like cotton-wool on Christmas trees; palm fronds rattled suddenly in hot gusts which darkened the sea, and were as suddenly stilled. The red-indian brown of the earth was warm underfoot and warm in colour where it showed amongst the jungle-green of the hills across the bay. I felt extraordinarily well, a suppleness of flesh and blood and bone, a *bien-être* like narcissism in its consciousness of being alive within my body. Now is the eternal life.

By the gatehouse, in a cottage, lived the negro Thomas who was supposed to look after the property—"seeing to your conveniences" he described it—and he strolled out on his floppy black feet, scarlet drawers sagging, his big jolly countenance smiling fit to bust under a baseball cap. He carried in his hand an island newspaper whose screamer headlines denounced the British Raj, but I was used to his theoretical politics, which in no way influenced his behaviour. He was delighted to hear that I expected guests, for the thought of anyone being alone for more than a few minutes terrified him. "Who's they who's coming, Mr Tilton?" he enquired.

"Oh—relations," I said. Halfway between England and Mexico it was hard to specify Amy's position more precisely.

"They is lucky folks coming along to this paradise we got here," said Thomas. He was only quoting the brochure, but it seemed indeed the earthly paradise, such fullness of life I felt. He had gone on to speak of my father, removing his baseball cap out of respect: "The colonel Tilton leave a sumptious amount of money, I heard on the paper," he said with awe.

Curiously enough the thought of the money did not contribute to my sense of well-being. Presently a taxi could be seen threading round the head of the bay and along the track towards us. I thought of the Land Rover descending through the wastes the morning Amy had met me. Here, the taxi sped through the green jungle of palms along the shore of a warm sea; and here the sense of tension included myself.

The taxi rattled up and stopped in its dust cloud. Amy sprang out—sprang rather as dancing girls are said to spring out of the pudding at stag parties, such a contrived gay leap onto the stage—and kissed me roundly. She was wearing a football jersey and high boots. Behind her George stepped out fastidiously as a grasshopper and looked round him with captious disapproval. He wore a cream tussore suit over a blue shirt, and a broad-brimmed white hat which shaded his saturnine face. Add a cheroot, and he could have been a plantation owner inspecting the estate. They were both, once again, dressed for charades. What word were they acting now?

"So these are the West Indies," George concluded when he had quizzed the prospect. "Well well."

His clothes might have stirred in the taximan atavistic memories of the slave owner, for the conventional quarrel about the fare from the airport became bitter, the taximan dashing to the dust Thomas's official charge-list and snatching instead the newspaper.

"You hear what that says on the paper," he foamed at George, banging the headline, "if you listening in you see what that says on the radio."

"You give me that," cried Thomas, tugging at the newspaper, "this not written for folks with limited intelligence to hear."

George watched the row with an air of surprise, his money extended.

"Come on my love," said Amy to me, swinging her bag, "George has been quarelling with the gollies ever since we landed."

"It isn't he who's quarrelling," I said as we walked down the hill into silence.

"Well, causing quarrels then, it's the same thing," she

said. "George is always in the middle of some row or other."

Amy ran excitedly about the house peering through windows. She wasn't quite the female form which heat had brewed in my mind: she wasn't any longer the happy phenomenon I remembered swimming fishlike in the Scottish river or running like a hind on the hill. It was contrived, the eeling and craning at windows so that her pants showed under her football sweater. Because she was tired, the scar on her face was a noticeable blemish. Her vivacity irritated me and I thought I would deflate her.

I said, "Amy is it true you tried to drown yourself? Did you jump in the sea that day?" I was sitting in a cane chair watching her.

She relaxed. All her slow grace came back when she smiled. "I tell you," she said, "if you end up in the sea and George is there, you think he pushed you."

I heard George's step approach the house, his voice still urging a liberal outlook towards fellow-blacks on Thomas, whose bare feet slapped along beside him. When he entered the sitting room he cast his white hat on a chair, extracted a bent cigarette from a pocket, lit it and sat comfortably down as if expecting the entertainment to begin. He was evidently in the best of spirits, but I felt irritated with him too. Their arrival, just like everyday guests, was an anticlimax.

"You'll never change Thomas's views," I said. "There's no point trying."

"Changing him isn't the point," George replied. "The point is to disagree with him, then he won't think there are more fascists around than there really are. Then he'll change so as to stay in the majority you see."

"Optimistic," I said briefly, my mind off the subject.

But George's was applied to it, as if his visit was a perfectly ordinary one from a nearby house. "You have to be optimistic if you're going to teach anyone anything," he said. "Against every shred of evidence, you have to believe that education improves people. You have to be prepared," he added, turning a pair of eyes as black as gun-muzzles suddenly on me, "you have to be prepared to travel halfway across the globe to teach people a lesson."

His eyes blazed, and I could not duck their aim. My heart thumped.

But Amy was complaining, "If all what you've done to me is education my love, I don't feel a bit improved."

"I know you don't. I know it doesn't work," he said equably, "and still with my boundless optimism I believe in trying."

"I've never found anything you believed in," she grumbled.

"That's because all you ever find is hysterical rubbish like Mrs Eddy and that woolly Mr Jefferies," he told her. "Of course I don't believe in that. What I have pointed out to you—with the help of Occam's razor—is that you don't either. That is education."

"But George," she protested, "you and Occam's razor have shaved off every hair of my head. I've nothing left."

"Ah well," said George, smiling serenely, "if you've nothing left then I don't believe in you either. 'All that you had I found. With the dead leaves on the ground'," he recited in his Grand-Guignol manner, "'I dance the Devil's dance'."

"Oh George," she said eagerly, "tell the what-you-may-call-it you made up on the plane. About the Bahamas, go on."

They were both in high spirits. Again, as I listened to George's limerick, I felt like pig-in-the-middle, unable to catch what they lobbed to each other.

> " 'My dear is it true the Bahamas
> Are simply quite full of old charmers?
> With their 'twenty-ish air
> Are they gay, debonair;
> Are their tastes so bizarre they'll alarm ours?'

—or possibly 'alarm us'," he finished, "I really don't know which would be best."

I tried to join in their mood. "Pyjamas would be a good rhyme in the last line."

"One doesn't want to be too obvious," he replied crushingly.

Amy said, "And we wanted to get in the bit about being alarmed because we are, aren't we George?"

"Extremely alarmed," he agreed. "One hears such stories of fandangos with the natives. And Amy expects to widen her circle. I suppose," he said to me, "I suppose Thomas pops down to oblige if a lady guest feels the need? Not? You hear that Amy? I shall have to see what I can arrange." He pursed judicious lips for a moment. Then springing up and rubbing his hands he exclaimed in jolly tones, "But gracious me! here I am speculating with the wife as though we were still on the plane, and all the time we have actually arrived, and the fun may begin at any moment. Now tell us your plan Ned. What have you got laid on?"

"Yes what shall we do?" rejoined Amy. "We don't mind, do we George? We're ready for anything."

They both looked at me. Just as one thought they had disagreed, they would act in unison, as if they were after all two syllables of the same word at charades. I couldn't make out their intention. In the silence the sea lapped on the beach. They seemed to share an expectation that what I said next would amuse them.

"We could go for a sail," I suggested.

Sure enough they laughed. "Yes, yes," said George, slapping his knee, "certainly boating would suit our book, wouldn't it Amy?"

I went down to the cove where my father's dinghy was drawn up on the sand. When I had it ready for the sea George and Amy joined me and we pushed it into the water and jumped inboard, Amy barelegged in only her football shirt, George in his white suit but barefoot. Over my swimming trunks I was wearing the suède shirt Amy had given me. At the tiller George worked the boat's head over till a breeze filled the sail; she heeled, the slap of water quickened under her stem and we drew swiftly off across the bay. First we ran a fast reach to the mangroves which fringed the lagoon's far shore, spray flying to leeward, the boat scudding and careering, Amy singing in the prow whilst the wind tattered her hair.

"Watch out George!" I turned to warn him as we flew towards the spider-legged roots of the mangroves. He held the course. I felt us rushing to destruction.

In the breakers he put up the helm. Our arrow-flight stopped short. The boat spun, wallowed, flapping the boom, came alive and urgent again as the wind snatched at the shortened sail, and slowly, stiffly, beat offshore. In the lifting, dipping bow Amy had nearly lost her balance.

"In *Swallows and Amazons* they used to say 'Ready About' before they played that trick," she shouted gaily to George.

He said nothing, watching the luff of the sail as he brought the boat closer on the wind. He was intent, in his element—almost was an element, leagued with wind and sea. Stronger blew the breeze now we faced it. Hurrying squalls strode across the sea and darkened it. Our own shore looked low and far off. I sat against the windward gunwale catching slaps of water the boat chucked up. She stood in irons, pitching. George let her head a point off the wind's eye and she leaped forward like a horse on turf, speeding for the reef and the glittering line of the horizon. Looking down into the water I saw sand and sea grass sliding swiftly under the waves, light running in the sea like quicksilver in veins: then I saw nothingness, the deep. I looked no more into the obsidian dark. Amy came and sat beside me, soaked, smelling of salt, her teeth chattering. It was unnaturally cold; her legs were pimpled with gooseflesh. When I looked at George in the flying boat his eyes were dark and intent with joy. His suit was soaked, I saw his knuckles white where the sheet pulled at his grasp. Faster and faster we flew towards the reef where the sea humped and boiled.

"That's where the sharks'll be," shouted George.

"I wish we could see one," Amy yelled back, the wind stripping the words off her lips.

"Lean out or we'll turn over," I urged Amy. I was perched out straining backwards myself.

"What, never upset in a gig?" George shouted.

I realized that only I was frightened. The boat careened and slewed on the bubbling dark green waves which lifted her and flung her onwards. George had let her off the wind, was sailing for the open sea. In the instant I realized this, pulling myself inboard from the sea ripping under my back, the boat gybed. Water with the violence of a cataract tore me off the gunwale. I smashed on the sea and plunged under.

There was a long falling terror to infinite depths of green silence. Treading the watery rungs of nightmare I fought upwards. At last I gasped air. The boat had gone. Then I knew why George had come to the West Indies. Fear like a weight sank me. When again I came up, I was in a trough between shale-grey waves which towered and toppled round my horizon, their flanks squall-wrinkled like scree: I was back in the viewless stone gulley where I had waited whilst George and Amy stalked above Drumnakeel, waiting for the shot. Sea water soaked into my bones bitter as frost. There was no ship or shore or rescue. That I was near the reef I knew. What cruel grey ghosts glided off the rocks I had seen from glass-bottomed boats. When the lift of a wave gave me a wider view I saw only dark sea and sky, and the low green land remote, before I sank into the viewless gulf again. I knew George was mad, I had always known: mad and a killer. In my heart I knew. I had let reason dissuade me. I splashed myself desperately round for a sight the other way when another wave lifted me.

I was only forty yards from the spit of rock which became the reef. The dinghy stood off the surf head to wind, her white sail rippling. Amy waved, and George let the sail fill to carry them in to the curving beach backed by palms. I swam to the spit and climbed out.

The idea of murder was at once absurd. It receded, as the roaring of the sea receded behind me on the reef, into its proper perspective viewed from safety. From firm warm sand what had seemed white-foamed breakers looked no more than the scud of catspaws. Reason ruled the elemental forces once again. As I approached, George ran the boat onto the beach and they both jumped out.

"That's just what that suède shirt needed, a good soaking," Amy called as she splashed ashore. "Doesn't it look better George?"

"Is that why he jumped out? Yes, I think the dip's done him good," George allowed.

We pulled the boat up the beach for Thomas to collect later, and set off walking along the sounding shore. On the land it was hot.

The air was tangible with heat, and full of the noise of the sea, so dense with heat and sound that it conducted a sense of touch, as if one's fingers touching the air touched also everything suspended in it—touched the wetness of the sea, touched the smoothness of pebbles, knew by touch as well as sight the satin of Amy's legs and the lean strength of George and the dry grainy heat of the sand between one's toes. I was aware of everything.

And everything was aware, was interconnected. What connected all creation was tension, when the wound clock ticks loudest: the avarice of time which thoughts of death inspire; the tautness of the drawn bow. The stalker stalking is stalked. The three of us without speaking approached the headland which divided the beach from the house.

"I'm going to swim round," Amy called from the waves where she walked.

"Goodbye Amy," George said.

She swam off with watery sounds. George and I struck over the headland, through grass and rocks which still gave out the heat of the day, though the sun was sinking into bruised clouds. We were suddenly inland, the sea unheard. Spent grass and the scrape of cicadas, rock and no water, the parched hillside; and along the hill's crest, palms sharp as shards of glass, bottle-green, spiked the uneasy sky. It would rain. The dust waited. In his white suit patched with sea stains George stalked ahead. "Where on earth did you get the suit George?" I asked.

"I got it," he said, "out of the acting cupboard. Just the ticket don't you think? One shouldn't take the Caribbean too seriously. Tell me, you going to keep the house here?"

"I wouldn't use it."

"Amy would like it."

"Would she," I said. "You mean I should give it her?"

"It might be prudent. Rather her handwriting, life in the acting cupboard. And her relationship with Terry would cause less speculation *dans cette galère*."

"Amy and Terry?" I repeated slowly. The implication had splashed like the first drop of the awaited storm, heavily. I tried to dodge it. "Don't be absurd George."

He laughed, walking on. "You draw a line round yourself and call everything outside it absurd. Why do you think she was so jealous of your friend Miss Tozer?"

"She wasn't." But I wondered. "She never said anything."

Again he laughed, saying over his shoulder, "It seems you don't live in a world where actions speak louder than words."

"What actions?"

"Foolish reflex actions like trips to Oaxaca."

I considered this. "You think she came to Oaxaca because she was jealous of Terry and Angela Tozer? I don't believe it."

He was walking rather cautiously ahead of me, apparently attending more to where he stepped in his bare feet than to what he said. "Well I know that was the reason she came back to Saradon. But you are evidently more confident of your charms—— Now who is this fine fellow?" he broke off to enquire.

A drunk negro slumped at the foot of a manchineel

tree arose unsteadily in his wellingtons and shambled towards us semaphoring messages. "You got some work for me? I go work for you man," he cried.

I waved the half-naked creature away, pressing on George's heels to make him hurry.

"I work for the boss, not you man," he retorted as he flailed past me. "I leave this place and follow you sir," he suggested in George's ear, squelching and stumbling along in his gumboots.

Even to a drunk negro George was boss of the two of us —the gloomy monarch, though improbably white-suited, whose realm underlay the world. That I owned the house made no difference: if I had owned Saradon it would have made no difference. Nothing eroded his power. Resentfully, I left the two of them talking by the door and walked through the house to the veranda.

The dark sea and the dark shore waited for the storm. Small waves broke yeastily on the beach, bubbling on the sand like champagne spilt on Creole skin. Then with liquid noises, trailing a wake of ripples, Amy came swimming out of the dark. In my mind she trailed George's suggestion of unnaturalness, a mermaid's fish-body under the water. She and her brother. I wouldn't believe the mutation. I walked out to meet her, the warm sea gushing into my beach shoes. Her floating nimbus of hair pushed towards me with the pulses of her breast-stroke. I wouldn't believe it was a wig. When she was close she arose streaming water. Because she stumbled I put out my hand—and saw the pool where we'd picnicked in the glen, Terry's hand pulling Amy under the bank: I saw it clear as I'd seen the scene through George's spy-glass, sharp and cold. She and her brother. But her hand in mine was wet and warm. It was George's spy-glass which distorted the world. When she kissed me her heat, the sun's heat, struck through her striped jersey and through her mouth, a greengage stolen from a south wall at Saradon liquefying in a child's mouth. Then she arched her back away from me and smiled, that slow, knowing smile of mischief. She waded through the water and I followed. George stood on the dark shore.

"George, George!"—she greeted him with her tireless optimism—"let's do our trick."

She ran towards him and hopped in the air. He made no move to catch her. She fell splash on her behind.

"Is that our trick?" he enquired.

Amy laughed in the waves at his feet. "George I trusted you," she shouted.

"And came a nasty cropper," he said drily.

She threw her arms round his legs in a welter of water. He withstood her struggle to pull him down and spoke to me above her. "Ned I hired that darkie for you."

"That drunk?" I was horrified.

"Yes I thought he'd come in handy."

"Where is he?"

"Having a rest in the kitchen with some of your rum."

Amy said, "And his feet in the Aga I suppose."

George lashed out at her like a heron fighting a pike. He lost his balance and fell. They fought and thrashed, fountaining water, one beached sea-creature in the surf. Or I thought they were fighting till I saw their mouths on each other's. Then I started to wade ashore. As I passed them George's hand gripped my ankle. He spat out sea and sand.

"Ned"—his voice was pained—"what is this I hear about you marrying my wife?"

I stopped. A tide of blood poured back into me. Like silk tearing his voice continued:

"Now I don't want to make an undue fuss. I don't when you come pestering me. You must face facts though. You really must be made to. What is it you want? You have to decide."

The two of them were on their feet, shaking the sea off them. They advanced crusted in sand as I retreated, their faces set in smiles like masks of comedy, lit in the light streaming on the water from the house behind me. There was menace in the tension. There was all the cthonian menace I had ever feared from sea or earth, and the tension connected it to myself. I mounted the steps of the house. They followed me, hunted me, their footfalls hollow on the veranda. In the sitting room I faced them.

"What exactly do you want?" George said again. "Well you choose Ned. Life or death. You choose." My heart pounded. I couldn't speak. Then he turned towards Amy like a ringmaster introducing an act. We were his creatures, in his circus.

When she moved I understood what he meant by life. Slow as a cat stretching she pulled up her jersey. Yes I would choose life. But with her jersey she pulled off her head—her head of hair like a cannibal trophy flopped on the tiles. A stubble sprouted from her skull. Breasts swelled like sores, putrid tipped, from flesh whose scars puckered as she moved towards me. Like maggots white in red meat the scars wriggled. The carnivore's mouth of her sex was hairy. It was George's lips in his beard. It was a volcanic meat-swallowing crack. I smelled the heavy rotten stench of the gralloch.

"No George!" It was the altar he had dug up to sacrifice me on. "No I can't."

Amy hesitated, her toes nibbling the tiled floor. She looked for orders to George. He opened the kitchen door like another trap loosing his creatures into the arena. Prowled in the negro. Amy fled. She fled from the raised black javelin set on her by George. In a bedroom the negro caught her. George strolled behind his gladiator into the dark. Amy cried:

"Get him off George! You know I didn't mean it about blacks."

Equably he replied, "Let this be a lesson to mean what you say. You must say what you mean Amy. You must speak the truth, and turn out your toes when you walk." *Through the Looking-glass.* I went to close the door on them. Out of the dark his face loomed near mine. He levelled two fingers at me. "Bang you're dead," he said. Like the bedroom door in Victorian fiction that door shut in my face, and out it seemed that I went—bang, just like a candle, out of his dream.

Or had they gone out of mine? Late in the morning I lay listening a long time before I dared enter the sitting room from the bedroom where I awoke. On the sheet beside me, as if I had fallen asleep reading and dreamed the whole episode, lay *Ten Thousand A Year*. When at last I entered the main room all its doors stood open onto silent bedrooms. The beds were neatly made into "coffins". That told me nothing. Both George and I had learned how to make coffins at our preparatory school. Of their visit the house bore no impress. Only in my head was there pressure.

Sunlight and the reflection of water made the house seem afloat, adrift, hallucinatory. The order which kept sea and sky apart seemed to hang by a thread. Supernatural stillness was charged with the imminence of collision. The pressure on the dam increased. The danger was of extreme vividness.

Chaos struck. Chaos like a tidal wave raged pell-mell into the house, into my head, as if the sky had fallen into the sea. The masonry of order collapsed into liquefaction. I knew what was happening to me: my intellect watched the onset of dementia. Like a bird above a dark sea it hung aloof.

In the middle of my mind's eye a picture stood firm. It was of the tufts of greyish hair which grew out of the ears of the psychiatrist who had treated my collapse when I was sixteen. They were as neatly clipped as topiary, fascinating. "You must get it out of your head that anything extraordinary has happened to you," he was telling me. "All right, you've been expelled from Eden. All children are, by growing up. Perhaps it comes later, and therefore more violently, to your class because of your protracted infancy, but there's nothing extraordinary about it and no-one's to blame. You know perfectly well your cousin isn't to blame, don't you? Tell me he's not."

"George isn't to blame," I told the sea and sky to make them part. My intellect knew that George was not guilty. My imagination had put the mark of Cain on him. Out of the facts my imagination made the mysteries it craved. Out of accidents it constructed crimes. Out of repression crawled horror like maggots from meat. I knew all this.

But what is the power of the intellect compared to the power of imagination? A white bird on the face of the sea.

There was time to catch my plane to Miami and Mexico. In the Embassy was protection. Even nearer, at the airport, once hospitalized by its uniformed staff, I would be safe. The fear of death in an air crash was nothing compared to the fear of life. I rang for a taxi, packed and hurried up the path. It was Sunday and Thomas was at church. I waited, looking down through the palms. Where I had imagined chaos, the beach by the blue water tempted me back. It was the outward face of paradise. The taxi came. The iron gate clanged shut behind me forever. I was safe in the taxi. Yes I had imagined—dreamed—the whole of George and Amy's visitation. That was the solution which left my concept of reality least shattered. True or false it was a solution: like a light held over silver it co-ordinated the random scratches of events into a pattern, for I saw that in my dream I had forced George and Amy to behave just as I had always feared or hoped they would behave. George's attempt to drown me; George's attempt to force upon me Amy's mutated body, in which my own moral repugnance was incarnate; George's punishment of Amy by making her accept the consequence of her whim: it all fitted, as the intellect can make a paradigm fit.

I remembered, moreover, as I settled back in the taxi, that in my dream, in the night, I had woken to the drumming of rain—rain gushing and splashing from roofs and waterspouts had awoken me, and I had looked through my window. The night was solid with rain which hissed on the sea. The sea smoked, and veiled in the smoke stood George, washing his hands in the sea. Now, in dry cane brakes beside the road as I was driven across the island, and in the dust blowing, there was no evidence that rain had fallen. It seemed that I could be sure that I had dreamed.

But circumstances have a habit of conspiring against certainty: reason flutters only a hand's breadth above the flux. Over his shoulder my driver told me that the body of a negro had been washed up on a beach that morning, murdered. That shot the white bird. It plunged into a raging sea.

X

TIME ELAPSED. DAY upon day, months of them,
floated down like leaves from the tree of life until a drift
of days a year deep covered over that flaw in the earth's
crust into which I had fallen like Alice into Wonderland.
I had been moved from Mexico. After a spell of rest in
Switzerland I had been transferred to Athens. Everyday
events had begun to construct their enclosure around me
once more, walling me in brick by brick. I had had no
contact with Saradon until Lea rang me up one day: with
time to kill between a yacht at Piraeus and her plane to
London she suggested meeting. "Heard you hadn't been
well again," she said. "I meant to drop in on the clinic
when I was at St Moritz for Christmas, but Switzerland
is such a tiresome shape. Are you recovered?"

"Oh Lord yes, there's nothing wrong with me," I
assured her.

When we met in Constitution Square she told me, over
the cup of coffee which was all she had time for, that
George was teaching History and Classics at a private
school in the Wirral. "Does he enjoy that?" I asked.

"Enjoy?" She appeared to wonder. "I don't think
George wants to enjoy himself. But he can tolerate himself as a schoolmaster, and that's an improvement on his
previous record."

"He's always been a bit of a pedagogue," I said.

"Yes he has. His trouble has been, trying to turn the
rest of us into a class. Now I suppose the wretched infants
have to listen." She laughed drily. "I tell you the sort of
thing he teaches them, poor George; when I was at Saradon
he was doing those dismal Indian wars, Tippoo Sahib and
what not, and do you know he told me proudly he'd made

250

the class learn the correct pronunciation of Seringapatam."

"Which is?"

"You're as bad as George—how should I know? Shreer-ingnapatama or something."

"Well, if it's correct I suppose that's what teachers are for," I said.

"Oh it's correct," she said impatiently, "but pronounce it like that and no-one outside the state of Mysore will have a clue what his pupils are talking about. It's typical of George."

I agreed. The correct lie: it was George's speciality. I wondered about his other half, the incorrect truth. "Was Amy at Saradon?" I asked.

"Poor little thing no, she's gone."

"Gone where?"

"Oh," she replied dismissively, "out of sight, under-ground, wherever people one doesn't see do go. Their marriage couldn't last, I knew that."

"She was an extraordinary creature."

"I never thought so," Lea claimed. "A very ordinary girl."

It annoyed me, such bland dismissal. For my peace of mind Amy had to be an aberration; if she was the norm, nothing was safe. Besides, I was sure that Amy and George were together, for I had come to see them as a unit, however fused—as two syllables of the same word, playing at Charades, or as premiss and antithesis in the same syllogism. Lea would not allow that they were to-gether because Amy had replaced her as George's hair-shirt. Such are the lies people tell in order to preserve as a uniformity their concept of the truth. Far from knowing everything, Lea preserved her equilibrium only by admit-ting nothing which upset it. I thought I would shake her balance. "How was Saradon?" I enquired.

"Mrs Winder is marvellous," she replied obliquely, as if I had asked a different question. "She holds it all together."

"Was the house shut up?" I pressed her, "or did they open it up for you?"

There was a quake of uncertainty in her eyes. I thought she might even ask me a question. But she didn't. "It was just as usual," she asserted.

"But they don't live in it you know," I told her. "They live in the kitchen and the servants' hall except when we're there. Perhaps George has never shown you the apartment he's made over the coach-house for him and Amy?"

By now her smile had stitched over the rent in her omniscience. "Oh I think you're imagining things again Ned," she said lightly. "Saradon is just as usual. George probably spun you some story when he went out to Antigua."

"George never came to Antigua." It was my view of reality, now, which quaked. Her expression remained serene, her mouth shaped into a small smile of disbelief. I edited my own features into a similar sketch.

So our two masks—our two views of the truth—faced one another across the table as if we were playing poker. Catching at a distraction, she looked over my shoulder. "Listen!" she said.

I had called her bluff. She didn't know whether George had come to Antigua, she didn't know whether George and Amy were still together, or how or where at Saradon they lived. My insistence had prevailed. As I had determined, so things were. I listened.

Came a pattering rush like hail on leaves swiftly nearing us through the streets. Just as a mob of youths and girls came running pell-mell into the square our waiter appeared and deftly picked up our table. Coffee and all he carried it into the shelter of the café as if, in an uncertain climate, a storm threatened. As we followed him I asked what was happening.

He too showed a poker face. "The students riot," he said. It was a censored statement betraying no views.

We watched through the penumbra of the arcade. In the brilliant light beyond, in a vivid clamour, the rush of runners swept across the sloping square like a freshet of rain flooding through. Colours, shouts; the flying crowd urged and herded by police in dark uniforms whose truncheons rose and fell. Hunters and hunted fled by. They were past before I could be certain of the face I thought I had seen.

Still the sight of her—the chance that she was near—made my heart turn over.

They were gone. The square drained dry, empty. The light in the dust lay dead. Slowly the square refilled with its everyday life of café tables and people like ourselves. Paying the bill I said to Lea, "You didn't see anyone you knew just then I suppose?"

"In that gallimaufry?" she disdainfully enquired, the choice of word reminding me of her indissoluble blood-link with George. "Hardly. Come, I must find a taxi—thank goodness the police are in control," she added, touching her lips with a napkin as she rose, "I thought for a moment I might miss my plane."

Fortunately nothing so untoward occurred. We found her a taxi, and I strolled through the well-policed streets towards the Embassy. Supposing it had been Amy in the flying crowd? After Mary Baker Eddy and Richard Jefferies she might have chanced upon Karl Marx on someone's shelf and picked him up, perhaps expecting Groucho. Or she might have picked up a student. Or, leaving a jeweller's shop to meet Terry at the Grande Bretagne for lunch, she might have been swept up in the mob and run with them for "the adventure". My view of things required that Amy was unpredictable, an aberration: part of George certainly, but with wilfulness and freedom enough to punish him as he deserved. Her absence or her presence would punish him equally. Yes, though my heart had missed many a beat in the last year at the glimpse of a blonde head, it might have been Amy I had seen in the square.

I took no chances. At the Embassy I concocted a story about an assassination threat and ordered that all my outside calls be intercepted. I took no chances with that voice like a rainbow, lancing in through my window to plant one foot in reality and the other on a pot of fairy gold. Amy *was* a threat to my life; in my lie there was the kind of truth she believed in herself, a justifiable impression that the facts might not support.

This done, I returned to my work. As it happened I was busy upon a peremptory minute—my move from Mexico had entailed technical promotion and had put me in a position to make local rules—which instructed all staff to connect pieces of paper with pins inserted only from left to right. Or from right to left, I don't remember which. It is the principle of uniformity which matters, if one's fingers are not to be pricked.

Philip Glazebrook

Philip Glazebrook was born in London in 1937 and was educated at Eton and Trinity College, Cambridge. He is the author of an earlier novel, *Try Pleasure* (1969). He lives in Dorset with his wife and two children.